DONATO CARRISI

INTO THE
LABYRINTH

Translated by Katherine Gregor

ABACUS

ABACUS

First published in Great Britain in 2020 by Abacus
This edition published in 2020 by Abacus

1 3 5 7 9 10 8 6 4 2

A CIP catalogue record for this book is available from the British Library.

ISBN 978-0-349-14395-8

Typeset in Horley by M Rules
Printed and bound in Great Britain by Clays Ltd, Elcograf S.p.A.

Papers used by Abacus are from well-managed forests
and other responsible sources.

MIX
Paper from
responsible sources
FSC® C104740

Abacus
An imprint of
Little, Brown Book Group
Carmelite House
50 Victoria Embankment
London EC4Y 0DZ

An Hachette UK Company
www.hachette.co.uk

www.littlebrown.co.uk

Donato Carrisi was born in 1973 and studied law and criminology. He won four Italian literature prizes for his bestselling debut *The Whisperer*. Since 1999 he has been working as a TV screenwriter, and he lives in Rome.

To Antonio.
My son, my best story

1

For most of humanity, that 23 February was just a morning like any other, but for Samantha Andretti it could have been the start of the most important day of her young life.

Tony Baretta had asked to speak to her.

Sam had spent the night tossing and turning like a possessed character in a horror film, trying to imagine why one of the cutest boys at school – and the world – should wish to speak to her of all people.

All this had begun the previous day. First of all, the request had not been issued to her directly or by him in person. Some things had to follow a specific protocol with teenagers. Naturally, the initiative would always originate with the interested party, but then a whole procedure would follow. Tony had used Mike, a member of his close circle, who had passed the request on to Tina, who sat next to Sam in class, and Tina had then told her. A simple, direct sentence which, in the unfathomable universe of secondary school, could mean a multitude of things.

'Tony Baretta wants to speak to you,' Tina had whispered in her ear during gym, skipping with joy, a glow in her eyes and voice – because a true friend is as happy about something nice happening to you as if it had happened to her.

'Who told you?' Sam had immediately asked.

'Mike Levin. He stopped me on my way back from the toilet.'

The fact that Mike had spoken to Tina meant it was a confidential matter and had to remain so. 'But what did he tell you exactly?' she'd asked to make sure Tina had understood properly – no one at school had forgotten poor Gina D'Abbraccio, nicknamed 'the widow' because when a boy had asked her if she had a date for the end-of-year dance, she'd mistaken his ordinary curiosity for an invitation and had ended up dressed in a long peach-coloured tulle gown, waiting in tears for a ghost.

'He said,' Tina had slavishly replied, '"Tell Samantha that Tony wants to speak to her."'

Naturally, while they were analysing all this, Samantha had made her repeat these words over and over again. Precisely to guarantee that Tina hadn't misquoted.

'When' or 'where' this chat with Tony would take place was not known, however, and that added to Sam's frustration. She figured it would perhaps happen in the science lab or the library. Or else behind the steps at the gym where Tony Baretta trained with the basketball team and Samantha with the volleyball team. Before and after school were ruled out, just like the canteen and corridors – too many prying eyes and ears. On second thoughts, having no further details, while being a kind of torture, was also what made it special. For Sam, there was no better way to describe this strange alternation between euphoria and depression that had followed that simple request, since the topic of the meeting could turn out to be a boon or a disappointment. Even so, she was grateful – yes, grateful – for what was happening to her.

Actually happening to her – Samantha Andretti – and nobody else!

Her mother was wrong to say that there are things you experience at thirteen which you appreciate more as an adult, with hindsight. Because at this moment, Sam was happy with a happiness that belonged to her alone and nobody else on the face of the Earth could have understood or felt. And that made her privileged ... Or else totally deluded and about to come smack up against a devastating truth: that, after all, Tony Baretta was famous for showing off with girls.

The fact was, she had never thought about Tony. At least not that way. Nature had started to change Sam's body and she had already got used to her period, but until now she hadn't had the opportunity to appreciate the positive effects of these changes. Samantha had never realised she was attractive – or perhaps she already knew it but before it was relevant in any way. She had begun to attract the curiosity of boys and it was a revelation to her.

Had Tony noticed? Was this what he was aiming at? To slide his hands under her top or – *Jesus, Mary and Joseph, forgive me* – elsewhere?

That was why, on the morning of 23 February – D-Day! – tired from lack of sleep and watching the glow of the dawn spread across her bedroom ceiling, Sam had convinced herself that Tony Baretta's words weren't real but merely the result of a hallucination. Or else she had probably thought about them so much that, amid the twists and turns of every teenager's fervent imagination, the prospect had lost all credibility. There was only one way to find out if she had deluded herself. And that was to lift her tired body from the sweat-drenched bed, get ready and go to school.

And so, having ignored her mother's chiding about not having enough breakfast – for God's sake, she couldn't breathe, let alone eat! – Sam put her rucksack over her shoulder and, intrepid but also somewhat resigned, quickly walked out of the front door to meet her destiny.

At five to eight, the streets in the area where the Andrettis lived were practically deserted. Anyone with a job had already gone a long time ago, the unemployed were busy getting over their hangovers, the elderly were waiting for the day to grow warmer before popping their heads out of their front doors and students would be leaving it till the last possible minute before setting off. For Sam, too, this was unusual timing. She wanted to drop by Tina's house, as she often did. But then she decided her friend probably wouldn't be ready yet and she didn't have the patience to wait for her.

Not today.

As she walked along the grey brick pavement, the only person she passed was a delivery man looking for an address. She didn't even notice him and he barely registered the girl who walked past him – to look at her, nobody would have imagined the turmoil inside her. Sam went past the Macinskys' green house, with that horrid black mutt who'd lie low in the hedge and give her a fright every time, then the small villa that used to belong to Mrs Robinson and was now falling apart because her relatives couldn't agree on the inheritance. She skirted the football pitch at the back of the church of the Holy Mercy. There was also a garden and a little playground with swings, a slide and the tall linden tree on which Father Edward would pin flyers advertising parish events. Although there was silence all around, at the end of the deserted street you could already see the main road hectic with traffic bound for the city centre.

But Sam didn't notice any of this.

The landscape before her eyes was like a screen on which Tony Baretta's smiling face was being projected. She was guided on her way only by the unconscious memory of familiar steps repeated hundreds of times before.

When she was halfway to her secondary school, Sam suddenly had a doubt about whether she was dressed appropriately for the meeting. She was wearing her favourite jeans – with rhinestones on the back pockets and small tears at the knees – and, under the black bomber jacket that was two sizes too large, the white hooded top her father had brought her from his most recent business trip. But the real problem was the dark rings under her eyes caused by the lack of sleep. She had tried to hide them with her mother's concealer but wasn't at all sure she'd managed it – she wasn't allowed make-up yet and hadn't learnt to apply it properly.

She slowed down and looked at the cars parked along the street. She immediately ruled out the silver-grey Dodge and a beige Volvo because they were too dirty and didn't meet her requirements. She finally saw what she was after. Across the road, there was a white minivan with reflective windows. She crossed to the other side and looked at herself. Except that, after ascertaining that the concealer did in fact cover the bags under her eyes, she didn't resume her walk. Instead, she carried on looking at the reflection of her face, framed with long brown hair – she loved her hair. She wondered if she was really pretty enough for Tony and tried seeing herself through his eyes. What does he see in me? And as she was wondering, her eyes focused for a moment beyond the reflective surface.

It can't be, she thought, and took a closer look.

On the other side of the glass, in the shadows, there was a giant rabbit. It was watching her, motionless. Samantha could have run away – part of her was telling her to run, and fast – but she didn't. She was fascinated, as though mesmerised, by this gaze emerging from the abyss. *This isn't happening*, she thought. *This isn't happening to me*, she repeated with the typical incredulity of some victims who, instead of fleeing their fate, are inexplicably drawn to it.

The girl and the rabbit stared at each other for an infinite length of time, as though driven by a morbid reciprocal curiosity.

Then, all of a sudden, the minivan door opened, depriving her of her reflection. As Samantha's face vanished before her, she saw no fear in her eyes. If anything, there was just a flash of surprise.

As the rabbit dragged her into his burrow, Sam did not imagine that this would be the last time she would see herself for a very, very long while.

2

First to surface from the darkness were sounds, like an orchestra tuning up before a concert. Chaotic and orderly but always light sounds. Electronic notes at regular intervals. Trolley wheels rolling from one side to the other and the clinking of colliding glass. The subtle ringing of phones. Quick but light footsteps. And all of that mixed up with incomprehensible, distant but nevertheless human voices – how long had it been since she'd heard voices? And she could hear her own breathing. Regular but muffled. Like breathing in a cave. No, there was something pressing on her face.

The second detail her mind registered was the smell. General disinfectant. And medicines. Yes, she thought, it smells of medicines.

She tried to find her bearings. She had no awareness of her own body, and only knew she was lying down. She kept her eyes shut because her lids felt heavy, ever so heavy. And yet she had to make an effort and open them. She had to do it quickly, before she could be overwhelmed by events.

Control the danger. That's the only way.

The voice that had just spoken was coming from somewhere inside her. It wasn't a memory but an instinct. Something that had taken shape over time, through experience. She'd had to learn to survive. That was why, despite the numbness, a part of her was always alert.

Open your eyes – open your damned eyes! Look.

A narrow slot opened in her field of vision. Tears flooded her irises, though it wasn't an emotional response – if anything, one of annoyance – by now she would rarely give the bastard the satisfaction of seeing her cry. For a moment, she was afraid of coming up against darkness but, instead, saw a blue light inundating the room all around her.

It was like being at the bottom of the ocean. Comfortable and peaceful.

This could be a dirty trick, though, she knew that only too well, having experienced first-hand how dangerous trusting could be. As soon as her eyes grew accustomed to the new setting, she began to move them, exploring the surrounding environment.

She was lying on a bed. The blue light was coming from fluorescent lights on the ceiling. She was in a large room with white walls. No windows. But, at the far end, on the left-hand side, there was a huge mirrored wall.

He doesn't like mirrors, the voice said again. How was this possible?

There was also a door standing ajar and, beyond it, a well-lit corridor. That was where the sounds were coming from.

It wasn't real. It didn't make sense. Where am I?

A human figure was standing outside the door, with its back to her, wearing dark clothes – she could make him out through the gap. He had a gun holstered at his side. Is this some kind of joke? What does it mean?

Only then did she notice a little table near her bed, with a microphone and recorder. There was an empty iron chair next to it, with a man's suit jacket hanging on the back. He's nearby, she thought. He's coming back. She felt a wave of fear sweep over her like a tide.

No, not fear, she told herself. Fear was the real enemy. I have to get out of here.

It wouldn't be easy, she didn't think she had sufficient strength. She tried moving her arms, lifted her elbows and pushed them into the mattress to pull herself up. Long brown hair fell over her face. Her limbs felt heavy. She managed to partly raise her torso, but immediately fell back. Something was clasped over her face: an oxygen mask connected to a valve on the wall. And a drip was attached to her arm. She yanked the tube and slid the needle out of her vein, but as soon as she deprived herself of the beneficial gas, she realised she had run out of breath. She coughed and tried to swallow the air around her but its consistency was denser than the fresh breeze she had been inhaling up to now. Her eyes filled with lively black dots.

Darkness was gaining the upper hand again but she didn't give in.

She pulled off the sheet that was covering her from the waist down and, through the shadows that obscured her eyesight, saw a thin tube coming out of her groin and ending in a transparent bag inside which yellow liquid had accumulated.

Still lying down, she moved her right leg, meaning to get out of bed, but something was holding onto her left. A weight. Caught unawares by the ballast, she lost her balance and realised she was falling down. She came crashing down on a cold, hard surface and knocked her face against it. Her left leg was the last thing to slide down onto the floor with a thud, like a stone.

The noise caught someone's attention and she clearly heard the door open and close again. Then she saw a shadowy figure running towards her: something was jangling at its side – a carabiner filled with keys. The figure put a steaming cup down on the floor and grabbed her under the armpits. 'Don't worry,' a male voice said encouragingly, pulling her up. 'Don't worry,' he repeated, gently handling her near-lifeless body. 'It's all right.'

She was almost suffocating and about to faint, so she let her head drop on the man's chest. He smelt of cologne and had a tie on, which she found cruel and absurd.

Monsters don't wear ties.

The man heaved her back onto the bed and, after brushing her hair off her face, placed the mask back over her mouth. The oxygen filled her lungs and brought relief. After making her lie down properly, he put a pillow under her left leg, which was in plaster from her ankle up to her knee. 'You'll be more comfortable like this,' he said caringly. Finally, he took the cannula she'd taken out and pushed the needle back into her arm. She watched him do these things with astonishment.

She'd grown unused to kindness. And above all to a human presence.

She tried to focus on him. Did she know him? She didn't think she'd ever seen him before. He looked about sixty and athletic. He had round glasses with dark frames and tousled hair. Besides the carabiner with the keys attached to his belt, there was a photo ID pinned to the pocket of his dark blue shirt. His sleeves were rolled up to his elbows.

Once the man had finished, he picked up the steaming cup he'd left on the floor and put it on the bedside table, on which there was also a yellow telephone.

A phone? It couldn't be a phone!

'How are you feeling?' he asked.

She didn't answer.

'Are you able to speak?'

She said nothing, staring at him, her eyes wide open, ready to pounce on him.

He came closer. 'Do you understand what I'm saying?'

'Is it a game?' The words emerged, harsh but muffled, from the oxygen mask.

'Excuse me?' he said.

She cleared her throat. 'Is it a game?' she repeated.

'I'm sorry, I don't know what you mean,' he replied, then added, 'I'm Dr Green.'

She didn't know any Dr Green.

'You're at Saint Catherine's. It's a hospital. It's all right.'

She tried to take in his words but couldn't. Saint Catherine's, hospital – it was information outside her reach.

No, it's not all right. Who on earth are you? What do you really want from me?

'It's understandable you should be disorientated,' he said. 'It's normal. It's still too soon.' He stared at her silently for a moment, with compassion.

Nobody looks at me like that.

'You were brought here two days ago,' he continued. 'You slept for almost forty-eight hours, but now you're awake, Sam.'

Sam? Who's Sam? 'Is it a game?' she asked for the third time.

Dr Green now looked worried. Perhaps he'd seen the perplexed expression on her face. 'You do know who you are, don't you?'

She thought for a moment, afraid to answer.

He forced a smile. 'OK, one thing at a time . . . Where do you think you are now?'

'In the labyrinth.'

Dr Green glanced at the mirror, then turned to her again. 'I've told you we're in a hospital. Don't you believe me?'

'I don't know.'

'Well, that's good enough for now.' He sat on the iron chair and leaned forward, resting his elbows on his knees and interlacing his fingers in an informal pose. 'Why do you think you're in a labyrinth?'

She looked around. 'There are no windows.'

'You're right, that's odd, but you see, this is a special room: we're in the burns unit. They brought you here because your eyes are no longer accustomed to natural light and it could be dangerous, just as if you had a burn. It's also why there are ultra-violet lights.'

They both looked up at the blue fluorescent lights.

He turned to the mirrored wall. 'Through there, doctors and relatives can look at the patient without exposing him or her to the risk of infection . . . I know,' he said, attempting a joke, 'it looks like a police interrogation room, like the ones you see in films or on TV. It's the first thing it made me think of.'

'He doesn't like mirrors,' she blurted out.

Dr Green turned serious again. 'He?'

'Mirrors aren't allowed.' She had avoided turning towards the left-hand wall until then.

'Who doesn't allow mirrors?'

She said nothing, thinking her silence would be sufficient. He gave her another sympathetic look. It was as gentle as a caress, but part of her felt angry. She wasn't sure of anything yet.

I'm not going to be taken in.

'All right, let's put it another way,' Dr Green said, not waiting for a reply. 'If mirrors aren't allowed and yet there is one here, then perhaps you're not in the labyrinth any longer, right?'

The argument was airtight, but after so many tricks – so many *games* – even just trying to trust someone was exhausting.

'Do you remember how you ended up in the labyrinth?'

No, she couldn't remember that, either. She was aware that there was an 'outside' but as far as she knew, she'd always been inside.

'Sam.' Again, he uttered that name. 'It's time to clarify a few things because unfortunately we don't have much time.'

What did he mean?

'Even though we're in a hospital, I'm not really a doctor. It's not my duty to treat you – there are far more qualified people taking care of your health. My job is to find evil men like the one who abducted you and kept you prisoner in the labyrinth.'

Abducted? What's he talking about?

Her head was spinning and she wasn't sure she wanted to hear any more.

'It's painful, I know, but we have to do this. It's our only way of stopping him.'

What did he mean by 'stopping him'? She wasn't sure she wanted to do this. 'How did I get here?'

'You probably escaped. Two nights ago, a police car found you on a road in an uninhabited area near the swamps. You had a broken leg and weren't wearing any clothes. Judging by your grazes, you may have been running away.'

She looked at her arms, which were covered in small wounds.

'It's an absolute miracle you made it.'

She couldn't remember anything.

'You were in a state of shock. The officers brought you to the hospital and informed the bureau. They looked for a match in the missing persons reports and identified you . . . Samantha Andretti.'

He put a hand in the pocket of the jacket hanging on the back of the chair, took out a small piece of paper and gave it to her.

She studied it. It was a flyer with the photo of a smiling girl with brown hair and hazel eyes. There was a word printed in red beneath the picture: MISSING.

She felt a pang in her stomach. 'That's not me,' she said, returning the flyer.

'It's understandable you should say that,' Green replied confidently. 'But don't worry, you've already made great progress since they found you. The abductor gave you psychotropic drugs to make you docile and control you. They discovered them in large quantities in your blood.' He indicated the drip attached to her arm. 'They're currently administering a kind of antidote and it's working because you're now conscious. Soon you'll also get your memory back.'

She wanted to believe it – *oh, God, how she wanted to believe it.*

'You're safe, Sam.'

A strange calm swept over her at these words.

'Safe,' she repeated to herself. She felt a small tear form in the corner of her eye. She hoped it would stay there because she couldn't allow herself to drop her guard.

'Unfortunately, we can't wait for the treatment to take effect fully, and that's why I'm here.' He stared at her. 'You'll have to help me.'

'Me?' she asked, startled. 'How can I help you?'

'By remembering as many things as you can, however insignificant.' Once again, he indicated the mirrored wall. 'There are police officers behind there who'll be present at our conversation and pass on every detail they consider relevant to the officers on the outside who are busy trying to catch your abductor.'

'I don't know if I can.' She was tired and frightened and wanted only to rest.

'Listen, Sam: you do want that man to pay for what he's done to you, don't you? And, above all, you wouldn't want him to do the same thing to somebody else . . .'

This time, the tear ran down her cheek and stopped at the edge of the oxygen mask.

'As you might have gathered, I'm a policeman,' he continued. 'I don't carry a gun and I don't go around chasing criminals or being shot at. To tell you the truth, I'm not even that brave.' He laughed at his own joke. 'But one thing I can assure you: together we'll catch him, you and I. He doesn't know it, but there's a place from which he can't escape. And that's where we'll hunt him down: not out there but in your mind.'

Dr Green's final words made her shudder. Even though she couldn't admit it, she'd always known that *he*'d got into her head – like a kind of parasite.

'What do you say – do you trust me?'

A moment later, she proffered her hand.

Green approved her decision with a nod, then gave her back the flyer. 'Good, well done, my brave girl.'

As she tried to familiarise herself with the face in the photo, he turned to the table and activated the microphone and recorder. 'How old are you, Sam?'

She studied the picture carefully. 'Not sure . . . Thirteen? Fourteen?'

'Do you have any idea how long you spent in the labyrinth?'

She shook her head. *No, I don't know.*

Dr Green wrote something down. 'Are you sure you don't recognise anything of yourself in that photo?'

She looked at it more closely. 'My hair,' she said, stroking one of the strands. 'I love it.'

In the labyrinth, stroking my hair is my favourite pastime.

The recollection came to her unexpectedly, like a quick flash out of nowhere.

I run my fingers through it to kill time, while waiting for a new game.

'Nothing else?'

I'd like a mirror but he won't give me one. She had a sudden doubt. 'Am I . . . am I attractive?' she asked timidly.

'Yes, you are,' he replied gently. 'But I want to be honest with you . . . I know why he wouldn't allow mirrors.'

She had a rush of anxiety.

'I'd like you to turn to the wall on the left and find out for yourself . . .'

During the silence that followed, all she felt was her breathing quickening in a frantic search for oxygen. She looked into Dr Green's eyes to see if she should be afraid, but he seemed unfazed. She understood that this was a test and that she couldn't avoid it. So she began to turn her head on her pillow. She felt the rubber band on the mask stretch over her cheek.

I'm now going to see the girl in the flyer and I won't recognise myself, she thought. But the truth was a thousand times worse.

When she met her reflection, it took her a while to focus on the image that was being sent back to her.

'You were abducted one February morning on your way to school,' Green said.

The much older brown-haired girl in the mirror started to cry.

'I'm sorry,' Dr Green said. 'It was fifteen years ago.'

3

'. . . *Fifteen years with no news, no clue and no hope. Fifteen years of silence. An endless nightmare with an unexpectedly happy ending, because until two days ago, nobody could have imagined that Samantha Andretti was still alive . . .*'

Bruno Genko was trying to follow the television news correspondent standing outside the entrance to Saint Catherine's, but he struggled to hear over old Quimby banging the bar's air conditioning unit, as old as himself, with a broomstick, in an attempt to get it to work again.

'Jesus, Quimby, will you stop that?' Gomez, one of the bar's most regular patrons, cried out from one of the booths at the far end of the room. 'It's not going to fix itself just because you're hitting it with a stick.'

'What the hell do you know about air conditioners?' the barman asked, annoyed.

'All I know is that you should put your hand in your pocket and make sure your customers get some fresh air,' the fat, sweaty man replied, lifting a half-full bottle of beer from the large stack in front of him.

'Naturally, I could if everybody in this place paid regularly.'

The lively arguments between Quimby and his customers were a frequent enough performance for anyone who frequented the Q-Bar. And it didn't take much for the owner to lose his temper. At that moment, however, the only audience, besides Gomez, was Bruno Genko, and on that particular afternoon he was in no mood for fucking around.

Genko was sitting on one of the bar stools, clutching a glass of tequila and staring at the television screen standing on an upper shelf. The blades of the fans above his head were moving warm humid air mixed with the smell of cigarettes. His drink hadn't yet been able to wash away the taste from having vomited his guts out in the back alley half an hour earlier. He hadn't used the bar toilet because he didn't want anyone to notice he was ill.

Even so, he looked awful and the nausea was threatening a comeback when he suddenly remembered what he had in the right pocket of his linen jacket.

The talisman.

Genko pushed the vision away and drained his glass in a single gulp. It's the heat, he told himself to pluck up courage while the recollection faded. Nobody must know. So he ignored the spat, the blows of the broomstick and the rattling air conditioner, and tried to focus on what they were saying on TV.

The news of Samantha Andretti's reappearance had been occupying the prime spot on all the local and national networks for the past forty-eight hours and had even relegated to the background the extraordinary heatwave afflicting the region, with temperatures way above average and a level of humidity never previously recorded.

'. . . *According to unofficial sources, twenty-eight-year-old Samantha Andretti is at present getting psychological support from an expert in the hope that she will soon be able to provide useful details that will help to catch the monster who abducted her and kept her prisoner . . . Some say there will be important developments in this matter before very long . . .*'

'Naaah . . . these reporters don't know fuck.' With a hand gesture, Quimby dismissed the correspondent on the screen and, with her, the entire journalistic profession. Then he resumed his seat behind the counter. 'And if you switch channels it's the same old tune. It's the fifth or sixth time this morning I'm hearing the same thing: they keep going on about "imminent developments" because they've run out of things to say.'

'And yet I could have bet the police would have fallen over one other to give tip-offs to the media,' Genko said.

'The chief inspector has put a news blackout on the investigation to avoid giving any advantage to the son of a bitch they're looking for . . . If they don't catch him somebody's going to make the bureau pay a heavy price for neglecting the fact that Samantha was still alive all these years. That really would make the police look good.' Quimby stopped, shuddering at a sudden realisation. 'My God, fifteen years . . . Doesn't bear thinking about.'

'No,' Genko agreed, shaking his empty glass.

Quimby took the bottle of tequila and administered another dose of the delectable medicine. 'The question is how she managed to survive this long . . .'

Genko knew the answer but couldn't tell him. But then

perhaps Quimby didn't actually want to hear it. Like most ordinary people, he wanted to believe the fairytale of the brave heroine who'd managed to resist and, in the end, even escape unscathed from the monster. In reality, she'd made it only because that was the way her jailer had wanted it. He had decided not to kill her, of course, but also to feed her and make sure she didn't get ill.

In other words, he had taken care of her.

Day after day, he had shown her a sick affection. Just like humans with zoo animals, Genko thought, raising the tequila to his lips. For all our kindness towards these creatures, deep in our hearts we know perfectly well that their lives aren't worth as much as our own. And Samantha Andretti had experienced this violent hypocrisy. She had been the caged animal, the creature to be admired. Having the power of life and death over her was her sadistic abductor's true reward. Every day, he'd made the decision to let her live. No doubt that had made him feel noble, magnanimous even. And maybe he was right. After all, he had protected her from himself.

But Quimby and ordinary people couldn't understand any of this. They hadn't visited the hell Genko had ventured into. Consequently, he felt sorry for them and would usually let them talk freely. Because a nugget of information could be lurking amid all that chatter, the kind of information that may become the turning point of an investigation.

As far as everyone was concerned, Bruno Genko was a private investigator. In actual fact, his job was to listen.

The Q-Bar was perfect for gathering rumours, indiscretions and simple tip-offs. It had been the point of reference for law officers ever since, about twenty years earlier, Lieutenant

Quimby had taken a bullet in the kidney during an ordinary search operation. Early retirement, career over, but he'd bought the pub with the insurance money. Ever since then, whenever police officers wanted to celebrate anything – be it someone retiring, the birth of an heir, a diploma or an anniversary – they would all meet up at the Q-Bar.

Although he'd never worn a uniform, Genko would regularly hang out in the bar and was by now considered one of the family. Of course, he had to put up with the banter and the nasty cracks but he was up to that. It was the price he had to pay to collect information that would be useful in his line of work. Quimby was his main confidant. All cops, even ex-cops, know you must never trust a private investigator. But the old man didn't do it for any kind of profit. It was a matter of vanity. Perhaps sharing confidential information with a civilian made him feel as though he was still part of the force. Naturally, Genko would never press Quimby to talk: the ex-policeman would never have breathed a word if confronted with a direct question. So he would simply lurk in the bar, sometimes for hours on end, and wait for the other man to take the initiative.

That day, too.

Except that today is different. There isn't much time left.

While waiting, he put a hand in the pocket of his linen jacket and took out a handkerchief to wipe the sweat from the back of his neck. His fingers brushed against the crumpled piece of paper – he'd called it the 'talisman' because he never parted with it. He felt a flush rise up through his stomach and was afraid he'd vomit again.

'Bauer and Delacroix were here last night, on their way to the overtime shift,' Quimby suddenly said.

Genko overcame his nausea and forgot about the piece of paper, because the cops mentioned by the barman were the officers formally assigned to the Samantha Andretti case. Here we are, he thought. He'd spent hours waiting for this moment and now he was being rewarded.

After mentioning Bauer and Delacroix, Quimby topped up his glass of tequila without being asked. A sign that he felt like chatting. Then he leaned across the counter. 'They tell me the story about an expert talking to the girl is true. Apparently it's a profiler with balls: a specialist in catching serial killers who's been called in specially from somewhere or other. Someone who uses unorthodox methods . . .'

Genko knew that surviving a psychopath was statistically unlikely. So, whenever it happened, the police had an invaluable witness and even a way into the twists and turns of a complex criminal personality. A multi-faceted web of fantasies, uncontrollable urges, instincts and obscene deviations. That was why they'd called in a professional to probe Samantha Andretti's mind.

Genko noticed that Quimby, too, kept referring to her as though she were still thirteen years old. He wasn't the only one. Many people, even on television, would say 'girl'. This was inevitable, since the last photo circulated straight after her disappearance was still in people's minds. And yet, even though the media hadn't got their hands on a recent picture to show the public, Samantha was now a woman.

'The girl's still in shock,' Quimby confided in a low voice. 'But the bureau's optimistic.'

Genko didn't want to appear overly curious, but he was certain that Quimby had found out something. 'What do you mean by optimistic?'

'You know what Delacroix's like: he doesn't say much and never commits himself ... But Bauer's convinced they'll catch the bastard ...'

'Bauer's a show-off,' Genko remarked, then, pretending he wasn't interested, returned his focus to the television screen.

Quimby rose to the bait. 'Yes, but apparently they've got a lead ...'

A lead? Could Samantha possibly have already supplied a crucial detail?

'I've heard they're looking for the prison set up by the abductor,' Genko said absent-mindedly, to add some fuel to the conversation. 'The police have surrounded an uninhabited area in the south, behind the swamps. Isn't that where they came across Samantha?'

'That's right, they've cordoned off a security perimeter and won't let anyone in. They want to keep onlookers away.'

'They'll never find the place.' Genko was trying to appear sceptical, so that the other man would feel the urge to contradict him. 'They haven't found it in fifteen years, so it must be pretty well camouflaged.'

Quimby seemed annoyed by his doubts. 'Samantha Andretti was on foot and even had a broken leg, so she can't have come a long way, right?'

The private investigator decided to throw the ex-cop's wounded ego a bone. 'I think she's the key to everything: if she cooperates, then there's a hope of catching the monster.'

'She'll cooperate,' Quimby replied confidently. 'But they've got something else, too ...'

So the lead didn't come from the girl. From where, then? Genko said nothing and sipped at his drink. This strategic pause gave the barman time to decide whether or not to tell him the rest.

'What they leaked about the way they found her isn't entirely true,' Quimby said. 'The police who saw her on the side of the road, with no clothes and a broken leg, weren't driving by there by chance.'

Genko quickly assessed the implications of this piece of information. Why should they have lied about the way they'd found her? What was it that wasn't supposed to be revealed? 'The police had been tipped off,' he said tentatively. 'Somebody reported seeing Samantha.'

Quimby merely nodded.

'A Good Samaritan.'

Quimby corrected him. 'An anonymous caller.'

4

Genko stepped out onto the threshold of the Q-Bar and was immediately assaulted by the mugginess, which constricted his throat and chest in a single grip. The heat was alive, an invisible animal that didn't give you a chance. Genko struggled to breathe, but still slid a cigarette between his lips, lit it and waited for the nicotine to kick in.

After all, what harm could it possibly do to him?

He looked around. At three in the afternoon, the city centre streets were deserted. An unusual sight for this time of day, this area and the fact that it was a weekday. The shops and businesses were shut. No passers-by. A ghostly silence. Only the traffic lights absurdly insisted on regulating the flow in streets void of traffic.

Because of the high temperature, the authorities had been forced to apply extraordinary measures to safeguard the residents' health. People were being advised to sleep during the day and leave their houses only at night. To make the transition smoother, the working shifts of police, firefighters and hospital staff had been altered. Government offices would open late in the afternoon and close at dawn. Even the courts began carrying out their activities in the evening. Firms and businesses had adhered to the change: at around 8 p.m., manual and office workers would crowd the streets to get to their workplace as if it was a normal rush hour. No one complained. On the contrary, shops and department stores had recorded an increase in sales, since people couldn't wait to leave their homes. As soon as the sun went down, they would all emerge from their hideouts, like rats.

For about a week now, days had begun at sundown.

Time has gone crazy, Genko thought, remembering what had happened a year earlier in Rome, where a storm had beaten down on the city, causing blackouts and devastating flooding. The result of pollution, global warming, the fucking way in which the planet was being treated. How long before the damned human race self-destructed without even noticing? Such a shame. Then he remembered the talisman in his pocket and decided that it was no longer his problem, when it came down to it.

So he decided not to give a damn and to contribute further to the general degradation: he dragged on his cigarette a couple of times, threw the butt down on the scorching pavement and crushed it with the sole of his shoe. Then he headed to his car, which was parked around the corner.

An anonymous caller.

As he drove his old Saab down the empty streets, Genko kept mulling over the information he'd obtained from Quimby. The air conditioning hadn't worked for years, so he kept the windows down. Sudden blasts would rush at him then pull back, as though he was advancing in the middle of a blaze. Genko needed a refuge, not to escape the heat but that thought. *Stop thinking about it, it's not your concern.* But he was tormented by doubt. Who had made the call? Why? Why didn't the informer help Samantha himself? Why omit his details? The stranger could have become the hero of these events, and yet he had preferred to remain in the shadows. What was he afraid of? Or what was he trying to hide? Genko knew his mind wasn't clear enough to think. Too much tequila or else that damned piece of paper in his pocket. He could hole up in the hotel room he had booked a week earlier, finish the binge he'd begun at the Q-Bar and fall into a deep sleep, hoping not to wake up again.

It's not going to be that painless, my friend, so get used to the idea.

He decided it was better for him not to be alone. And there was only one person who could stand him in this condition.

When Linda opened the door, her expression told Genko he must look awful.

'Christ, are you out of your mind going out in this heat?' she chided him, pulling him indoors. 'And you've been drinking,' she added with a disgusted grimace. Linda blamed the temperature and the drink for his pallor and the rings under his eyes.

Genko didn't contradict her. 'Can I come in?'

'You're already in, you idiot.'

'OK, then, can I stay awhile or are you busy?' His clothes were soaked in sweat and his head was spinning.

'I have a client in an hour,' she replied, adjusting her dark blue silk kimono over her bronze skin.

'I just need to lie down for a few minutes, that's all.' He

went on into the apartment, looking for the sofa. Unlike the Q-Bar, the air conditioning here was working and there was a nice semi-darkness because the blinds were down.

'You know, you stink of vomit. You could have a shower.'

'I don't want to be a nuisance.'

'It'll be more of a nuisance if you make my apartment stink.'

Genko sat down on the white sofa, which matched the carpet and took up prime position in the living room, amid black-lacquered furniture and unicorns. They were all over the place and in various forms – posters, figurines, cuddly toys and a few even trapped inside snow globes. They were Linda's passion. 'I'm a unicorn,' she'd once said. 'A beautiful, legendary creature: no one in their right mind will ever admit to believing in unicorns, and yet men have always insisted on searching for them in the hope that they really exist.'

She was right on one thing. She truly was beautiful. That was why men wanted her. And they were willing to pay a high price for the privilege of being with her.

'Come, let me help you,' she said when she saw he couldn't even remove his jacket. She took off his moccasins and stretched his legs on the sofa, then plumped up a cushion and placed it under his head. She caressed his forehead lightly. 'Hey, you've got a temperature.'

'It's just the heat,' he lied.

'I'll get you some cold water. It's easy to get dehydrated in this heat . . . Especially when you drink tequila in the afternoon. And I'm putting this wretched thing in the dryer,' she added, picking up his linen jacket. 'I might be able to get rid of some of the stench.' She vanished down the corridor.

Genko took a deep breath. His head hurt and he felt numb. And even though he wouldn't admit it, he was scared. He hadn't been able to sleep properly for weeks. The stress was eating away at him and when his body couldn't take any more anxiety, he would collapse into sleep. It wasn't slumber but a kind of yielding. After half an hour's oblivion at most, reality would rouse him again to remind him his fate was sealed.

He could talk about this to Linda, and share his burden with her. It might even be liberating. After all, he couldn't deny that part of him had wanted to come here because of that. She wasn't just a good friend. Even though there was a boundary between them which they had never crossed, Linda was the closest he had to a wife.

When, six years earlier, she had called him in tears, asking for help, she had already been a prostitute for a long time, but her name was still Michael. The metamorphosis was not complete, this beautiful woman was trapped in a male body and five o'clock shadow framed the angelic face, with its high cheekbones, full lips and blue eyes. Michael had turned to Genko to escape persecution by a client. Back then, he would sell himself for not very much and go with anybody. And so he had come across a guy who would first fuck him then beat him up, accusing him of having forced him into an act that was against nature. And yet he would keep going back to him, full of remorse. So the story would start all over again, always with the same outcome.

Michael didn't know how much longer he could resist. He had tried pushing away his persecutor but without success. It became harder and harder to conceal the bruises from the beatings. He was scared to death.

With a job in hell himself, Genko could picture how it would turn out. Transsexuals were the favourite victims of violent misfits with pent-up anger. So when he looked deep into Michael's eyes, he immediately realised that the situation was serious and that no policeman would help him. If he didn't intervene, this frail, frightened angel would certainly die.

Threats and even violence wouldn't be enough to persuade the persecutor to disappear; an obsession with physical pain cannot be eradicated: it's like trying to put out a fire using the art of persuasion. The surest way of stopping this man was to kill him, but Genko was no murderer, so he came up with a plan. Since the guy worked as a broker for a well-known merchant bank, Genko paid a hacker to break into the firm's computer system and transfer enormous sums of money from investors into the man's personal account. Then all he had to do was wait for somebody to notice the theft. The guy got a ten-year sentence for fraud and embezzlement. In jail he could freely vent his instincts or be prey to those of others. Michael was free at last.

'What does this mean?'

There was a slight tremor in Linda's voice and, even without looking at her, Genko immediately knew she was upset. He turned his head a little and saw her standing still in the doorway, his linen jacket over her arm, a sheet of paper in her hand. Suddenly, it was all clear: before putting the jacket into the dryer, she had emptied the pockets so their contents wouldn't be damaged.

'What is this?' she asked again, almost angry this time.

Genko propped himself up. Here we are, he thought. He hadn't told anyone because he was afraid of the idea materialising: if words remained trapped on a page, then perhaps there was still hope of escape.

No, there is no hope.

'It's a talisman,' he said, but Linda looked disorientated. 'Do you know what a talisman is? It's an object to which we attribute the power to protect us. A bit like your unicorns.'

'What the fuck are you saying, Genko?' She was angry. 'It says here that you're going to die.'

He knew what had happened. After she'd realised it was a medical report, she had quickly scrolled down the text but the words were incomprehensible because her mind was desperately looking for something else. And she'd found it only on the last line. The answer to a terrible question. Two words.

'Prognosis: fatal.'

The same thing had happened to Genko when his own eyes had explored the document. What was written before the last line didn't matter. As a matter of fact, anything at all could have been written. After all, what difference did it make? Those words belonged to a time that was over, and the whole of the past wasn't worth anything any more, the life that had preceded that moment didn't make any more sense. These two cold, official words were a watershed. Nothing would be the same again.

'What's going on?' she asked, fearful. 'Why?'

Genko got up and went to her, because she was unable to move. He took the report from her hands and brought her back to the sofa with him. 'Listen, I'm going to try and explain but you have to listen. All right?'

She nodded, although she was about to cry.

'I have a sort of infection,' he said, indicating his chest. 'Some bacteria's got into my pericardium, I don't know how and neither do the doctors.' An alien monster was eating away at his heart. 'They say there's no cure because we found it too late.'

Linda was confused. 'You should be in hospital. They should at least try to do something . . . I can't let you die like this without doing anything.' Her voice was growing strident, almost hysterical.

Genko gave her hands a squeeze and shook his head. He didn't have the courage to tell her that when he'd asked if there was a cure, the doctor had recommended admission to a hospice. But Genko didn't feel like shutting himself away in a place where people go only to die.

'The positive side is that it'll happen suddenly, so I practically won't notice it. A small explosion in my chest and I'll be gone in a few seconds. Like a gunshot.' An invisible bullet, shot straight through the heart – he rather liked the image.

'And how long . . .' She couldn't quite ask. 'I mean how much time—'

'Two months.'

'Is that all?' She was upset. 'And how long have you known?'

'Two months,' he said without really thinking.

The news knocked Linda off balance. She was incapable of saying anything.

'The deadline's today.' Genko laughed but an acidic pellet of terror plummeted to his stomach. 'Strange: until yesterday I had a finishing line before me, and all I had to do was wait for the end of the countdown. But today . . . What happens from today?' He bowed his head, staring blankly at the carpet. 'I feel like a man on death row who hasn't been told the time of his execution.' He laughed again, this time in earnest. 'I was watching the clock yesterday, expecting something to happen

at midnight. You know, like in *Cinderella*. What an idiot ...'
He was actually angry: he had spent sixty days getting ready
for the crucial moment. And now there were no more rules.
Events were being decided by a silent anarchist. 'That's why
this piece of paper is a talisman,' he said, carefully folding the
report again. 'It protects me from chaos. Because you can also
go crazy waiting to die.'

Linda, however, couldn't manage to be this lucid. 'And
you're only telling me now?'

'I couldn't admit it even to myself ... If I'd confided in
anyone it would have all become real: I was about to die.' He
corrected himself: 'I am about to die. Or perhaps I'm already
dead, depending on your point of view.' It would make an
interesting philosophical conundrum. When does one start
dying? When one contracts the deadly disease or when one
discovers it?

Linda got up from the sofa. 'I'm just going to make a couple
of phone calls and cancel my appointments,' she said with
renewed determination. 'You're not going anywhere today.'

Genko took her hand gently. 'I didn't come here to die, even
if in practice it could happen this very instant.' He was trying
to defuse the tension and ease the sense of guilt.

'Then why did you? To say goodbye to me?' She was
angry with him.

He approached and kissed her on the forehead. 'I see: you're
afraid I'm going to stick a gun in my mouth and put an end to
it immediately, without waiting. I admit the idea has crossed
my mind, and I'm not ruling it out if things drag on. But you
won't avoid the worst by keeping me here, because the worst
is already written on that piece of paper.'

'You can't expect me to give up, you understand?'

He understood because he knew she loved him. 'Have you seen the news? About that woman who forty-eight hours ago managed to escape her jailer after fifteen years of imprisonment?'

'Yes, but what's that got to do with you?'

'I was thinking that if a thirteen-year-old girl can resist horror for so long, then everything is possible ... Even a miracle.'

She looked at him, confused.

'No, I don't think I'll get well,' he said, dismissing any illusion on the subject. 'But perhaps it's not a coincidence that it's all happening now.' He remembered: an anonymous caller. But he couldn't reveal the tip he'd received from Quimby to Linda.

'Promise me you won't kill yourself.'

'I can't. But I can assure you that right now it's the last thing on my mind.' He changed the subject: 'I need a favour,' he said. 'A week ago, I booked a room at the Ambrus Hotel, a small place near the railway bridge.' He took his wallet and pulled out a business card. 'Room 115 and it's paid for for another seven days.' In fact, he didn't think he would be staying there that long. He'd moved there because he was afraid that if he died at home, nobody would find his body. He was terrified by the idea of slowly rotting on the floor because he didn't have friends or relatives who cared about him. It was simpler in a hotel. One morning, the cleaning woman would come into the room and find him stone cold dead. But he did not explain this part of the plan to Linda. 'There's a safe in the room. The combination is 1107.'

'It's my date of birth,' she said, surprised.

'I know. That's why I chose it. Now listen carefully: when

you hear that . . .' He couldn't say it. 'Well, anyway, when what has to happen happens, go there and open the safe. You'll find a sealed envelope.'

'What's in it?'

'Never mind and it's no concern of yours,' he said in a warning tone. 'You absolutely mustn't open it. Just get rid of it as soon as possible, all right? And don't throw it away. You have to destroy it and make sure nothing's left.'

Linda couldn't understand the need for such a subterfuge. 'Why don't you do it yourself?'

He dodged the question. 'The porter has already received my instructions, and will let you in.'

Linda didn't insist, but Genko was certain she would keep her word. He stood up and put on his linen jacket, then checked the time. Four p.m. – he really had to go.

'Will you call me later?' she asked with doe eyes.

Genko came closer and stroked her face. 'I guess if I forget you'll think I've dropped dead . . .'

'Just as long as you don't forget you're still alive,' she replied, taking his hand again, lifting it to her lips and kissing it. 'Remember: as long as you have air in your lungs, it's not over.'

He liked this simple yet enlightening notion contained in her words: for as long as he had air in his lungs, he would not forget that he was still alive. 'Don't worry, there's something I must do before the irreparable happens.' He headed to the door.

Linda didn't know what to think. 'Where are you going?'

Genko turned and smiled at her. 'To hell.'

5

'The house of things' was a warehouse in an industrial district on the outskirts of the city. Someone had noticed a former storage area and converted it into a large private depot. For a modest annual sum you could rent a locker and store in it stuff you no longer needed – in most cases old furniture or assorted junk.

Genko reached the entrance and, hunched over in the Saab, rummaged in the glove compartment for the fob to open the automatic barrier. He groped around, finally found it and inserted it into the appropriate lock affixed in a small pillar, hoping it still worked.

The barrier lifted.

He went down a series of alleys between the rows of lockers. That was how he discovered that the place was no longer a home just to objects, since a few shutters were partly rolled up and inside you could detect clear signs of human presence. The renters had turned the lockers into makeshift homes. Genko wasn't surprised. He was familiar with this phenomenon. The population of the 'house of things' consisted mainly of males. Men with no families, who had lost their jobs because of the crisis, or else divorced husbands who, in order to pay alimony, were no longer in a position to afford a room, let alone an apartment. Sometimes neither. Poor, desperate people. People who'd turned nasty. Genko felt on him their eyes full of shame and resentment – hiding in the shadows of their lairs, watching the Saab with suspicion as it drove past. Above all, they were frightened, because outside this place, all that was left was the street.

He reached the locker he had rented many years earlier.

He got out of the car and bent down to open the heavy padlock. The shutter had been down for too long and when he pulled it up to the level of his head, it made a loud metallic clang. The blinding light of the sun stopped at the exact edge of this den, as though it lacked the courage to cross it. Genko took advantage of the time it took for the noise and dust to subside to wipe his grease-stained hands on the sides of his linen jacket and let his eyes grow accustomed to the semi-darkness.

Gradually, a series of shelves reaching up to the ceiling appeared. On one of them there was a row of five grey cardboard boxes, each of them with a label indicating a year, a code and the contents.

He didn't like coming here. He had exiled to this hole the dishonourable proof of his few failures. When it came down to it, a piece of his life was also shut up in these boxes. There were the errors he could no longer make up for, the wasted opportunities and the sins for which nobody could or would forgive him.

But perhaps something could still be done, he told himself. Because he had made up his mind to leave a mark.

He picked a box, the third one, pulled it out of the mosaic formed by the others, lifted the lid and began to look through the documents. At last, he found what he needed.

A thin file that contained just one sheet of paper, only one.

Even so, as he had partly told Linda, this piece of paper could be the key to access hell.

6

The hands. The hands were different. These aren't my hands. These hands belong to somebody else.

And yet she was the one who commanded the movements of the fingers, so there simply had to be an explanation. She hadn't turned to the wall with the large mirror again. She didn't have the courage. But she kept staring at her hands, trying to understand how this could have happened.

Fifteen years, and she hadn't noticed.

'Sam.' Dr Green's voice travelled across a desert of silence to bring her back from these thoughts. 'Sam, you must trust me.'

She shifted her gaze to the tape recorder. Here I am.

'I know everything seems absurd at the moment, but if you let me do my work, we'll put everything back in its place, I can guarantee it.' The man was still sitting by her bed and had given her a little time to process the revelation that she was no longer thirteen years old. 'The treatment is working and your body's getting rid of the drug you've been given. Your memory is already coming back.'

Her eyes drifted to the drip connected to her arm. That slowly flowing liquid contained the answers, the details of a very long nightmare.

I don't know if I want to remember.

Dr Green seemed to have great expectations of her. Strangely, she realised, she didn't want to disappoint him. Was that a good sign? After all, she barely knew him. Yes, it was a good thing. Because every time he told her to trust him, she believed him a little more. 'All right,' she said.

Green looked pleased. 'We'll take it in stages,' he explained. 'A person's memory is an odd mechanism. It's not like this recording, it's not enough just to rewind the tape and listen to it. On the contrary, memories are often recorded one on top of another and get mixed up. Or else the recording is incomplete, or there are gaps or flaws: the mind repairs them in its own way by putting in patches that are actually false memories and can be confusing. That's why it's essential to adopt a few rules so we can tell what's real from what isn't. Is everything clear so far?'

She nodded.

Green waited a few seconds before continuing. 'Now I want you to go back to the labyrinth with me, Sam.'

This plan terrified her. She didn't want to go back there. Never again. She wanted to stay in this comfortable bed, surrounded by the sounds of a fast-paced world outside the door to her room, and the hospital noises mixed with muffled human voices. *Don't take me back to the silence, please.*

'Don't worry, this time I'll be there with you,' he said, trying to reassure her.

'All right . . . Let's go.'

'Something easy to start with. I want you to remember the colour of the walls.'

She closed her eyes. 'Grey,' she replied without hesitation. 'The labyrinth walls are grey.' Their image had flashed in her field of vision.

'What kind of grey? Pale or dark? Is it even or are there, for instance, cracks or damp patches?'

'It's always the same. And the walls are smooth.' She felt as though she were stroking them. She opened her eyes and saw Green writing notes in his pad. She found his presence comforting. Just like the white hospital walls – a white softened by a blue fluorescent light that suggested the bottom of the ocean.

'Do you remember if there are any sounds?'

She shook her head. 'No sound can come into the labyrinth.'

'Smells?'

She tried to identify the sensations that were quickly flowing into her memory. 'Soil . . . There's a smell of wet soil. And mould . . .' She combined all the information: no windows or sounds, a smell of damp. 'It's a cave.'

'Do you mean the labyrinth is underground?'

'Yes . . . I think so . . . Actually, I'm sure of it,' she said finally.

'Who called it that?'

'I did,' she admitted straight away.

'Why?'

She saw herself walking down a long corridor with various rooms leading into it. *It's a place that's well lit, with fluorescent lights on the ceiling. She's not cold but not warm either. She's walking barefoot and exploring her surroundings. Two parallel rows of iron doors. Some are open and lead to empty rooms, while others are locked. She reaches the end of the corridor and turns right: it's the same scene. More doors, more grey rooms. All identical. She keeps walking and comes to a fork. No matter which direction she takes, she ends up at the starting point again. At least so it seems. It's impossible to find her bearings. There doesn't appear to be an exit. Or an entrance. How did I get here?*

'The place where I am has no end. And no beginning.'

'So nobody lives there except you,' Dr Green concluded.

'No, it doesn't look like a house,' she replied categorically. 'I've already told you, it's a labyrinth.'

But Green wanted to know more. 'Does it have a bathroom, for instance?'

It's a small, narrow cupboard. And there's only a toilet bowl. And it stinks. It stinks so badly. You can't even flush it. She doesn't want to use it.

'I don't want to use it,' she said, slightly embarrassed, gauging Green's reaction. 'So I hold it in. I'm always holding it in.'

Except that it's impossible to hold it in for so long. She holds her belly and can already feel the warm drops wetting her pants.

'Why don't you just go ahead and let it out?' Dr Green asked. 'What's stopping you?'

'I'm ashamed,' she admitted.

She's standing and staring at the toilet – the ceramic is yellowed and chipped, with rust trickling down into the hole. The stagnant water has an opaque coating. She's disgusted. She's skipping from one foot to the other, unable to bear it.

'Why are you ashamed?' Then he asked, 'Are you really alone?'

The question sent a chill through her.

She's crouching precariously over the bowl, and her bladder empties with a powerful jet. The sound of pouring urine gets lost in the empty space.

'Can you see or hear anyone?'

'No.'

Green simply took note and made no comment.

Perhaps she'd disappointed him. Perhaps she should have been clearer about what was happening. 'The labyrinth is watching me,' she blurted out and noticed that her statement instantly aroused his attention again. He turned very slightly to the mirror, as though to send a signal to the police officers watching the scene. 'The labyrinth knows everything,' she stressed.

'Are there any cameras?'

She shook her head.

'Then how does it do that? Explain it to me, please . . .'

'It's the cube,' she said, but realised immediately that he didn't follow. 'That was the first game.'

'Tell me about it.'

'It was there when I woke up . . .'

After wandering for hours, searching for help, she goes into one of the rooms and lies down on the floor. Exhausted, she falls asleep straight away. When she opens her eyes, she takes a while to remember where she is – a few seconds of peace before fear kicks in again. And the object is on the floor, a metre away from her face. A familiar sight that belongs to the past. A colourful cube. Green, yellow, red, white, orange and blue.

I know what it's called. A Rubik's Cube, that's what it's called.

'Six sides. Nine squares on each side. Every little square is a different colour.'

'I know,' Green said. 'It was a very popular game when I was a child. Believe it or not, people were crazy about cracking it.'

'I can well believe that,' she replied, because she, too, was going crazy. Except that there was nothing fun about her associations with that object.

Green seemed to notice her anxiety and looked apologetic. 'Please, carry on . . .'

'The colours were all mixed up when I found it.'

What is she meant to do with it? Kill time? It's absurd. She doesn't know where she is or who brought her here. She's frightened and hungry. 'Please, I want to go home.' But nobody answers.

'I sat curled up in a corner, looking at that thing for I don't know how long. I didn't even want to touch it. Something bad would happen if I did, I could feel it. But I kept thinking the same thing, that I was there and couldn't get out. It was an upsetting thought and I couldn't get rid of it.' She paused. 'Or maybe I could.'

'So what did you do?'

She looked up at him, her eyes filled with tears. 'I picked up the cube.'

She studies it, then starts to turn the multicoloured sides. Anything to do away with the problem of time that won't pass. Her mind won't focus, distracted by fear. But gradually the pressure relents and her terror takes a step back – withdrawing, but still close by. She can now keep it at a distance. All her attention is on this combination of colours, and a few minutes later she manages to complete one of the sides, the orange one. She puts it back on the floor and fear comes back to stalk her. She looks at the object. She has corrected part of the imperfection. The finished side is order and cleanliness. It makes her feel safe. There must be an explanation for what is happening to her. And at that moment, her heightened senses pick up on something.

A change.

It doesn't take long for her mind to decipher the new signal. A smell. That, too, like the cube, is familiar. She gets up from the corner and goes out into the corridor. She looks around. Nobody there. She starts to search, cautiously. She lets herself be guided by her sense of smell but is afraid it's just a hallucination. But it's not: it's for real. She reaches the entrance to one of the rooms. The door is ajar and she pushes it open with the palm of her right hand. There's a paper bag in the middle of it.

McDonald's.

'A burger, Coke and fries,' she said, then added for Green's benefit, 'Lots of fries.'

It doesn't occur to her to be prudent. Hunger makes the decision for her. She rushes to the food and wolfs it down. She doesn't ask herself how it got here or who bought it. She's learning her first lesson.

Survival.

It's only once she's had enough that she begins to rationalise what's happened. She goes back to the room where she left the cube: she must carry on solving the puzzle. She strolls down the long corridors, her head bowed over the game. With some difficulty, she has completed another side – the green one – and is working hard on the third – the red one. *Tackling three different colours is far from easy. She walks past one of the rooms and notices something out of the corner of her eye. She goes back and freezes.*

The prize for completing the second side of the cube is a mattress with blankets and a pillow.

In a short space of time, she's made huge progress: her stomach is full and she doesn't have to sleep on the floor any more. But finishing the third side is harder than she thought.

'I think days went by and I realised I couldn't finish the red side. I wasn't as clever as I thought. Meanwhile, no food and no water.'

'So what happened?' Green asked. 'How did you survive?'

She's lying on the mattress. Her clothes have become loose on her and she's got hardly any strength left. When was the last time she had a drink or some food? She spends most of her time sleeping and having nightmares. Sometimes, she doesn't even know if she's asleep or awake. What torments her most isn't hunger as such, because it doesn't manifest itself as a craving for food. It's sudden stomach cramps, as though her belly was trying to come out and was digging a route inside her.

A little later, perhaps a couple of days later, the pangs stop. But then it's worse, because that's when the thirst starts. Nobody's ever told her that thirst is worse than hunger. Because it makes you lose your mind. Because as you feel yourself drying up, all you can think of is drink. And you're ready to tear at your own veins with your teeth and suck your own blood just so you can quench this need . . .

She knows there's a way to put an end to this craving but she hasn't applied it yet. She finds the very thought of it too revolting.

But she has no choice if she wants to survive.

And so, with what little strength she has left, she drags herself to the cupboard. She looks at the smelly, slimy slop in the dirty bowl. First of all, she puts a hand into it and tests the texture. Then she shuts her eyes and brings it up, while the prospect of it makes her retch. Don't think about it. You mustn't think about it. Like when she used to scrape her knee as a child, and if she concentrated, the pain would go away. Now she must forget about the taste. So she sinks her mouth into her cupped hand and starts to suck. The liquid filters through her lips and teeth, and she swallows it without holding it in her mouth ... When she goes back to her room, she feels dirty inside. She's still alive, but this isn't a relief because she knows she'll have to do it again.

Meanwhile, the cube is on her pillow, staring at her.

But she's so angry that she grabs it and starts taking apart the sides she has completed ...

'I was immediately sorry and started to cry. I was at the end of my tether and tried to put all the colours back where they'd been.'

'I'm sorry,' Green said. He seemed to mean it.

'I managed to finish only the green side, then I fell asleep. When I opened my eyes, there was a basket in the room, with cold soup and warm fizzy water.'

The doctor nodded. 'And how did you account for this gift?'

She corrected him. 'It wasn't a gift. Whenever I needed something basic, like food, clean underwear or a tooth-brush, all I had to do was finish the first side. I couldn't see the point in forcing me to play that stupid game, since completing just one side was relatively easy. Then I understood.'

She closed her eyes and a tear rolled down her cheek, sliding under the oxygen mask. 'If I'd completed all six sides, it would have let me go.'

'*It*?'

'The labyrinth,' she replied.

'Is that what happened? You completed the game and the labyrinth set you free?'

She shook her head. She was crying now. 'I never got past the third side.'

7

For the world, the news item of the day was Samantha Andretti's reappearance. For Bruno Genko, on the other hand, it was the fact that the end of the world hadn't come to him yet.

As he drove his Saab with the windows down, the radio was broadcasting 'Take the Money and Run' by the Steve Miller Band. However desperate his situation, hearing this track cheered him up. But not for long. The song wasn't being played for him but for those who could still picture their future. Whereas Genko was stuck in the present, and would soon become the past. Many people think that a dying man regrets all the things he hasn't done or that he's postponed doing in life. Instead of which, the hardest thing for him was to no longer be able to enjoy small pleasures, like a carefree song on the radio.

Because every time was the last time.

Brimming with venom, Genko turned off the radio and focused on the road. He'd left the city to go inland, to the swamp area. As he gradually drove away from the coast, the heat became less oppressive. But he realised that, even though he felt sad, he was no longer afraid.

Samantha had changed everything.

In fact, the extra time granted him without his asking for it was not a gift – rather, it was torture. That was why he needed something to make this pause meaningful, before the inevitable finale.

One last task ... While he still had air in his lungs, he thought, recalling Linda's words.

On the passenger seat next to him, the wind kept blowing open the flap of the file he had just taken out of storage. The document it contained was his only hope.

It wouldn't be long now before he reached his destination. He wondered if the profiler dealing with Sam had already revealed to her how much the world had changed during her absence. He wondered if she'd enquired after her family. Had they told her that the grief had been too much for her mother to bear? Had anyone found the courage to tell her that a nasty illness had taken her away six years earlier?

The patient admitted to Saint Catherine's had been officially identified as Samantha Andretti partly thanks to a DNA sample stored in the missing girl's file. Without that, the police would have had a big problem on their hands, since after her mother's death, Sam's father had moved away to build a new life for himself and had left no record of his whereabouts. They still hadn't been able to locate him to tell him his only daughter was alive. And the news, although constantly repeated on television, had obviously not reached him.

It was crucial for Genko that the man not reappear in the hours to come.

As he drove along the motorway, he passed only two other cars, heading in the opposite direction. Once the road penetrated more deeply into the swamp area, Genko no longer saw a soul. The strip of asphalt seemed suspended in mid-air, because everything around it was only green marshland, as still as the low vegetation that covered it. Then he went through a dense forest of dead birches, their darkened trunks mirrored in the putrid water, the reflections performing a spectral dance on the surface.

Genko noticed the first patrol car in the distance, one of many roadblocks surrounding the area where Samantha had been found. There were two officers inside, one of whom got out and raised a traffic sign, motioning to him from a distance to turn back. But Genko drove on. In order to avoid causing unnecessary alarm, he slowed down and kept his hands on the wheel in full view. As he drew close to the police officers, he waited for the one with the sign to approach the window of the Saab.

'You can't come through here,' he said in a tone that brooked no argument. 'You have to turn back immediately.'

'I know, officer. But it's important, please let me explain.' He knew that a compliant tone was music to the ears of law-enforcement agents. Genko hated himself for all the arse-licking he had to do with the police.

'I don't care about your explanations,' the man replied, moving a hand to the holster at his hip. 'I suggest you do as I say.'

He was a tough guy, so Genko had to play it gently. 'I'm a private investigator, my name's Genko. I can show you my licence, if you like, it's in my wallet.'

'Nobody's allowed through,' the uniformed man answered stubbornly.

'But I don't want to go through,' he replied, wrongfooting the policeman for a moment. 'I'm here to speak to officers Bauer and Delacroix. Could you call them for me, please?'

'I don't think they'd want to be disturbed.'

'I'm sorry, officer, but I beg to differ.' Elaborate words sometimes helped confuse those with limited cognitive skills. 'I think I have information on the Samantha Andretti case which the officers I've just mentioned will no doubt find very useful.' Then he nodded at the file on the seat. 'I have with me some documents I feel they should see straight away.'

The man put out his hand. 'Give them to me, I'll make sure they get them.'

'I can't, they're confidential.'

'If they're important, you have to give them to me.'

'I'm telling you again, I can't do that.'

The officer was running out of patience. 'You know, I could arrest you for obstruction of justice.'

'No, you couldn't,' Genko said, casting off the disguise of the mild-mannered citizen and giving him a stern look. 'The law says that a private investigator in possession of material useful for solving a police matter is personally responsible for it until he can pass it on to the authorities in charge of the investigation. So, with all due respect, I can't just give it to the first officer I come across. You do understand that, don't you?'

The officer said nothing for a few seconds, without losing his military air. Then he went to the patrol car.

*

There was a long, silent quarter of an hour during which Genko smoked a couple of cigarettes, leaning on the bonnet of the Saab while the officers stared at him from across the road. The only sound was the marsh cicadas.

Then the horizon began to alter its shape at the end of the road.

Shortly afterwards, the front of a brown saloon car emerged from the hot, shimmering air. It was like a mirage. Although one couldn't yet hear the noise of the engine, the car was coming very fast, raising a cloud of dust in its wake.

The people inside it must be pretty pissed off, Genko guessed.

The car braked abruptly and two solid-looking men in shirts and ties got out. One of them, a blond, looked straight out of a magazine and the other one, a black man, had an angelic face – like a typical pair of cops in a TV film, Genko thought when he saw them.

'I don't know whether to kick you up the arse or smash your face in,' Bauer said immediately. 'If you've collected evidence without consulting us, I can throw you into jail without even going through a judge.'

Delacroix was happy to let his colleague do the talking, content with monitoring the situation, ready to intervene. The two patrol officers were watching the scene, amused. Genko knew what they were thinking: now it's up to you, private eye.

Genko displayed the most conciliatory of smiles. 'Calm down, guys. Nobody's taken the initiative here, OK? I'm just doing my duty as a law-abiding citizen.' He knew how annoying a smart-arse attitude could be to a policeman, but he had to make them believe he'd got his hands on something big.

'Genko, I suggest you take out what you have, give it to us and get out,' Delacroix intervened. 'This day's awful enough without you adding to it.'

'Please,' he pretended to beg.

'We haven't got time to waste.'

'I'm only asking for five minutes.'

Bauer's face was scarlet from anger and bathed in sweat. 'You'd better hope it's something important.'

Genko stepped to the passenger side of the Saab, put a hand through the open window and picked up the folder from the seat. On his way back towards them, he opened it and took out the sheet of paper it contained. He handed it to Delacroix.

'What's that supposed to be?' Delacroix asked contemptuously, without even looking.

'It's a contract.'

The two policemen seemed taken aback, and they looked down and read the few lines.

Genko decided to get straight to the crux of the matter. 'Fifteen years ago, while you cops were hunting for butterflies, Samantha Andretti's parents came to me to help them shed some light on the disappearance of their only daughter.'

He could still remember meeting them in the booth of a crowded diner, one Monday morning. Sam had been missing for weeks and they hadn't slept for several nights. They were holding hands. They explained they'd got his contact details from a policeman in the bureau. He had implied that if they didn't try other avenues in addition to the official one, there might not be any hope of finding out what had happened to their girl.

The compassionate policeman had been telling the truth: the chances of solving a missing persons case grew increasingly slim as the hours went by. After three days, they were practically nil. Unless, of course, there was a lead. But there were no clues with Samantha, no witnesses. She seemed to have evaporated in the bleak sun of a cold February morning on her way to school.

Genko didn't deal with finding missing children, and besides, it had been too long now. It had been weeks, the evidence had been compromised and people's memories were vague. He'd tried to tell them this but they'd insisted. 'We know you're very good at what you do, we've had excellent references,' Sam's father had said. 'We beg you, don't leave us alone like this, not knowing.'

One of the basic rules of private investigation is not to empathise with your clients. It sounded cynical, but Genko knew perfectly well that it was essential not to let himself be influenced by the emotional reasons that drive a client to request an investigation. Hatred and pity are contagious. They often constitute an obstacle to reason, which has to remain clear and impartial. At times, feelings actually become a danger.

There was a guy who had stolen money from his boss in order to pay for treatment for his wife who had cancer. Genko had tracked him down but, moved by compassion, had granted him time to get the stolen sum back and return it to its lawful owner. Except that he had underestimated the thief's determination. In order to save the woman he loved, he hadn't hesitated to cheat him and flee again.

Genko was aware of running a serious risk with the Andrettis. That was why he had accepted the case but only with clear boundaries. 'You'll pay me double my usual fee, in advance. You won't call me to ask how the investigation is going and I'll be under no obligation to give you regular updates. I'll contact you when I'm ready to communicate something. If you don't hear from me within a month, you'll know I haven't found anything.'

They'd both seemed confused by these conditions. Genko was hoping he'd put them off. Instead, much to his surprise, they'd signed the contract without a word – the contract which, years later, was now before Bauer and Delacroix's eyes.

Bauer gave Genko a fierce look. 'What the fuck does this mean?'

'It means that according to this paper, I've been instructed to follow the case.'

'This is an old contract,' Delacroix said calmly, holding it out. 'It's been too long.'

But Genko didn't take it back. 'You're joking, right? It doesn't have a use-by date: the assignment is valid until revoked.'

Bauer was about to attack him again, but Delacroix stopped him with a hand gesture. 'Well, since Samantha Andretti has been found I don't see there's any more need of you. But if you want to keep looking for her, be my guest.'

At this quip, his blond colleague calmed down and burst out laughing. Delacroix tried once again to return the sheet of paper.

But Genko ignored his gesture again. 'The newspapers are saying that Sam was found by chance two nights ago by a car patrolling the area. How come I hear it was because of an anonymous tip-off?'

Bauer's smile suddenly vanished. No reaction registered on Delacroix's face, though.

'I can understand that the police might be unpopular for not having looked for the girl properly back then,' Genko said, driving the message home. 'But actually taking the credit for finding her and turning two passing officers into heroes frankly seems a bit much.' As he said this, he looked at the two officers by the patrol car – hearing him refer to them in this manner, they looked away, embarrassed.

'We're under no obligation to confirm anything or to share confidential information with you.' While maintaining his aplomb, Delacroix was trying to make it clear to him that the joke was going too far.

'That's where you're wrong,' Genko replied, indicating the contract. 'In article eleven, section b, Samantha's parents gave me the mandate to represent them with the police, and even appointed me their daughter's guardian in the absence of other relatives.' The clause contained the stipulation that, should he find the girl, then underage, he would be responsible for her safety until he had brought her back home. This had never come about, but the technicality could now serve a different purpose.

'The agreement is no longer valid,' Bauer protested with his customary vehemence. 'Samantha is of age. Besides, her mother's dead and her father can't be traced.'

'Even if she's no longer underage, we must establish if she's of sound mind. Frankly, I doubt it, since she's in a state of shock . . . So that just leaves her father. But for as long as you haven't tracked him down, and for as long as he hasn't personally revoked my assignment, my duty is to represent the needs of my client, Samantha Andretti, to the best of my ability.'

Delacroix was less impulsive than his colleague and much more pragmatic. 'We'll go and have the contract declared void by a judge. I don't suppose it'll take much to persuade him: he'll just need to take one look at you.'

It was true, and Genko knew it: a judge would mistake his good intentions for an attempt to profit from the case after fifteen years. So he pretended to give it some thought, although he already knew his next move. 'All right, guys, in that case, let me propose a deal.'

The two men said nothing, just waited.

'I have in my archives a nice thick folder with the results of my investigation fifteen years ago.' He was hoping that such a well-constructed lie might win the two men over. Actually, all the boasted-about file contained was the sheet of paper in front of them. Because the Samantha Andretti case was the most troublesome case he'd ever had. Like the police, Genko hadn't found anything.

There's no human action that doesn't leave traces. Especially when it's a criminal act.

It was a lesson in its own right in the training of every private investigator. It might even be said that the profession depended on this simple premise, which came as a pair with another golden rule.

There's no such thing as the perfect crime, only an imperfect investigation.

That was why, of the few failures in Bruno Genko's career, the Andretti case was the most resounding. Because, in all that time, he had even got to the point of doubting that there was an abductor.

The monster's most successful trick had been to convince everyone that he didn't exist.

'Are you offering us an exchange?' Bauer asked. 'Did I get that right? You give us your file and we let you stick your nose into our investigation – is that what you want?'

'No,' Delacroix said, correcting him, having sensed the nature of the deal before his colleague had. 'What he's offering is to help us in saving our arses . . .'

Genko nodded. 'My file contains the statements of witnesses never questioned by the police, clues that were never gathered and a series of important leads that were inexplicably ignored at the time. In other words, evidence that the bureau dropped the case too soon.' He'd laid his cards on the table. 'It would be a real shame if the media got their hands on these papers. On the other hand, as Samantha's guardian, I'm obliged to use any means I can to shed light on the shady aspects of this unfortunate business.'

The two police officers clammed up in a stiff silence.

Genko knew that it was never advisable to get cops' backs up, because sooner or later they'd make you pay for it, and Bauer and Delacroix's attitude didn't bode well. It was sheer madness asking to take part in the police investigation. Apart from being legally inadmissible, such a request would bring him nothing but trouble, if nothing else because it was based on a bluff. That was why he decided to reopen negotiations. 'I have no intention of disclosing the material in my possession,' he assured them calmly. 'I know perfectly well that if I did, I'd have nothing to stop you from slaughtering me. I'm not that stupid . . . All I ask is a favour, then I'll disappear, I promise.'

'I wouldn't give him anything,' Bauer said, addressing his colleague. 'As a matter of fact, I'd like to see if this arsehole really has the balls to spill the beans to the press.' No doubt he was already enjoying the prospect of getting his hands on the detective.

Except that you can't do anything to me, Genko thought, staring into his bovine eyes. This was one of the few advantages of being about to die. An imminent end is like a superpower. It makes one invulnerable.

'All right,' Delacroix said unexpectedly. 'What do you want?'

Genko turned to him. 'I want to hear the recording of the anonymous call.'

8

The base camp from which the search for Samantha Andretti's prison was being coordinated had been set up right in the middle of the swamp area, in a clearing with the skeletal remains of an abandoned service station. Every year, the marshes would claim a substantial portion of the soil, driving away anybody trying to challenge the hostile environment.

Even with the police presence, Genko thought, it was a gloomy place.

When he got out of the car and looked around, he was immediately bewildered by the frantic to-ing and fro-ing of technicians and police officers coming in and out of tents and caravans.

Several teams of searchers were busy in the swampland, using amphibian equipment and sniffer dogs. In addition to the forces in the camp, there were groups of specialists analysing every collected clue in mobile labs. Where petrol pumps had once been, there was now a helicopter about to take off again to search the area from above.

Bauer and Delacroix, who had driven him here, got out of the car and came up to him.

'You know how lucky you are to be here, don't you?' Bauer reminded him. 'Police officers shouldn't get involved with filthy blackmailers.'

Genko smiled and was about to respond with a quip when they were interrupted.

'Delacroix!' an angry voice called out.

Genko turned and saw a man in a navy blue suit and a tie approaching with a far from friendly expression. He had a large shaggy dog at his side.

'I'll only be a second,' Delacroix said, and walked towards the stranger.

Bauer pulled Genko by his jacket sleeve. 'Let's go,' he said.

As they walked away, Genko kept an eye on what was happening between the other two men.

'Nobody answers my calls any more,' the stranger was complaining. 'When are you going to start looking for her?'

Genko wondered for a moment whom he meant. Look for whom? Samantha Andretti had been found. But the dog started to bark and drowned out their voices.

'Quiet, Hitchcock,' his master commanded.

Genko slowed down, watching the conversation, which was growing more heated.

Meanwhile, Bauer was waiting for him on the steps of a caravan. 'Well, are you coming?'

The inside of the caravan had been equipped with highly sophisticated devices which at this moment were in the process of analysing the recording of the anonymous call. The audio file was split into different coloured graphs on the computer screens. Four technicians were trying to detect sounds buried in the background noise, in the hope of finding some clue as to the identity of the man who had made the call.

Any of the spikes in the graph could conceal another voice or the tolling of a bell or, if they were really lucky, even a name. The aim was to discover the location of the call and identify possible witnesses who might provide a description of the stranger.

Genko had been looking around for five minutes, arms crossed, unable to keep still on the swivel chair. Bauer was standing there, keeping an eye on him, evidently annoyed by his constant fidgeting. But neither of them said a word until Delacroix returned.

'I'm sorry,' he said, dripping with sweat, as he came into the vehicle. He helped himself to a glass of water from the dispenser and turned to his colleague. 'Have you already explained it to him?'

'No, not yet.'

Delacroix took a chair and sat down opposite Genko. 'Naturally, what we're going to tell you has to be confidential.' He took a sheet of paper and a pen from Bauer. 'If a single word of this gets out, I'll come straight after you.'

'In that case I'd better hope none of the police officers around here take bribes from the media,' Genko said to provoke them, before signing the form and returning it to Bauer.

'The mobile phone that was used had been stolen,' Delacroix began. 'After the call it was either switched off or destroyed, so it's impossible to track down the user.'

'Whereas Samantha Andretti was about twelve kilometres

64

away from the unit that picked up the call,' Bauer added. 'Which means that whoever found her had ample time to decide whether or not to call the police.'

'So you don't think it was the abductor?' Genko asked, although he had already discarded the theory that the monster could have been moved to an act of pity after keeping her confined and brutalising her in heaven knows how many ways for fifteen years.

'We've ruled that out because the voice frequency is that of a young person, who would have been barely a teenager at the time of the abduction,' Delacroix explained. 'But it could be an accomplice who had repented or else was afraid of being discovered.'

There were many options on the table, Genko thought. He had the impression that the investigation was at a standstill. The two officers were being quite cooperative, and he wondered whether it was just a tactic to conceal something important. 'Can I hear the call now?'

Bauer gave one of the technicians a sign and the man played the recording. The loudspeakers immediately diffused a hiss, interrupted by the usual rhythmical sound of an incoming call.

'Police emergency,' an operator replied.

'Um . . . I'd like to speak to the police . . .' a hesitant male voice said.

'What is it regarding, sir?' the operator replied calmly. 'Tell me what kind of emergency it is and I'll put you through to the police.'

There was a brief silence. 'There's a naked woman, I think she might be injured. Her leg might be broken and she needs help.'

The operator was trained not to panic, so she maintained a neutral approach. *'Has she had an accident?'*

'I don't know but I don't think so ... There were no cars.'

'Do you know this woman? Is she a relative?'

'No.'

'Do you know her name?'

'No ...'

'Where is this person?'

'Um ... On Route 57, I'm not sure where exactly. It's the road that goes through the swamp, northbound.'

'Is she conscious?'

'Yes, I think so, she looked conscious ...'

'Are you with her now?'

Silence.

'Sir, did you hear me? Are you with this woman now?'

There was a moment's hesitation. *'No.'*

'Could you give me your details, please?'

The man grew impatient. *'Look, I've told you about it, the rest is none of my business.'* The call was suddenly disconnected. He'd hung up.

The technician stopped the recording. Bauer and Delacroix turned to Genko as though to make it clear to him that now he'd got what he wanted they had nothing more to say to one another.

But Genko hadn't had enough. 'If it's not the abductor or an accomplice, why didn't he come forward?' He'd already asked himself that same question. 'Why stay out of the limelight?'

'If we knew that,' Bauer replied, 'we certainly wouldn't tell you.'

Genko ignored him, because Delacroix suddenly looked

66

interested in his opinion. 'She was found in the middle of the night,' he continued. 'And who goes to the swamp in the middle of the night? And with a stolen phone?' Only two categories of people really came under suspicion, and those present in the caravan had reached the same conclusion as Genko. 'Drug dealers and poachers.'

'Somebody with something to hide,' Delacroix confirmed, 'and who's better off not telling the operator his name.'

Genko, however, was only partly persuaded by this. He'd picked up on something else. 'Can I listen to the recording again?' he asked, surprising everyone.

'Why?' Bauer snarled, unwilling to make any more concessions.

Genko turned directly to Delacroix and opened his arms. Delacroix was more reasonable and gave the technician a nod.

The recording started again from the beginning.

This time, Genko tried to memorise the stranger's voice as best he could, picking up on every detail, inflexion and texture.

Local accent, the typical gravelly voice of a heavy smoker, a definite subsidence in the palatal consonants.

He wasn't wrong. There was something strange about the way he spoke. A vibration that no technology could have ever picked up on. It wasn't just a fear of being discovered because he was guilty of illegal activities, like drug dealing or poaching. It was something else, Genko had no doubt about it.

It was terror.

9

'How are you?'

'Fine.'

'Really?'

'Nothing's changed since this afternoon.' At nightfall, crickets had taken over from cicadas in the swamp. The heat was still unbearable, but there was a full moon. The Saab was parked at the side of the road, hidden by the long foliage of a willow. Genko had taken advantage of the break to call Linda.

'Have you had something to eat at least?'

'Not yet, but I promise I will.' His friend's concern was a pleasant novelty for Genko: nobody had ever taken care of him. Perhaps because he'd always kept everyone at arm's length. He'd never regretted his choice, not even after learning from the doctors that he had no way out. No soul-searching for Bruno Genko. No regrets. Only one thing he felt remorse over.

'What's in the safe in Room 115 of the Ambrus Hotel?' Linda unexpectedly asked.

Genko said nothing, wishing he could end the call there and then. Linda, though, had no intention of dropping the subject.

'I've been thinking about it all day ... If I'm supposed to destroy it, then you should tell me: what's in the sealed envelope?'

Genko put one hand on the steering wheel while holding the phone with the other: it had suddenly become very heavy. 'Nobody's forcing you to do it,' he said with unusual harshness. 'Only I thought I could trust you.'

'I know the room number and the combination: I could go there now and open the envelope,' she replied stubbornly.

'That envelope has nothing to do with you.'

'Why do I get the feeling there's a lot you're hiding from me?'

Because it scares me, it's true. But he didn't tell her that. Instead, he closed his eyes and took a deep breath. He realised that Linda was starting to cry.

'You saved my life, do you have any idea what that means? And now I can't do the same for you. Can you imagine how I feel?'

No, he definitely couldn't imagine it. Feelings had never been his strong point. At that moment, a black van drove past his window. Genko immediately looked at his watch and made a mental note that it was 9.06 p.m. 'I have to go,' he said into the phone.

'For as long as there's air in your lungs ...' Linda reminded him with a sniff.

He imagined her, wrapped in her silk kimono, curled

up on the bed, in the half-light of a candle. 'Of course,' he said gently and hung up. Then he looked up, past the windscreen.

A hundred metres or so in front of him stood the Duran, a bar with neon signs that promised billiards and satellite TV for watching sporting events. There were twenty or so vehicles in the car park, mostly Jeeps and pick-up trucks. It looked like a full house.

Genko had spent the last three hours monitoring the situation. Car stakeouts were the most difficult part of his job. They could go on for weeks. In films, private investigators always had a crossword and a flask of coffee to pass the time. But true professionals knew that even the briefest moment of distraction could invalidate hours and hours of surveillance, and that caffeine is a diuretic.

Patience wasn't enough; you needed discipline. Because the problem wasn't boredom but routine. Having the same scene before your eyes for such a long time could create a dangerous habit.

Genko never imagined he would waste part of the time his sick heart was granting him on a stakeout. The hollow in the front seat of the Saab was proof of how much of his life he'd wasted waiting in his car. He'd once been assigned to track down a debtor. Unlike the creditors who had hired him, he was convinced the man had never left town. So he'd taken up position outside his home and for twenty long days had done nothing but watch his windows and front door. The man's family members came and went at all hours of the day and night, but there was no sign of him. So he decided to flush him out. Human beings are all motivated by two things to the point of losing their minds over them.

Sex and money. All it took was for him to make a phone call to the debtor's wife, pretend to be an official from a foreign embassy and tell her that her husband had inherited a sum of money from a distant relative who'd emigrated abroad many years earlier, but that it was necessary for the beneficiary to go to the office in person in order to accept the bequest and complete the usual forms. An hour later, the debtor left his house.

While he was recalling this, the black van that had driven past him a little earlier came back, heading in the opposite direction. This time, it slowed down, almost stopping, outside the Duran's car park. A few seconds later, it sped up and drove away. As it passed the Saab, Genko checked the time: 9.31 p.m.

According to his calculations, he had twenty-five minutes at most.

He parked outside the Duran, got out of the car and headed to the entrance of the bar.

As soon as he stepped inside, at least thirty pairs of eyes shifted towards him and examined him with suspicion. It was understandable. With his pale linen suit and his dejected expression, Genko stuck out amid checked shirts, boots and baseball caps.

There was a grey cloud of cigarette smoke hovering above the bar counter. Every so often, you could hear the sound of billiard balls colliding over the folk songs streaming out of the stereo.

To put a name to the stranger who'd found Samantha Andretti, the police were bound to look among the men who usually hung out in the swampland. During the meeting with Bauer and Delacroix, it had been established that it could only be a drug dealer or a poacher. Genko's money was on the latter, partly because for drug dealers, the risk of being discovered and getting several years in jail wasn't usually worth any woman's safety.

'What can I get you?' a young waitress asked. She was wearing an army green vest and was covered in tattoos.

'A wheat beer and a tequila.' Genko didn't sit down as he waited to be served, but went and stood in front of the large screen, which was broadcasting a football match. The sound was muted, so he could pretend to be interested in the game and at the same time assess what was happening around him and, above all, give the other patrons a chance to get used to his presence. The waitress brought his drinks soon afterwards. Genko immediately downed the shot of tequila, paid the girl, and started walking around the bar, holding his beer.

He could sense the hostility of the other customers: people of the swamp, accustomed to the harshness of a difficult life and not particularly inclined towards good manners, especially where strangers were concerned. He took a stroll around the billiard table and watched a couple of shots, just so he could study the players' faces better.

Besides being the only place of entertainment in the area, the Duran was a hangout for poachers and illegal fishermen. Genko could in no way be certain that the man he was looking for was in this room, but the black van that had twice driven past the bar was practically confirmation that he was on the right track.

'We've ruled that out because the voice frequency is that of a young person, who would have been barely a teenager at the time of the abduction,' Delacroix had said. So Genko began to discard all those present who were over thirty-five. That left about ten people, but that was still too many. To narrow it down even further, he walked past a few of them who were chatting, and kept an ear open, listening for a familiar sound in their voices.

He'd listened to the telephone recording only twice and wasn't sure he would be able to recognise the man he was looking for by ear alone. But a voice could reveal many things: a person's origin, habits and even appearance.

Local accent, typical gravelly voice of a heavy smoker, a definite subsidence in the palatal consonants, Genko recapitulated. But the first two traits were practically irrelevant, since these were people born and bred in the area and the percentage of smokers here was very high. Moreover, the third wasn't an anomaly: the speech impairment could be caused by missing teeth or simply by the fact that the man had been chewing gum while talking on the phone.

Genko turned to one of the tables by the window and had a revelation.

There was a sturdy young man sitting there, alone and apart, looking out of the window, lost in thought. On first impression, he looked under thirty. There was a bottle of beer and a half-empty plate of fries in front of him. He was drawing patterns in his ketchup with a toothpick.

It was his hands that had attracted Bruno's attention: they were entirely covered in old blisters. His skin looked like melted wax. A burn, he thought. There was an even longer scar on his neck, stretching to the bottom of his face, and he had tried to conceal the burn with patches of sparse beard.

Genko decided to bet everything on him.

'May I sit down?' he said, putting his glass on the table.

The young man looked up. 'Do we know each other?' he asked in a gravelly voice. It wasn't the tobacco and too many cigarettes, Genko mentally corrected himself, but the effect of breathing in smoke in a fire. This explained the definite subsidence in the palatal consonants he'd noticed in the recorded voice. The scar probably extended into the mouth as far as the larynx.

He's breathed in flames, Genko thought. Only kerosene could do that to a man. And poachers used it to start fires and flush out ducks from the bushes.

Genko sat down even though he'd not received permission. Before the young man could protest, he stopped him dead with a few specific words. 'The police know it was you who made the call.'

'What the—' the young man snapped.

Genko didn't give him time to respond. 'They're going to arrest you and charge you with being an accessory to that woman's abduction, you do realise that, don't you?'

The young man didn't reply. He was dumbfounded.

From his reaction, Genko knew he'd hit the bull's eye. 'A black van has already driven past a couple of times, which means the Duran is under police surveillance. I wouldn't be surprised if this place was crawling with mics: they have a recording of the call and they have equipment that can identify a voice in the middle of a crowd. If I'm right and they know you're in the bar, then the cops are already in position around here and will burst in any minute now.' He looked towards the exit.

The young man did the same and the mere prospect was enough to petrify him.

'When the unmarked van drives past out there,' Genko said, pointing at the window, 'that'll be the signal and all hell will break loose.' Then he checked his watch. 'We have less than ten minutes.'

The young man was as dazed as a boxer who's just received a volley of punches right in the face.

Good. He mustn't give him time to think.

'I don't care about your name – only in what you have to say.'

'What do you want from me?' the young man replied, and once again stared out of the window, in a state of shock

Genko had to imply that he was his only hope, and he was succeeding. 'I need to ask you a few simple questions, and all you have to do is tell me if what I say tallies more or less with how it all went.'

The young man with the wax-like face turned to look at him with bewildered eyes.

'Two nights ago you were coming back from a hunting trip in the swamp when you noticed a woman in the middle of the road.'

The young man nodded.

'You stopped and got out of the car.'

'The pick-up truck,' he corrected him, although it wasn't necessary.

'All right, the pick-up truck,' Genko said. 'You spoke to her, she was upset.'

'She kept begging me to stay with her.'

Genko pictured the scene for a moment. He saw Samantha – naked, vulnerable, frightened – clinging to the legs of the first human being she'd seen in a long time, who wasn't a monster. For all she knew, the world outside her jail might have ended some time ago.

'She was covered in scratches and had a broken leg,' the young man continued. 'I thought she might have had an accident.'

'An accident?' Genko repeated to make it clear he wasn't buying it. 'Then tell me, why did you drive away and leave her in that condition?'

'I have a criminal record,' he said, looking down. 'I didn't want any trouble.'

He wasn't just lying, Genko thought. He was ashamed. 'What kind of accident is it where you break a leg and end up without your clothes?' He remembered the dark note he'd heard in the man's voice on the recording.

Terror.

'What you're saying is bullshit,' he said. 'The truth is, you wet yourself.' He felt strangely sorry in uttering these words. With a face like a piece of burnt toast, he couldn't have had an easy life.

The young man looked around, frightened. 'Look, I didn't—'

With every minute rushing by irrevocably, Genko couldn't afford the luxury of compassion. 'You got scared because the woman told you someone was chasing her.' The young man said nothing so Genko thought he'd guessed right.

But then he shook his head.

'There was someone chasing her, though, wasn't there?' Genko insisted, to be sure he'd understood correctly, the adrenaline rising inside him.

More silence. But this time, his hesitation was as good as a confession.

Genko hadn't expected this. Was the young man really claiming he'd seen the face of the monster who had abducted Samantha Andretti? The man whose identity had been a mystery for fifteen years? Genko could feel his sick heart beating wildly and hoped it wouldn't let him down just at this moment. He had to control his emotions, try to keep calm and manage this new situation as best he could. 'Would you be able to describe him?' As he asked, he took a pen from the pocket of his jacket, then pulled out the medical report, the only piece of paper he had within easy reach.

The young man seemed agitated.

'Don't worry, we'll take it in stages,' Genko said, ready to write everything down. 'Did he have long or short hair?'

'I don't know ...'

'Was he tall, short, slim or fat? What was he wearing?'

The young man shrugged but avoided his eyes.

Meanwhile, time was flying, flying too fast. Genko would shortly have to leave the bar if he didn't want to find himself in the middle of a police blitz.

'How can you not remember? Don't you realise the police are going to kick the shit out of you?' He sensed that the young man was still frightened. But it wasn't the police that had this effect on him. His eyes filled with tears. Terror, Genko repeated to himself. He had to know what had happened – he simply had to. 'Was the man armed?'

'I don't know ...'

'Because you had a weapon, didn't you?' A simple deduction, since he was a poacher.

'The shotgun,' he confessed in a whisper.

'So, if the worst came to the worst, you could have defended yourself. Why did you run away, then?'

The young man had locked himself in an obstinate silence.

Genko checked the time. The ten minutes were almost

over. He was no longer sure he could stay here, but he couldn't leave without knowing. 'Listen, you've already abandoned a wretched woman who was begging you for help, and for that alone you deserve to rot in jail for twenty years. Don't do it again . . . Did you think you could cleanse your conscience with an anonymous phone call? Even the worst criminal never forgets he's a man, and trust me, I've met quite a few. What I'm offering you is probably your last chance to put things right.'

'You won't believe me if I tell you . . .' The young man looked up at him, imploring mercy.

'What wouldn't I believe? For fuck's sake tell me.' He was running out of patience – three minutes: outside the window, the road was still deserted.

'He came out of the woods. I knew he was looking for the woman. When he saw us, he froze.'

'And then?'

'Nothing, he stood there, staring at us. He made my blood curdle.'

'Why?'

'Because the guy . . .'

'What was the matter with this guy?'

But the young man was evasive. 'I couldn't tell the police emergency number: they would have thought I was crazy and nobody would have come to help the woman.'

What was he talking about? What couldn't he say? As he tried to find a way to draw out the information, Genko saw a black patch driving past the Duran's window.

The unmarked van. Time up.

Genko leaped to his feet, intending to leave as soon as he could. He was about to put the medical report and the pen back in his pocket when the young man grabbed him by the arm.

'Are you here to help me?' he asked, his lip trembling.

'No,' he confessed after having lied to him. Disappointment and fear appeared on the young poacher's face but Genko didn't care any more. He glanced at the door of the Duran, did a mental calculation of how long it would take him to reach it before the bar lights suddenly went off and the sound of crashing glass preceded the blinding roar of stun grenades used by special forces to knock out likely enemies and neutralise any potential threat.

'It was a rabbit.'

Genko was about to disengage his arm from the young man's grip when he stopped. 'What?' he said, surprised by his own question.

The young man snatched the medical report and the pen from his hand and began to draw. It was a rough, very childish sketch. Then he returned the piece of paper with a trembling hand. Confused, Genko looked at it.

It was a man with the head of a rabbit and heart-shaped eyes.

10

Dr Green leaned over to remove the oxygen mask. Then he looked at her and smiled. 'How are you feeling now?'

She was still struggling to breathe on her own.

'Let your lungs get used to it.' He mimed what she had to do by putting his hands on his chest.

Her breathing was improving with every mouthful of air. 'Thank you,' she said, then turned to the bedside table.

The yellow telephone was still there, and not a figment of her imagination.

'Is there someone you'd like to call?' Green asked, noticing her movement.

'May I?' she asked, incredulous.

He laughed. 'Of course you may, Samantha.'

She tried to sit up.

'Wait, I'll help you.' He took her by the arms and put a pillow behind her back. Then he placed the telephone on her lap.

She lifted the receiver and put it to her ear. But she couldn't hear anything.

'To make an outside call, dial nine,' he explained.

She did and the line cleared. It was a pleasant sound that sent a joyful frisson of freedom through her. Then she looked at the keypad and her face darkened.

'What's the matter?' Green asked, noticing something was wrong.

'I can't remember any phone numbers.'

'That's understandable,' he said, trying to comfort her. 'It's been too long. Besides, the numbers might have changed, don't you think?'

This thought cheered her up.

'So many things have happened in the world while you were away, Samantha.'

'Like what?'

'You'll have a long time to discover it, trust me.' He took the telephone and put it back. 'It's right here. As soon as you remember a number, all you have to do is dial it.'

She nodded, grateful for his explanations – polite, calming. 'They've forgotten about me, too, haven't they?' She meant her family and friends, although she couldn't remember them.

'Well, it hasn't been easy for anyone,' Green said, sitting back down. 'You come to terms with death: after a while, memories take the place of grief. But when you don't know what's happened to the person you love, all you have left is doubt. And it doesn't leave you until you obtain some answers.'

'Then why aren't my parents here now?'

'Your father will come soon. He moved away but they're

looking for him to give him the good news. As for your mother ...' Green's expression saddened. 'I'm sorry, Sam, you mother passed away six years ago.'

She should have been upset. Because that's how a daughter feels when she's told that her mother isn't there any more, doesn't she? And yet she felt nothing. 'OK,' she heard herself say with lucid coolness, as though implying that her heart didn't need to 'come to terms' with the death of the woman who had brought her into this world, that she had already accepted it as a fact.

'Once you recover your memory,' he reassured her, 'you'll find grief waiting for you along with your recollections.'

'Wouldn't it be better if I didn't? You're saying it as though it's something that would actually be good for me.'

'Nobody can avoid suffering, Sam. It wouldn't be healthy.'

'And you don't think I've suffered enough?' She was suddenly angry. 'Besides, what do you know about it? What do you know? I suppose you have your nice family, children and a wife. But what about me? Fifteen years have been stolen from me. In fact, worse than that: somebody's taken a part of me.'

'Does the name Tony Baretta mean anything to you?'

Who is he? And what's he got to do with this?

'Probably not,' Green replied to himself. 'When you disappeared, your friend Tina – the girl who sat next to you in class, although you might not remember her either – told the police that on that February day you had a meeting with Tony: you were at the same school and he'd let you know that he had something to say to you.'

She was afraid she wouldn't like the rest of the story.

'For that alone, the boy ended up at the top of the list of

suspects,' Green continued. 'The police even considered the possibility that he'd killed you then got rid of your body.' He gave her a serious look. 'But what I think is that Tony Baretta had a crush on you and simply wanted to declare it to you . . . And, like you, Tony was only thirteen.'

There was a few seconds' silence.

'I'm sorry, I didn't want to upset you. I'm not saying it was your fault. But what happened to you affected a lot of people. Innocent victims, exactly like you. And they deserve our grief. Yours, too, believe me.'

She felt a pang of guilt tighten her stomach. 'And what can I do for them now?'

'Help me catch that beast.' Green changed the tape in the recorder. 'You must make more of an effort, Sam,' he said with unexpected calm. 'We don't have much time and you need to at least give me something. You do understand, don't you?'

'I don't know . . .' her words trailed off into uncertainty.

'Perhaps it's still too soon to remember everything, but at least a detail: how tall he was, what kind of voice he has . . .'

She stared at him. 'He never talks to me.'

Green didn't reply immediately. He first switched the tape recorder back on. 'Not a single word in fifteen years?'

'You think I'm mad, is that it?'

'Not at all,' he quickly replied. 'It's a matter of *belief.*' He looked her in the eyes. 'You see, Sam, many people are convinced that their lives are constantly watched over by a higher entity. They call it God and accord Him power over Earthly things. They know He's there even if they can't see Him. And they're also convinced that God is connected with their presence on Earth and the purpose of their lives. They'd feel lost and abandoned without Him. God is a need.'

'Are you saying I need that bastard? That I'm protecting him?'

'No. You're asking me to believe in the existence of somebody you've never seen or heard, and I'm all right with that: I'm with you. But some things require a rational explanation. For instance, how did you manage to escape after such a long time?'

She couldn't understand what Dr Green wanted from her. What was he trying to do? At that moment, something vibrated softly in the background.

He took a mobile phone from the jacket hanging on the back of his chair. He'd received a text message. 'In a little while, the antidote we're giving you to counteract the psychotropic drugs will help you remember,' he said, reading the message on his phone. 'But now please excuse me for a moment.'

He stood up, glanced at the drip connected to Samantha's arm, then headed to the exit.

'Dr Green,' she called. 'Could you leave the door open?'

He smiled. 'I'll leave it ajar, is that all right?'

She nodded. The doctor left a narrow gap through which she could see the corridor. She couldn't tell whether it was day or night but the duty policeman was still there, with his back to her, beside the door. There was a pleasant silence – the hospital sounds were present but distant. She wanted to close her eyes but was afraid of falling asleep. Because she was sure that he would come back in her dreams.

Just then the yellow telephone rang.

A jolt of fear went through her body, nailing her to the

bed as though there were a huge magnet beneath her. She slowly turned her head to the bedside table. It was demanding her attention.

Out of the corner of her eye, she checked the reaction of the policeman outside the door. He hadn't even stirred. She wanted to call him, beg him for help. But fear was constricting her throat, preventing her from speaking.

Meanwhile, the phone kept ringing, time and time again in the muffled silence. Like an appeal or a threat.

Part of her rejected the evidence. Another part, though, was whispering something she didn't want to admit. That at the other end of the line there was an old acquaintance – an old friend who was calling to let her know that he would soon come and see her.

To take her back home, to the labyrinth.

She wanted to get up, get away from the phone. But her leg, being in a cast, prevented any movement. So she turned to the wall with the mirror. Green had told her that there were police officers behind it, listening to their every word. Could there possibly be no one there now? She raised a hand to attract their attention. At the same time, she turned to the door and finally, in a whisper, started calling the policeman. 'Excuse me ... Excuse me ...' she said in terror but also shyly – aware that fear makes one stupid.

But the ringing went away just as it had come.

All she could hear now was her own panting and a whistling in her ears, an annoying vestige of that diabolical sound. She turned to the phone again to make sure it really had stopped. Yes, it really was silent again.

Luckily, a familiar sound came to her rescue: she recognised the jangling of the keys Dr Green had on a carabiner clipped to his belt. Shortly afterwards, the door opened and he came back into the room. 'Are you all right, Sam?'

'The phone,' she said, indicating it. 'It was ringing.'

'Don't worry, it was probably a mistake. Somebody must have dialled the wrong number.'

But she paid no attention to what he was saying. In fact, she didn't even listen to him. A hazy thought had formed in her mind. The ringing of the phone had opened a chink in her memory, through which something – an intangible recollection – was emerging.

A sound memory.

'*Excuse me . . . Excuse me . . .*'

It was her voice, the same words she'd uttered a little earlier, trying to attract the duty policeman's attention. But now she could hear them only in her mind because she herself had uttered them at another time, in another place . . .

She's walking in the labyrinth. The long grey corridor ends with an iron door. The door is shut. It's always been shut – she remembers this with absolute certainty. But now there's a sound coming from behind it.

As though someone was scratching its metal surface.

It's an insignificant sound, like the nibbling of a mouse or an insect chewing. But in the silence of the labyrinth the softest sound becomes huge. She heard it from her room, and immediately came to see where it was coming from.

As she slowly approaches the iron door, she wonders what it could be. She's scared of finding out but realises she cannot avoid it. It's not simple curiosity. She has learnt to check out every detail, investigate every alteration in the prison routine.

Because she never knows when or how a new game may begin.

And her instinct is telling her that something behind that door is waiting for her.

'Excuse me ... Excuse me ...' she continues to call with absurd politeness, hoping to receive an answer.

'You're right,' she finally said, looking at Dr Green. 'I wasn't alone.'

11

He left the Duran in time to see the start of the special forces blitz in the rear-view mirror of his Saab.

He hadn't even reached the suburbs of the city before the radio broadcast the news of the arrest of the first suspect in the abduction of Samantha Andretti. As Genko drove, he was thinking about what had happened in the bar. He was still finding it hard to believe the story about the man with a rabbit head.

'We still don't know on what grounds Tom Creedy has been arrested,' the broadcaster said. 'He is being taken to a secret location as we speak, and there he will soon be questioned by the police.'

So the young man's name was Tom Creedy. They'll take it out on him, he thought. He was the perfect candidate to divert the attention of the media and public opinion from the pursuit of the real abductor. And if they failed, then only the poacher would suffer.

But if Tom also told Bauer and Delacroix the story about

the rabbit man, then perhaps he would get away because they'd think he had mental health issues. Genko pictured the two police officers' faces when they discovered they couldn't use the poor wretch as a scapegoat, and that made him laugh.

The laughter was stifled by a coughing fit and he suddenly felt a weight on his sternum. The Saab swerved dangerously into the other lane just as another car was coming. Genko managed to move back in time. When he thought the end had come, the pain went away just as it had come.

He realised it had been an alarm bell. His heart was trying to remind him to spare himself. But spare himself for what? The police possessed the means and resources to investigate further, while his own research was inevitably limited. And his only lead ended with Tom Creedy and his useless visions.

He felt a huge sense of emptiness and despondency. He no longer had a purpose. All that was left for him was to die.

He reached the city at about one o'clock in the morning. The streets were clogged with traffic. Because of the heat, people were now living only by night and had poured out into the streets in search of entertainment. Some were also working: skyscrapers filled with offices were lit up, and there were workers coming and going inside.

It occurred to Genko that everybody had something to do except him. Moreover, he didn't know where to go. He could return to Quimby at the Q-Bar and try to take his mind off things or chew the fat with someone over a drink. Or else he could hole up in Room 115 at the Ambrus Hotel, lie down on the stained bedspread and wait for something – sleep or maybe death. And then there was always Linda's

apartment. He would find human warmth amid her unicorns, but his relationship with her was now contaminated
with sadness and he didn't want to feel sad. Not tonight. He
wanted a day like any other from his old life, a day like so
many other days, the kind you forget the morning after. An
ordinary day, when you don't remember you're alive. How
many days like that had he had? To be shelved in the past
without wondering if they'd been any use. And yet right now
they were the most desirable ones. If he could have relived a
single day of his existence, he wouldn't have chosen the best
one but the most normal.

I want to go home, he thought. Because he no longer gave
a damn whether or not someone would find his body.

As usual, he parked his Saab two blocks away and continued
on foot, checking that he wasn't being followed – a precau-
tion that had become essential over the years: nobody must
know where he lived.

The area was just before the city centre. It still had an
old-fashioned charm, and hadn't yet been discovered by
the nouveaux-riches. Their money would probably have
swept the streets clean of the dregs that populated it, but
for the time being, the only money around was linked to the
drugs trade.

Genko reached the building where he'd been living for
almost twenty years and immediately had to dodge a homeless drunk in order to access the front door. Since the lift was
always breaking down, he took the stairs. He felt suddenly
exhausted. He had to stop and catch his breath every five or
six steps because of the stifling heat.

There was the noise of rows on every floor. Fortunately,

his neighbours chose to fight in the privacy of their homes. The police would come and take someone away every so often, but when all was said and done, it was the perfect hiding place.

Genko reached the fourth-floor landing and inserted the key in the lock. He went in and quickly closed the door behind him. He stood still, in the dark, for a few seconds, enjoying the welcoming coolness of the air conditioning, set to come on at specific times. He took a deep breath and let the smell of home permeate him.

A smell of order, of cleanliness.

He switched on the light and saw the few pieces of furniture that decorated his living room. Only the essentials. A sofa, a television, a dining table. There was an open-plan kitchen and everything was properly arranged – utensils, espresso machine, juice extractor with a bowl for fruit and vegetables next to it. All the provisions were on the shelves and the fridge was full.

Before going any further, Genko removed his shoes, clothes and underwear until he was completely naked. Then he put his faded linen suit and his shirt that smelled of sweat on a hanger and placed them in a garment bag which he zipped up and hooked onto the coat rack.

He walked barefoot on the floorboards to the bedroom. There he also kept his gym equipment – a treadmill and a bench with weights and bars. He couldn't wait to lie down on the orthopaedic mattress, the freshly laundered sheets. But first he went into the bathroom and stepped into the shower.

Outside his home, Genko made a show of scruffiness and sloppiness, but within these walls he was reconciled to his true nature.

The first rule of a private investigator's job wasn't to go unnoticed. On the contrary, appearance was of paramount importance, because strangers immediately had to focus their attention on the crumpled clothes that stank of sweat and nicotine and the bristly, neglected beard. His humble look was really a suit of armour, because other people had to make do with the surface. When they saw a poor wretch, they usually felt superior and inevitably dropped their guard.

Faking it – that was the trick.

As the hot water from the shower washed away his sweat and tiredness, Genko closed his eyes and tried to make peace with his anxieties. I have failed a second time, he thought. After fifteen years, the thought of Samantha Andretti had come back only to torment him. Why now? He'd forgotten about her, buried her with other unsolved cases in the box in 'the house of things'. If only she had reappeared a week later, he would probably have never known. How stupid of him to have thought he could fix things. After all, what could he do? Catch the monster? What would be the use?

None to Samantha, who certainly hadn't needed him to save herself. She'd managed it on her own.

But did he really believe that finding the abductor would absolve him of his guilt towards her? Because what was eating away at him most at that moment was that, when it came down to it, he had made himself that bastard's accomplice. When Sam's parents had come to ask for his help, he should have refused. Instead, he had accepted the assignment. He'd taken their money and been hard on them.

To be honest, from the very beginning, Genko hadn't entertained any hope of solving the mystery of the disappearance. Then why had he lied? Was it just one of the absurd tests of self-discipline he inflicted on his own will-power and sometimes on his soul? If he'd managed to shed his pity for a thirteen-year-old girl and her pleading parents, could he have said that he'd passed the test? Was that the whole truth of it? Had he merely been looking for another trophy in honour of his damned self-control?

He opened his eyes, determined to punch tiles in the shower cubicle, but stopped himself. No, he told himself. It's the exact opposite.

I didn't believe in the case. That's my only fault.

True: I should have declined the assignment but I wasn't able to be rational. Did I do all I could fifteen years ago? I don't know. I can't do anything else now. Is it too late?

A man with a rabbit's head was the mocking answer he deserved.

He wished he could laugh about it with someone – oh, God, how lovely it would have been to bring somebody here tonight. A woman, or a friend. But no one had ever set foot in this apartment. This wasn't a regret; he'd had to make choices.

Solitude sharpens your perception of things, he reminded himself.

It was essential to have a sixth sense in his work. To get into people's minds. But in order to think somebody else's thoughts you had to be always focused. And family and friends were dangerous distractions.

He went back into the bedroom and finished drying himself in front of the mirror. His body showed obvious signs of rapid weight loss. The muscles chiselled by long daily workouts were quickly disappearing. When he wasn't play-ing the part of the private investigator with a cursed look about him, he neither smoked nor drank and kept to a strict diet. This hadn't prevented his body from getting ill, but this degree of self-denial had certainly made him into one of the best in his field.

My field is hunting. And the hardest animal to hunt is man.

Genko repeated that in front of the mirror, as though to convince himself of his mission.

In order to catch a man you needed particularly honed skills. Intelligence, a power of observation, a proficient knowledge of technology, quick reflexes, calm, resistance to stress, courage.

Above all, you needed an in-depth understanding of human nature.

Hardened debtors, small- or big-time swindlers, blue-chip criminals, professional thieves. These were his prey. In order to catch them and make sure they paid back what they owed or returned what they'd stolen, Bruno Genko was given a generous fee by important private companies. Money he had hidden in bank accounts abroad, intending to spend it once he had divested himself of the filthy clothes he'd been wearing for ages.

But he had put that moment off for too long.

The saddest thing was that nobody else would be able to enjoy his wealth. Of course, he could give it to charity or leave it all to Linda. But then other things would come to light, things he'd had to do in order to earn this money. Tricks, lies, compromises and subterfuges of which he wasn't proud. In addition, if anyone started to ask questions about the origin of the money, his clients' privacy would be compromised.

Better leave things as they are, he thought.

On his death, his accounts would become 'dormant', as the jargon went. Then, after a number of years, the bank would come into possession of the money.

The only legacy he could leave now was a monster. And the beneficiary of the bequest was a former thirteen-year-old girl called Samantha Andretti.

Could the envelope in the safe at the Ambrus Hotel change anything? Its contents were too dangerous. In that case, why hadn't he destroyed it immediately? Why had he asked Linda to do so?

He knew the answer but chose to ignore it.

He pulled back the sheet and sat on the side of the bed where he normally slept. Before going to bed, he opened the drawer of the bedside table. There were three orange bottles of pills, part of the palliative care his doctor had prescribed 'to make things easier', he'd said. They were basically anti-depressants. Genko opened one of the bottles and let a couple of pink tablets slip out into the palm of his hand. He stopped for a moment, then decided to increase the dose and the couple of pills turned into five. He had no intention of committing suicide, partly because he wouldn't have been able to with these drugs. But there was no harm in giving death a helping hand. He poured himself a glass of water from the pitcher standing on the bedside table, but, before swallowing the lot, he thought again about Samantha Andretti.

She was safe. In fact – as he'd thought earlier – she had saved herself. *But how had she managed to escape from her prison?*

It was unlikely that she had been able to overpower the abductor, since fifteen years of torture and privation were bound to have undermined her body. So much so that maybe all it took was a run through the woods for her to break a leg, he thought. Then had she cheated her jailer? Or else taken advantage of an instant of absent-mindedness? Perhaps, after such a long time, the monster was feeling too sure of himself and she had grasped the right moment to run away.

But he still wasn't convinced by this theory. The reconstruction lacked something.

He tried to picture the scene of her fleeing through the trees, pursued by her jailer. The irrational image of the abductor with the rabbit head flashed through his mind for a second, but he immediately dismissed it. Sam was naked. *Why was she naked?* In her desperate flight towards a dubious salvation, she had fallen and broken a leg. Perhaps she'd managed to drag herself to the road. *What advantage did she have over her pursuer?* Although incapable of moving, Sam was hoping – praying – that somebody would come by. But no one came. And the abductor would soon catch up with her.

But then she had heard something: a sound in the distance, a familiar sound. The engine of an approaching vehicle. She had seen the pick-up's headlights appear, and started to wave to attract attention. She had probably seen the look of astonishment on the driver's face. She was afraid that, instead of stopping, he would speed up and leave her there. It would have been an unbearable insult.

But the vehicle had stopped. A disfigured young man had got out. A monster who didn't, however, seem like a monster. She deluded herself into thinking he wanted to help her, take her away from there – wake her up from the nightmare. But then the young man had noticed that someone was coming out of the woods. 'I knew he was looking for the woman. When he saw us, he froze.' That was what Tom had said. 'He stood there, staring at us. He made my blood run cold ...' Sam had seen a familiar terror in her saviour's eyes – Genko was certain of it, he had heard the dark tone of that terror in the recorded voice. Sam had realised that he would leave her alone again. And indeed, Tom had got back into the truck and driven away. Shortly afterwards, he'd called the emergency number.

From then on, while a profiler listened to her story in hospital, the police had begun to comb every inch of the swamp, searching for Samantha Andretti's prison.

Why haven't they found it yet?

Genko hadn't realised he was staring into space, the glass in one hand, the pills in the other. He suddenly shuddered.

They haven't found the prison because it's not in the swamp, he thought. It was the abductor who took the girl there.

But why?

'For the same reason Tom had gone there,' Genko said softly. The young poacher had suggested the answer. The swamp was perfect hunting ground ... and the hardest animal to hunt is man, he repeated.

Sam didn't escape, it was the abductor who had freed her.

It was a revelation for Genko. The monster had taken her there then let her go. Naked and lost in the woods surrounding the swamp. He had granted her a small advantage. Then he'd followed her trail.

A kind of test, Genko thought. *A sadistic game.*

While running away, the prey had injured her leg. The predator would certainly have caught up with her but there had been an unforeseen event.

The poacher's pick-up truck.

Genko put the glass and pills on the bedside table and forgot about them. He even forgot that death was pursuing him, too. He got up from the bed and started walking around the room. Adrenaline had taken hold of his mind. The pieces of the puzzle were coming together and he would soon be able to see the whole picture, he was sure of it.

What else didn't add up in the reconstruction? There was something.

Because after Tom drove away, why hadn't the abductor taken advantage and gone to Samantha? He could have dragged her away. Maybe he was afraid the young man would call the police immediately, Genko thought. Maybe he didn't think he had sufficient time to run away with her.

But he could always have killed her.

Right now, she was providing clues that would be useful in catching her jailer. Why take such a risk?

There was only one explanation for such inexplicable behaviour. The abductor had got frightened. Just like Tom, he had decided to run away. But why? What had frightened him? He had to go somewhere safe. Safe from what? Perhaps he was afraid of being recognised. Or that Tom would soon provide information that would lead to his being identified. But that would only make sense if Tom had looked him in the face. Instead, the young man had seen only . . .

'A rabbit,' Genko said out loud, to his own surprise.

Why would a masked man need to run away?

Because the mask itself was a clue.

12

However absurd, this theory had to be checked out. Genko had no choice, partly because he had given little credence to solving the mystery of Samantha Andretti's disappearance once before. And that had cost the girl fifteen years of oblivion.

He rushed into the hallway, opened the garment carrier and took the medical report from the pocket of his linen jacket. If it weren't his precious talisman, he would probably have thrown it away immediately.

He gave Tom's drawing a closer look.

Despite the childish doodle, the man with the rabbit head seemed to have a normal build. There were no details that attracted particular attention except perhaps the heart-shaped eyes.

Genko thought about this. The time had come to open the third room in his apartment again.

He hadn't set foot in it since the doctors had diagnosed his imminent demise two months earlier. He keyed a seven-number code on the pad next to the bulletproof door.

The electronic lock clicked.

Once, Genko had loved to shut himself in his office. Besides being the place where he kept his most sensitive secrets, it was a refuge for his thoughts. There was a filing cabinet and a bookcase with law books, manuals on investigative techniques and military tactics, as well as the complete works of Machiavelli.

The walls were painted green. One of them was dedicated to an indecipherable collage by Hans Arp.

Genko loved the Dadaists and had bought it at an auction for an astronomical sum. One of the few follies in his life that had been worth committing. He went into his office and walked past the masterpiece, ignoring it with a pang of regret because he couldn't take it with him to his grave. Instead, he headed straight for the stereo. He picked out a record and placed it on the turntable. As soon as the stylus hit the groove, Bach's 'Goldberg Variations', in a 1955 recording by Glenn Gould, filled the room.

Then Genko went and sat down at a circular desk.

There was a MacBook Air connected on the internet, through a secure line, to an external server where Bruno's precious archive was stored. Sensitive data collected over twenty years of practising his profession. It would spell trouble if that ended up in the wrong hands.

Furthermore, from this location, Genko was able to access the database of every government office or police department. He could stage incursions into the computer systems of private organisations and companies, and tap into sensitive information in the lists of banks and insurance firms. And all without any risk of being identified.

He secured the medical report with the young poacher's

drawing on the back to the Anglepoise lamp with a piece of sellotape, so that he could have it in front of him, almost on a level with the screen. 'Let's see if I can find you,' he said to the strange animal figure with the heart-shaped eyes. Then he began a search by typing the keyword 'rabbit' into the terminal.

The first place Genko scanned was the police data banks. Samantha's abductor may have committed other crimes, even small ones, in the past. Perhaps even using a mask to conceal his identity.

A long list of felonies appeared on the screen. From the theft of rabbits to the ill-treatment of rabbits, to the story of a guy who'd dress up as a giant rabbit to molest women in the street. Genko quickly glanced at the list but nothing leaped out at him. He decided to refine his search by inserting a second word.

Children.

A new list opened before him. There was no limit to human cruelty. Poisoned Easter bunnies given out outside a school by a psychopath. Minors used as drug mules, with substances hidden in soft toy rabbits. Not to mention 'bunny girls', children who would pose naked in front of a webcam in exchange for an online purchase or mobile phone credit.

Here again, Genko found no interesting connection. So he tried to widen the field by gradually going back in time.

That was when the file of a certain 'R.S.', a child in the 1980s, caught his attention. The minor's name had been covered up because the case had implications of a sexual nature.

'R.S.' was ten years old at the time. He had disappeared one Monday morning, then reappeared three days later as though nothing had happened.

There was an interval of almost twenty years between this case and Samantha Andretti's abduction. It was unlikely that the same person was responsible for both disappearances.

Moreover, the keyword 'rabbit' did not feature in the brief story in the police report, but rather as a simple note at the bottom of the page – it could have been a typo.

'Disappearance of minor-rabbit-psychological support-social services-maximum discretion.'

Otherwise, there was a note referring to the Missing Persons Bureau.

Limbo.

It was the most obscure section in the police department. Information relating to the disappearance of innocent people was always a mystery. According to statistics, there was approximately one incidence a day, but official figures were not available. The reason for this was simple: although it was true that many vanished ones returned of their own free will, the fate of others remained an unsolved conundrum. And that was certainly not a good advertisement for the bureau's reputation.

For that reason, the Limbo archive had never been digitised and there was no trace of it on the internet.

'Twenty years,' Genko thought, tempted to move on. But the 'R.S.' case was the only handhold he had, so perhaps it was worth looking further into it anyway. He had two options: going to the Missing Persons Bureau, requesting the paper file and risking being sent away or else trying a more cunning approach, starting with a simple phone call.

He chose the second option.

He logged onto the department website and searched for

the Limbo contact details. The bureau manager's name was María Elena Vasquez, a name he'd heard before.

He wrote down the number and dialled it on his phone. It rang and rang in vain. Impossible, he thought. Although it was night-time, following the new directives, they were in the middle of working hours.

'Hello?' a male voice finally answered.

'Hello, sorry to bother you . . . This is Special Agent Bauer. Can I speak to the manager?' The man at the other end of the line said nothing and Genko immediately had an unpleasant feeling.

The silence was interrupted by a dog barking. 'Quiet, Hitchcock,' the voice said.

As soon as he heard the dog's name, Genko realised he'd made a wrong move. The man on the phone was the same one who had had an argument with Delacroix at the swamp base the day before. So the stranger in the navy blue suit and tie was a policeman. And he was also bound to know Bauer well.

'The manager isn't here at the moment but I can help you, if you like,' he stated in a neutral voice. 'I'm Special Agent Simon Berish.'

Genko knew keeping up the act was risky. 'It's about an old missing persons case,' he said tentatively. He then gave the details of the file and held his breath until he made out the sound of a keyboard as the other man entered the data into the computer.

Berish muttered something. 'There isn't much in the database: just the copy of a report written by the police closing the investigation.' Then he read out, '"R.S, age ten . . . Missing for three days . . . Returned home of his own accord . . ."'

'How come the little boy's real name isn't mentioned?' he asked, surprised.

'Actually, there isn't even a hint of what happened to him during the seventy-hours he was missing.'

'How's that possible?'

'The complete file is in paper form and apparently catalogued in the oldest part of the archives ... I'm afraid you'll have to come here in person, Officer Bauer.'

Genko ignored the suggestion. 'Could you tell me what else is in the report you have in front of you?'

'All it says is that after the events, his mother and father relinquished their parental authority and the child was put into care at the Wilsons' farm.'

The Wilsons' farm. Genko noted in his pad.

'There's a psychiatric report, if you're interested,' Berish said. 'Would you like me to send it to you?'

'Don't worry, just read it to me ... As long as you don't mind.'

'No problem,' he replied and began to read. '"Although the minor doesn't have any mental defects, he shows a limited emotional range which often manifests itself in an over-anxious attitude as well as an absence of sexual inhibitions, pica and bedwetting."'

Pica was the repeated eating of non-nutritional substances, such as soil or paper. As for the bedwetting, Genko wondered if it was an after-effect of the shock. But what alarmed him was the lack of sexual inhibition. What did that mean?

'"To make this psychological picture even more complex, there are sleep issues that often generate morbid fantasies on waking, which the child conveys in drawings that show a clearly immature view of reality.'" Berish paused. 'Some of the drawings are attached to the report,' he said unexpectedly.

This detail caught Genko unawares. An immature view of reality, he repeated to himself. 'I've changed my mind: would you mind sending me a copy?'

'Give me your email address.'

If he didn't supply a police department email, Berish would realise immediately that he wasn't speaking to Bauer. 'I'll give you a fax number.'

'You're even worse off than we are,' Berish said.

Genko wasn't sure if it was just a joke or a way of making it clear to him that he hadn't believed in his little bit of play-acting from the start. 'Absolutely,' he replied with a forced little laugh, then gave him contact details that could not be traced.

'I'll switch on our old fax machine and send you everything,' Berish promised. 'In any case, as I said, you're welcome to come here because the archived files always contain interesting surprises.'

'I might pop in,' Genko lied. 'In the meantime, thank you very much.' He hung up and stared at the machine in his office, waiting for it to start.

He wondered if Simon Berish wouldn't send him anything at all.

He'd tempted fate by introducing himself as Bauer. But he'd done it partly because Limbo didn't handle cases of any particular importance to the department. And in any case, the 'R.S.' case dated back to the 1980s and had had a positive conclusion with the reappearance of the missing boy.

His imminent death had made him unprepared. He

would have never been so careless in the past. But while he was torturing himself with this, the fax machine started and soon began to spew out a series of sheets.

Genko's relief didn't last long.

To start with, he thought there had been a transmission error because all the pages were identical. Then he realised that they were different drawings with the same elements repeated, reproduced obsessively.

A sky full of birds, a city or perhaps just a district with council housing. In the centre of the page there was a large church and, behind it, a football pitch.

But what struck Genko and left him breathless was the way in which 'R.S.' had drawn people.

An immature view of reality. The little residents of that place all had rabbits' heads with heart-shaped eyes.

13

Dawn wasn't yet a hint on the horizon as he drove through the countryside. The moon had already vanished from the sky but you could still see the stars. Within three hours at most, the sun would rise and the heat would start scorching the world again, forcing humans to hole up to escape that apocalyptic summer.

Before he left, Genko put on the crumpled, smelly linen suit again. The talisman on which Tom had sketched the portrait of the rabbit man was back in his pocket.

He was going to see the foster family who had cared for the ten-year-old boy after his parents had given up on him. He'd found the address online, and the farm didn't look like it had been active for ages.

After leaving the main road and taking a dirt track, the Saab drove along a maze of paths through fields of sun-flowers. Genko was afraid he'd got lost when his headlights finally lit up a sign indicating the way to the Wilsons' farm.

About six kilometres further ahead, he made out the

outline of a house against the starry sky. It stood on a hill, with two cypresses for sentinels. The Saab drove through a wooden arch and stopped in the open space on the other side, next to the barn. Genko got out of the car and looked around, trying to work out if there was anybody about. The lights were off. Maybe people in the countryside, he thought, hadn't adopted the expedient of inverting day and night. He reached into the car and sounded the horn to attract attention.

Two dogs started barking inside the house. A light came on at a window on the second floor. Shortly afterwards, the front door opened and someone came out. Genko didn't have time to make them out because a torch was immediately aimed at his face.

'Who is it?' a female voice asked while the two dogs kept barking at her side.

'Mrs Wilson?' Genko said, shielding his eyes with his hand to avoid being blinded. 'I'm sorry to land on you like this but I need to speak to you.'

'You still haven't told me your name,' the woman objected.

'You're right. My name is Leonard Muster,' he lied, taking a fake ID out of his pocket. 'I work at the Public Prosecutor's office.'

The woman lowered the torch and said nothing for a moment, probably studying the unexpected visitor, wondering if she could trust him. 'What does the Public Prosecutor want from a wretched old woman at this time of night?'

Genko laughed. 'It's just a formality.'

'All right, come in, we'll talk in the house.' Tamitria Wilson and her two mongrels walked ahead into the farmhouse. She was wearing a nightgown that came down to her ankles. Although her hair was grey, she still wore it long, down her back. She walked leaning on a stick she had probably carved out of a tree branch herself. She led her guest into a spacious kitchen with a large oak table.

She motioned to the dogs and they went and lay down by the hearth. 'What can I do for you, Mr Muster?' she asked while turning on a ring to warm up a pot of already made coffee.

Leonard Muster was a made-up identity Genko had used before. The document of a grey bureaucrat didn't have the intimidating power of a policeman's ID, but it did have the advantage of not raising a barrier. Genko had learnt that people would sometimes give misleading information to law enforcement agents because they secretly despised their authority. In order to obtain full cooperation, a skilful private investigator had to put himself on a level with his interlocutor.

'Once again I apologise for coming so late,' he said, 'but in the city, because of the heat, offices have changed their shifts and they're now making us work at night. I did try calling but it just rang and rang.'

'My phone has been out of order for over a year, actually,' the woman replied sharply. 'But the telephone company doesn't give a damn.'

Genko had no trouble believing her, since he'd seen no other houses on his way there. 'I'm here because the Prosecutor has asked me to go over the files of a few cases of missing minors just in case something has been overlooked ... Since Samantha Andretti's reappeared, we're all under pressure in the department, you know. Our bosses don't want any more skeletons popping out of the cupboard.'

'I see,' the woman replied without much conviction. 'But how can I help you?'

'Of the children you fostered at the farm, could you tell me how many had had experiences like Samantha Andretti?'

She turned to look at him. 'All of them.'

Genko tried to control his astonishment; he hadn't expected this kind of response. 'All?' he finally asked.

The woman put her stick down and took the coffee pot from the stove. Limping, she carried it and two red enamelled tin mugs to the large oak table, invited Genko to sit down on one of the stools, then did the same. 'My husband and I built this place many years ago,' she said, indicating something behind Genko.

He turned and saw that she was referring to a framed photo on the mantelpiece. In it, a man was posing with a shotgun, smiling, surrounded by children.

'We didn't have children so we decided to devote ourselves to other people's unfortunate ones.'

'A worthy mission.'

'I hope so . . . I used to call them my special kids . . . I've loved each and every one of them as though I'd given birth to them myself. And they never let me down. Even though I don't know where they are now, I'm sure they still think of me and that everything I've taught them has been useful to them in their lives.'

She talked about them as though they truly were extraordinary beings and not just problem children. Only the power of love can transform a flaw into an asset, Genko thought.

'Have you ever heard of "the children of the dark", Mr Muster?'

'No, I haven't,' Genko confessed, her definition making the hairs stand up on the back of his neck.

'They're minors who go missing and are then found by the police or inexplicably reappear, like Samantha Andretti,' Tamitria Wilson said. 'They're kidnapped by unscrupulous men who abuse them. Some run away and others they let go. But the time in captivity marks them for the rest of their lives.'

'Why "children of the dark"?'

'Because often they're kept shut in underground lairs, buried alive. And when they see daylight again, it's as if they were born a second time. But they'll never be the same again.'

During the silence that followed, the elderly woman poured the coffee into the mugs and gave one to Genko.

He sipped the black liquid and quickly asked, 'Among the cases I was sifting through in the office before coming here, there was the one of a ten-year-old boy listed in the documents only with the initials "R.S."'

The woman thought for a while. 'I'd need to know when he was staying here on the farm.'

'Early Eighties, more or less.'

Tamitria Wilson froze, struck by a recollection. 'Robin Sullivan,' she suddenly said.

'It was a brief disappearance,' Genko reminded her. 'Just three days. Afterwards, his family no longer wanted to look after him.'

'His mother was no good,' Mrs Wilson stated with a hint of contempt, 'and his father even worse. I don't know why those two insisted on staying together. Robin would always get caught in the middle whenever they rowed, and he was the only one who would suffer in the long run. I don't think his parents loved him.'

Her last sentence and the certainty with which she had uttered it made Genko all of a sudden feel sad for the child. 'What do you think happened to Robin during those three days?'

'He never wanted to talk about it,' she replied, her gaze lost in thought. 'He was a vulnerable boy, who needed a lot of love, compassionate ... The perfect prey for anyone with ill intentions.'

'But how can we be sure he was abducted and didn't run away from home?'

'They lure them with attention they don't get elsewhere,' she replied, staring at him. 'They pretend to take an interest in them but all they want is to take them to a dark place.'

Genko tried to argue. 'Yes, but Robin—'

The woman slammed her hand on the table and glared at him. 'You really want to know how I can be sure that Robin was the victim of a monster?'

Genko did not reply.

'I know from experience Robin Sullivan was a normal kid before he went missing. Perhaps a little challenging, like many children who are left to their own devices, but normal. After those dreadful days he never wanted to talk about, he changed. You'll know what I mean if you've read his file.'

'Pica, bedwetting ...' Genko listed, remembering the thin file Officer Berish had read out to him over the phone.

'He'd eat soil, plaster, toilet paper. We constantly had to keep an eye on him, and he had to have his stomach pumped at least six times. Then he started eating insects.' She sighed at the memory of it. 'He even lost control of his sphincter, it was a total regression to early childhood. We were forced to make him wear a nappy and that didn't help with his interaction with other children: they made fun of him and beat him up.'

The weakest of the weak, Genko thought. 'Was he uncommunicative and solitary?'

'On the contrary,' the woman replied. 'Robin displayed disturbed emotional responses from the start.'

Genko remembered the absence of sexual inhibition mentioned in the medical report. 'What do you mean?'

'He was always looking for physical contact with people. Family members at first, then the other children at the farm. Even with me and my husband ... But his search for love would often turn into something morbid. Robin's every gesture had unusual malice for someone his age.'

'Is that why his parents didn't want to look after him any more?'

The woman stared at him gloomily. 'He was infected by the dark.'

Once again, Genko shuddered. He was infected by the dark, he repeated in his mind, memorising the phrase, certain it was a key to accessing Robin's secret world. 'I'm sorry to bring back these memories,' he said after taking another sip of the terrible coffee. 'But, as you can understand, my department would be in an embarrassing position if it transpired that we'd ignored the case of another abducted child.'

'So what else do you want to know?' Tamitria Wilson asked, puzzled.

'Robin Sullivan's psychiatric assessment says that he suffered from sleep disorders.'

'You mean nightmares,' she said mockingly. 'I can't understand why some doctors use big words to describe something so simple.'

Genko pressed her. 'Was there a recurring element in Robin's nightmares?'

'Children use dreams to convey reality. Whenever they feel uncomfortable or ashamed, they say it was a dream.'

Genko noticed that this was an evasion on the part of Mrs Wilson. 'Robin would draw after he woke up,' he added, watching her reaction. 'And in these drawings, people looked like rabbits.'

Tamitria Wilson stared at him for a moment. 'I know why you came here tonight, Mr Muster.'

Genko feared his cover had been blown. 'Really?' he said with an amused expression, trying to keep calm.

'Yes,' she replied sternly. Then she added, 'Maybe the time has come for you to meet Bunny.'

14

'Follow me and watch where you step.'

Tamitria Wilson had opened a hatch in the floor of a storage room, revealing a staircase leading to the basement. Equipped with a torch, she started slowly going down the steps with the help of her stick. Genko walked behind her, afraid she would fall.

'I'm sorry, there's no electricity down here,' she said, directing the light. 'The farm is falling to pieces and I no longer have the energy to run it. I tried, but one day I decided that the house would grow old with me. We're both full of aches and pains and there's nothing anybody can do about it.'

Genko mentally made the connection between an old lady alone in a big house and the telephone being out of order. If she were ever unwell or had an accident, Tamitria Wilson couldn't even have called for help. Her beloved dogs would have feasted on her body.

'I should have moved out ages ago,' she said, 'but it's the only place I know.'

Meanwhile, Genko was holding on to the handrail and could hear the floorboards creak at every step. He couldn't work out where they were going. What worried him most was the reason Tamitria Wilson hadn't wanted to provide an explanation: he had to see it with his own eyes or he wouldn't understand – that's what she'd said. Who was Bunny? Hadn't the old lady just told him she was alone in this house? Maybe her long isolation hadn't benefitted her, he thought. Maybe she wasn't all there any more. All Genko wanted was to gather information on Robin Sullivan's fate then leave, but now he had no choice but to follow her into the basement.

When they finally reached the bottom of the stairs, Tamitria ranged over the room with her beam of light.

It was a storeroom stacked with rusted iron beds, mattresses, furniture, boxes and various knick-knacks. There was so much stuff that it was impossible to tell how large the room was.

'I carried on for a while after my husband died,' Mrs Wilson said as she shuffled deeper among cramped cupboards and piles of things. 'But then the government stopped helping us and I could no longer hire staff, so I had to give up.'

'When did this happen?' Genko asked.

'Our last special boy flew the nest about nine years ago.'

'And what about Robin?'

Tamitria leaned on Genko's arm to step over a heap of boxes that had fallen down from a stack. 'He left when he turned eighteen, just like the others. At least I helped him get his high-school diploma,' she added proudly.

Genko was afraid the woman would trip up in the middle

of all that junk. 'And you never heard from him again? You don't have an address or phone number?'

'He once sent me a postcard from a tourist resort in the south of the bay,' she replied as they went around a mountain of old, discoloured magazines. 'And then nothing.'

The two mongrels hadn't followed them down here and would bark occasionally from the top of the stairs. Their yelping grew increasingly distant and Genko didn't blame them for their cowardice. Bunny, he mused again. He hoped it was worth it.

They came to a brick wall blackened by the damp. Tamitria stopped and pointed the torch at its base. Genko took a step forward and saw, standing on the floor, a large trunk with brass trimmings, like something from the old days. The lid was secured with a padlock.

'Here it is,' the old lady announced. 'Bunny is inside here.'

Genko got the unpleasant feeling he was standing before a coffin. The woman said nothing else. She handed him the torch, put her stick on the floor and knelt with difficulty in front of the chest.

He saw her fumbling with her necklace. She took it off and he figured there was a key hanging on it because immediately afterwards, Tamitria went to work on the padlock. Once she'd removed it from the iron rings, she lifted the lid. Genko did not move.

'Shine some light here, please.'

He approached and illuminated the contents of the trunk.

All there was were white sheets and embroidered towels. An old trousseau.

'I decided to keep Bunny inside here because I didn't know where else to put him,' Mrs Wilson said, rummaging through the linen. 'Maybe I should have thrown him away but part of me told me not to.'

What was she talking about? What was in this box?

Tamitria suddenly stopped searching and Genko realised she'd found something, but her back was still obstructing his view. The old woman was looking at the object she was holding. 'Bunny,' he heard her say softly, as though she'd just met an old friend she hadn't seen for a long time.

At last she turned to him. She was clasping a little book to her chest.

'Bunny arrived here with Robin. We always used to check the new children's luggage because we didn't want them to bring into the house items that were dangerous to them or others, like slings or knives. As soon as I opened Robin Sullivan's suitcase and saw this, I immediately knew something wasn't right.' She handed it to Genko. 'Have you ever had a nasty feeling but been unable to explain it, Mr Muster?'

Genko was surprised at his own brief hesitation. Something was holding back his curiosity – a foreboding. Then he took the little book from Mrs Wilson's hands and looked at it.

It was just an old comic book.

The colours on the cover were faded and on it was the picture of a large blue rabbit with heart-shaped eyes. The animal had a playful, very sweet expression. It was smiling. The title of the book was printed between his ears. A single word.

BUNNY.

'May I look through it?' he asked.

'Of course, go ahead.'

Genko looked around and noticed a stack of suitcases. He put the torch on top of it, so his hands would be free, opened the comic book and started leafing through it. The black-and-white drawings were of average quality. The story was equally childish. Bunny leaves the forest and moves to a park in a big city. There, he meets a group of children who become his friends. He plays and has fun with them.

Neither the story nor the illustrations revealed anything abnormal. However, instead of inspiring joy or calm, they conveyed something disturbing. The more Genko turned the pages, the more uneasy he felt.

The old lady was correct, something about the comic wasn't quite right.

One thing in particular worried him: the adults in the story were not aware of Bunny's existence.

Only children could see him.

Genko forced himself to read more closely. He sensed he was nearing a fine line and even if he couldn't see beyond it, he knew something evil awaited him on the other side.

He was concentrating so hard that he didn't notice that the old woman hadn't said anything for some time. He didn't even notice the long shadow rising over his head, or the quick movement in the air as Tamitria Wilson's stick came down heavily on the back of his neck.

The last image he saw was Bunny smiling at him.

15

He got the proof that he was still alive when he felt the taste of his own blood.

He explored his mouth with his tongue and discovered he had lost a tooth. He must have broken it falling on his face on the floor. Old bitch, he thought. He was surrounded by darkness but he gathered from the smell of dust and mould that he was still in the huge basement beneath the Wilsons' farm. He tried to stand up but felt dizzy and nauseous, with cold sweat and palpitations. Strangely, though, this time he wasn't afraid that he'd reached the end of the line.

It was almost worse than dying.

Trapped underground, with no way out and no light. Buried alive. A child of the dark, as Tamitria Wilson had described the abducted children.

His monster was a limping, solitary old woman.

Before he could be overcome with panic, Genko tried to analyse what had happened. He could remember reading the comic, Bunny's face, then the sudden blow to the back of his neck. Why on earth had the Wilson woman struck him? She could have used an excuse to get rid of him and not let him into the house. Instead, she'd brought him down here to show him Robin Sullivan's comic book. It made no sense. Maybe she was simply mad.

He groped for a support and clung to the edge of a chest, put one knee on the floor and heaved himself up. He felt his neck stiffen and a sharp, stabbing pain sent flashes across his eyes. He let out a brief, deep cry: it was his stomach settling. Then he reached out, searching for the stack of suitcases on top of which he'd put the comic and found it there, still open. He closed it and put it in his jacket pocket, together with his talisman. That was when he realised he no longer had his wallet, his mobile phone or the fake ID he'd shown the woman on arrival.

They didn't fall out. She took them.

The first thing to do was go back to the staircase leading to the surface, but he couldn't remember which way they'd come to the green trunk. It would be difficult to find the path back in total darkness, but he didn't want to give up without even trying. So he put out his arms and began to probe the darkness, searching for a way.

As he advanced, he tried to recognise the objects that came up before him. A cupboard door, a coat rack, a lamp. Every so often, his knees would knock against something and he nearly tripped a couple of times. All he was focusing on, however, was his own breath.

He reminded himself of the promise he'd made Linda – *for as long as there's air in my lungs* . . .

The plan was to get to the hatch that led to the storeroom. He was certain it would be shut and that he would have to shove it open with his shoulder. He wasn't sure he'd manage it as it had seemed quite sturdy. Once out, he was confident he'd find himself faced with Tamitria Wilson and her stick. Or perhaps she had a gun in the house – he remembered the shotgun held by Mr Wilson in the picture on the mantelpiece. Bruno Genko didn't like guns. He'd needed one only a couple of times in his work and hadn't fired a single shot on either occasion. Even so, he knew how to use them and would practise regularly in a private range. He owned two pistols. A Beretta, kept in his office safe, and a semi-automatic stored in a plastic case hidden under the spare wheel in the Saab. Neither was accessible at this moment.

He slowly went forward, not knowing what to expect, until the tips of his fingers touched something hard and slimy. He realised he'd reached a dead end, because what he had before him was a brick wall. 'Shit!' he said. But he was wrong to get angry. Perhaps this situation was a taster of what awaited him after death. A dark hell just for him. A rightful punishment for the sins he'd committed throughout his life. For the contents of the safe in Room 115 at the Ambrus Hotel, he thought, and felt ashamed. Then he heard soft, muffled sounds coming from his left.

A moan. No, a voice.

He moved in that direction, felt the wall, then came across a kind of pillar. He examined it with his touch. It was a thick, cast-iron pipe connected with the surface. He knew because the same voice he'd heard earlier was echoing in the hollow interior.

It was coming from the house above him.

Unable to hear well, Genko pressed his ear to the metal. The sounds were unclear but he thought he recognised

Tamitria Wilson's voice. Her words would vanish before they could make sense. Genko tried to concentrate more but it was no use. The thickness of the pipe prevented him from making out that sort of guttural chanting. Then, all of a sudden, the pipe began to conduct the voice better and the words grew clearer. The woman must have come closer to the area under which he was standing, and he was finally able to catch the odd sentence.

'. . . he showed me a fake ID. But then I took his wallet and from the documents in it I discovered his name's Bruno Genko and he's a private detective. Bastard . . .'

She was furious. He couldn't work out who she was talking to because nobody was responding to her ranting. The crazy old woman is talking to herself, Genko thought, or perhaps to her dogs.

'. . . I took him to see Bunny – what else could I do? I couldn't think of anything else. Then I figured I could give him a blow on the head down there. But actually, I took advantage as soon as he turned his back to me . . .'

Genko didn't know whether to be angrier with her or with himself for getting caught in such a stupid way.

'. . . I'd never seen him before tonight. I don't know if someone sent him . . .'

This last sentence didn't seem to have been uttered randomly but sounded more like a reply. He felt a sudden chill, like the kiss of a ghost. She's not talking to herself, he thought.

'. . . I decided to tell you straight away . . .'

She was on the phone to somebody. The landline was out of order, so the old woman must have a mobile phone. 'I locked him in . . . Don't worry, he can't get out of there . . .'

Who wasn't supposed to worry? Who was the old woman talking to? Genko had a nasty feeling. He'd wound up in this trap by his own doing and things were about to get worse. Who was Tamitria Wilson's mysterious interlocutor?

'. . . All right, I'll wait for you then . . .'

Genko stopped trying to figure out an answer. Whoever it was, they were on their way.

16

He's coming for me.

His breathing was laboured and he felt like a mouse trapped in a box. How long would it take the person on the phone to reach the farm? How long did Genko have to come up with something? He wandered through the storeroom, no longer paying heed to where he was stepping. He wanted to find an object with which he could defend himself, but it was difficult to get his bearings in the dark.

Until a couple of hours earlier, the notion that he didn't have long to live had been a kind of superpower that made him feel invulnerable. After all, how much worse could it get? But now he was surprised by how strong the survival instinct inside him still was. The fear he felt was proof of that.

He'll come and that will be the end.

He slipped and collapsed on a heap of tin boxes that came crashing to the floor, and something made of glass also broke into a thousand pieces. He found himself lying with his stomach on the floor, his arms stretched forward. His right hand had inadvertently slipped into something soft, which felt like the lair of a big insect. He lifted his arm, pulled at a few spider's web-like threads and, repelled, immediately tried to extricate himself. But after a closer examination by touch, he realised it was only wool. There was a basket of yarns under him.

As he tried to calm down, he realised he'd finally lost control. To make up for it, he noticed a pale glow in front of him. He'd found the staircase that led to the hatch in the storeroom.

He climbed it.

At the top of the stairs, the light from the ground floor above filtered through the gaps in the wooden door, interrupted every so often by passing shadows. It was the dogs guarding his only way out. Genko pressed his right shoulder against the hatch and pushed in an attempt to lift it. As expected, there was a catch on the other side – a bolt, judging by the metallic sound. The illness had weakened his body: he wasn't strong enough to take it off its hinges.

From his position, however, he could better sense what was happening on the surface. He recognised the sound of Tamitria Wilson's stick, accompanied by the dragging of her limping leg. Together they produced an obsessive, mesmerising beat – knock and quick swish, knock and quick swish, and so on.

There was a smell of freshly made coffee and biscuits. The old witch was fussing in the kitchen while waiting for her guest.

He thought he recognised the sound of a car arriving and heard Mrs Wilson walking away and, a couple of minutes later, coming back. He gathered from the number of steps on the floor that she was no longer alone.

'I decided to call you because I immediately realised there was something wrong,' she was explaining. Her voice no longer had its earlier harshness and was gentle now. 'As I mentioned on the phone, Mr Chatty asked me lots of questions about the children who stayed here, but actually he was interested in only one of them.'

Apparently, all it had taken to worry the woman was bringing up Robin Sullivan. Genko realised he'd flung open a dangerous door to the past. From there, he'd fallen into an unfamiliar abyss, and now the only way out was being quickly shut behind him.

'I've searched him thoroughly: he's not armed. Here's the mobile and the ID,' she said, probably showing him the items she'd purloined.

Genko felt like a fool. Usually, when he made house calls, he always hid his phone and wallet somewhere – in a neighbour's post box, or else in the engine compartment of the Saab. Now these two knew too much about him.

'He's down there. He's come to – I heard noises a little while ago. But now he's been quiet for some time, so perhaps he's hiding and plotting something.'

Tamitra's guest listened and still said nothing.

'I've no idea why he came and stuck his nose here,' Mrs Wilson continued.

At this point, Genko heard footsteps coming towards him. His ailing heart was like a piston in his chest, as though about to explode at any moment, just as the doctors had predicted.

Having reached the hatch, they stopped. Genko drew

closer to one of the gaps, hoping to see the face of the man with Tamitria Wilson, but his position prevented him from having a clear view.

'What do you want to do with him?' she asked.

That's a good question, Genko thought. He, too, wanted to know.

But the guest didn't reply.

Not a good sign, Genko decided. Then there was a gunshot, followed by a few seconds of total silence. He wondered what was happening when, suddenly, the old witch's eye appeared in the gap.

He immediately pulled away but it was too late.

He expected Tamitria Wilson to start screaming but she said nothing. She continued to stare at him and a thin trickle of blood ran over her motionless eye.

She was dead.

Genko slowly walked backwards down the wooden stairs, trying not to make too much noise, at the same time watching the hatch, expecting it to open any second now. He managed to reach the darkness of the underground storeroom and waited behind a piece of furniture.

We'll both be in the dark down here, but he won't want to take risks. He'll flush me out with smoke. Or, even worse, he'll set the farm on fire and let the flames take care of me and the old woman's body. But Genko quickly discarded this idea. He won't do it, he told himself. He must first retrieve something very dear to him. He put a hand on his hip and caressed the comic book in his jacket.

Bunny. He would never let him burn.

He prayed he was right, while more interminable minutes passed. Then, finally, something happened. He heard the sound of the bolt opening. The hatch began to lift. The light from upstairs slid in through the opening, gliding down the steps like a stream as far as the floor, then gathering around a long dark shadow. Here he is, Genko thought. Come on, come down here.

Come to me.

But the man was undecided. Genko recognised the sound of the trigger of a semi-automatic pistol. It was a warning: the guest wanted him to know that the next bullet would be for him. Finally, he took a first step towards the opening. Then another, and another. Genko leaned out from behind his hiding place and saw that the man was halfway down the stairs. He took from the floor the end of the wool he'd found in the yarn basket and yanked.

He saw the spider's web tighten at the very moment the prey ended up in it.

The stranger on the stairs tried to free himself from the trap but, caught unawares, lost his balance and fell forward. Genko watched the arc of his flight as though in slow motion, and saw him land on the floor with a loud thud and a moan. It wasn't pain, he thought, but rather rage.

He took advantage of this, burst forward and ran to the stairs.

He stepped over the man on the floor as he was trying to disentangle himself. He reached out and Genko felt his fingers try to grab his ankle but they lost their grip. He climbed the steps two at a time, running towards the hatch that awaited him like an open mouth. Before diving into the light, he heard the unmistakable sound of a gunshot. The bullet brushed his ear. Genko grabbed the edges of the floor and heaved himself through the hole in one leap. He came up against Tamitria Wilson's petrified stare. He was about to fall back but managed to avoid the worst, landing on his side. He was winded, but turned immediately to try and close the hatch and trap the man in the basement. A second shot made him hesitate. The bullet hit the timber and Genko's face was showered with splinters. He panicked. He gave up on the hatch and ran away without looking back, heading for the front door.

The short distance seemed endless. He finally reached the door, clasped the handle, pushed it down and pulled it. But the door didn't budge. He hadn't considered the possibility that it might be locked.

He heard heavy footsteps climbing the steps behind him.

He didn't turn to look, absurdly convinced that if he did he would die on the spot. He started kicking the door hysterically, revealing an urge to save himself that was peculiar for someone who had almost exhausted his life bonus points.

The steps behind him stopped.

He's taking aim, he thought, expecting to feel a bullet tearing his flesh. But, just in time, he noticed a window in the living room. Fuelled by despair alone, he ran towards it, pulled it up and climbed out of it.

Once out, he headed for the Saab. It was still where he had parked it, just twenty metres away from the porch. Fifteen, ten, five. *No shot – how come?* Genko ran around the car, crouched next to a wheel, and sliding towards the driver's seat, opened the door and dived in. Keeping his head down for fear of a bullet hitting him through the rear windscreen, he looked for the key he'd luckily left in the ignition. He slammed his foot on the accelerator. The engine produced a prolonged rattle, as though flooding, but then the carburettor drew fuel and the car started with a jump. Only then did Genko sit up in his seat. He gave the house one final glance in the rear-view mirror and glimpsed a figure behind the window through which he had just managed to escape.

Bunny the rabbit was waving goodbye.

17

'Tell me about the door, Sam.'

She can hear Dr Green's voice but is unable to answer him. Her mind is trapped in the labyrinth, outside the iron door behind which a relentless sound is concealed.

Like a mouse nibbling or an insect chewing.

'Who's behind the door, Sam?'

'There's someone in the labyrinth with me . . .'

Another voice comes over Dr Green's but it's not from within the hospital room. It's a little voice. Another little girl. She's scratching at the door and crying.

'Hey, you,' *she says,* 'can you hear me?'

No reply.

'Can you hear me?'

She sniffles.

'What's your name?'

Nothing doing.

'Are you deaf?' *No, she can hear perfectly well. She's just frightened. Frightened to death.* 'Listen, don't be afraid. I

don't want to hurt you. I'm like you. The same thing's happened to me. And now I'm here and I don't know where I
am.' She feels oddly euphoric. It's selfish, she knows that. But
she's glad she's not alone any more. 'I promise I'll help you.'
She's lying, she knows she is, because she, too, needs help.
What she should tell her is: 'Nobody will help us down here.'
Instead, she lies. She doesn't want to lose her new friend. 'It's
just a game,' she says. 'It's easy, all you have to do is play by
the rules.' She should tell her that it's he who makes up the
rules, but she doesn't. 'It took me a while but once you get
how it works then it's all much simpler ... He just wants to
play with us.'

'Who is he?' a faint voice behind the door finally asks.

I don't know, she thinks. Maybe it's God. Because down
here, he's God and he decides whether you can be OK or not
OK, or if you have to die. And he puts you to the test with
his games. 'He never answers my prayers. It all depends only
on us ... We can choose to play or not. But if you don't play
you don't get food or water ... If you don't play you don't
survive ...'

'How many games have you played?' the voice asks.

'Many ...' She's lost count by now. 'But you'll see, you'll
enjoy them.' It's absurd – how could she enjoy them? Why
did she say such a thing? There's nothing 'enjoyable' about
being here, and 'enjoyable' is the least appropriate word to
describe what happens in the labyrinth. You'll hate it, is what
she should have said. You'll hate everything, even yourself,
for what he's going to force you to do. 'All we have to do now
is work out how to get you out of there,' she says, feeling the
sturdiness of the iron door.

'I have the key.'

She's taken aback by this piece of information. 'Then what are you waiting for? Open it and come out.'

Silence.

But she doesn't give up. 'Are you hungry? I have some food back there.'

No reaction.

'Don't you trust me?' Perhaps she's right not to, given how many lies she's told her. 'Don't be silly.' She's running out of patience. 'I've already told you I won't hurt you.' It's frustrating. 'But if you want to stay in there, go ahead . . . You know you'll die there, don't you?' She feels terrible for having said that. She still remembers her first day in the labyrinth – she was terrified of everything. 'OK, I'm sorry . . . But it's been such a long time since I've spoken to anybody. I can't believe you're here now. I—' She's crying, crying and she hates herself for it. 'I – I just want us to be friends.'

A metallic sound breaks the silence. It's a key turning in the lock – two, three times.

She can't believe it: she's managed to persuade her.

The iron door opens but just a little. She hears footsteps walking away – backwards, gingerly. She slowly pushes the door open with one hand, revealing a frightened little girl standing in the middle of the room. She's wearing a nightgown that's torn in several places. She's barefoot and her feet are bleeding. Her blonde hair and her face are soiled with mud. She looks at her with bright blue eyes. She's holding her arms behind her back and rocking, just like a little girl.

'Hi,' the girl says.

'Hi,' she replies and tries to approach her but the little girl steps back. She realises she's still wary – all right, trust takes time. 'Come with me, I have some clean clothes that'll fit you.'

She proffers a hand but the little girl doesn't reciprocate. 'I'll show you where I am, the room where I keep all my things. There's also a mattress, so you can lie down if you like.' But the prospect clearly doesn't appeal to her, because she's still not moving. 'You must eat and sleep. Otherwise, you won't be ready.'

'Ready for what?' she asks.

'For a new game,' she replies. 'You never know when it might start, but I'll explain everything to you, I promise.' She turns her back on her and walks down the corridor, hoping the little girl has finally made up her mind to follow her.

'I know everything,' the little girl says.

She's surprised. What does she mean, she knows everything?

'I am the game.'

These last words bounce around her head like a pinball. She is turning and has already noticed a change out of the corner of her eye. The little girl unclasps her arms from behind her back and she sees something flash brightly by her hip. It's the fluorescent light bouncing off the revealed blade.

'He said I have to do it,' she says, lifting the knife. 'Because if I do it, I can go home.'

How many paces lie between them? A dozen? The instinct she has developed during her long imprisonment tells her she only has three options. Run away. Fight. Give in. She's about to go for the first but changes her mind. Instead, she darts to the little girl, and the latter does the same because she's worked out her intentions. They're both heading for the door – the iron door that is all the difference between life and death. She has an advantage but she has to get the key. She reaches out, bends her wrist, curls her fingers. She takes it out and holds it in her fist. She pulls the door shut just as her adversary clings *to the edge with both hands and drops the knife. They both follow it with their eyes as it falls to the floor. Then she pulls as hard as she can while the other girl stamps her feet and shouts, 'No! No! No!' The door shuts with a loud clang that echoes throughout the labyrinth. She has the presence of mind to put the key into the lock. Her hands are shaking but she manages to turn the key once, twice, three times. Meanwhile, the little girl keeps screaming and crying. And she hates her. She hates her so much. And she also starts screaming.*

'It's over . . . Sam, can you hear me? It's over.'

Dr Green had his arms around her but she kept struggling.

'Listen, Sam, you're safe now. Nothing's going to happen to you.'

She was trembling with despair and couldn't stop.

'I want you to take a nice deep breath . . .'

She tried and, for a moment, seemed to manage it.

'Don't give up now, Sam.'

She was, indeed, feeling better. 'I didn't want to . . .' she whispered.

'What didn't you want?' Dr Green asked, holding her tight.

'Please forgive me . . .'

'Forgive you for what, Sam? You didn't do anything.'

Dr Green didn't realise it wasn't her speaking but the little girl in the labyrinth.

'Open the door, please. Forgive me,' she begged behind the door. 'Please don't leave me here!'

She can hear her from her room but has decided not to respond. She's sitting on the mattress, her knees up to her chest, staring into space. She's ignoring her.

'Trust me, I won't do it again.'

But now she's the one who doesn't trust. The little girl has given her no choice. These are the rules of the game. And the game now stipulates that the little girl locked in the room carries on screaming and crying until she runs out of energy.

'I don't know how long this went on for . . .'

'What are you talking about, Sam?'

'Days, or weeks, maybe . . . Meanwhile, I knew what was going on behind that door. At first she wanted me to let her out. She begged, sometimes cursed me. Then she began to ask for food and water. Then nothing . . . She didn't say another word . . . But I knew she was still alive – I knew it . . . But I did nothing, I didn't lift a finger . . . I should have opened the door . . . But he was testing me, he wanted to know if I was able to resist, if I would feel sorrier for her or for myself. That was the point of the game . . .'

Dr Green had let go of her.

She noticed and looked at him. 'And when I started noticing the smell, I knew I'd won.'

18

'Robin Sullivan was ten years old in the early Eighties, so he should be less than fifty.' It wasn't dawn yet and the heat was already unbearable. The ceiling fan was turning too slowly to move the stagnant air in the small office at the police station. The blades produced a sad squeaking sound, like a bird call. Genko found it annoying but even so was trying to explain what he'd discovered. 'You should issue an arrest warrant.'

Bauer was leaning on the table, wiping the sweat from his neck with a paper handkerchief. Delacroix was opposite Genko, sitting astride a chair, his arms crossed under his chin. The two men weren't even trying to look interested.

'Come on, guys, I had a hell of a night ...' Genko tried to protest. His face was scratched from the wood splinters spewed by the hatch. The image of Bunny, watching him leave through the farm window, kept flashing through his mind.

Bauer scrunched up the tissue, threw it at the bin and

narrowly missed. Delacroix sighed, as though mulling over this information. 'Let's see if I've got this right. You claim that this Robin Sullivan killed a woman and then tried to murder you, too?'

It had only been two shots, actually. Because then he'd stopped shooting at him. *Why had he done that?* 'If you go and check, you'll find the old woman's body.'

'Why would he have tried to kill you?' Bauer said. 'I still don't understand ...'

It was disheartening. 'Because I got to him,' Genko replied as though it were the most self-evident thing in the world. 'He's the man you're looking for, Samantha Andretti's abductor.' He was expecting a little more enthusiasm after a revelation like this. 'Think about it, Robin Sullivan was a "child of the dark",' he said, quoting Tamitria Wilson. 'He was kidnapped for three days as a child and hasn't been the same since.' The little boy had never wanted to reveal what had happened to him, Genko remembered.

'And?' Bauer asked once again.

Genko looked at them both. 'You're joking, right?' He spread his arms. 'You just have to open any psychiatry text-book: anyone who was a victim of abuse as a child is more likely to display the same behaviour towards innocent victims as an adult.'

He was infected by the darkness, Mrs Wilson had said about Robin.

'But if I understand correctly, this is just a theory,' Bauer replied. 'Because you didn't get a good look at the man who shot at you.'

He remembered the moment he had kicked the front door in order to escape from the farm. He heard once again the sound of footsteps behind him. Terror had even prevented him from turning to look at his pursuer, while the latter was hesitating to shoot. Why had he hesitated? 'I told you: his face was covered.' He specified that it was a rabbit mask. And given the little credence they were giving the rest of his story, it was just as well.

'So, even if we did find Robin Sullivan, you wouldn't be in a position to identify him.' Bauer shook his head. 'Tell us again how you got to this Tamitria Wilson?'

'Do I have to remind you that I'm not obliged to reveal my sources?' But Bauer knew that very well, he was just toying with him.

'The strange thing is, next door we have a poacher called Tom Creedy who claims that he was recently approached in a bar by a guy who stank like hell and who asked lots of questions about Samantha Andretti and then went as far as to intimidate him.' Bauer turned to Delacroix. 'Do you think that's enough to charge them both with complicity in an abduction?'

Genko smiled in disbelief. 'And did he also mention the guy with the rabbit head?' he asked, point blank. 'Because, let's be frank about it, if you're planning on using dear Tom against me, then you'll have to also make public the business of the rabbit-man and the fact that your principal witness needs a psychiatric assessment.'

The two men weren't fazed. 'What do you know about that?' Delacroix asked.

Genko had not mentioned Bunny and the comic book. They were the weakest elements in the investigation and he still hadn't grasped their role or significance.

Only children can see the rabbit, he remembered.

'If Tom Creedy led you to Tamitria Wilson, then he must have told you something he hasn't told us,' Delacroix said.

'Or should we believe that all he fobbed you off with was this nonsense about the rabbit-man?' Bauer added with contempt.

Believe it or not, that's what happened, Genko thought but said nothing.

Delacroix was trying to be conciliatory. 'Perhaps Creedy involuntarily gave you a detail he then forgot because he didn't consider it important.'

'You're wasting your time,' Genko interrupted. 'I haven't come here just to report a murder, is that clear? I'm here to give you a hand, I've told you what I know and suggested you check it out. I've done my duty as a citizen, and I didn't even have to. And as legal guardian of Samantha Andretti—'

Bauer leaped at him and grabbed him by the scruff of his jacket. 'Listen, arsehole, we've tracked down her father. When we mentioned your name, he said that fifteen years ago you took a load of money from him and then vanished.'

He wasn't far wrong, Genko thought.

'So I know what's on your mind: you're trying to get some publicity by bragging about an assignment no one's given you. You're just a shitty parasite.'

Genko didn't even try to refute the accusations. After a few seconds, Bauer let go of his jacket and went back to his place.

Delacroix's mobile phone began to ring. He answered and listened briefly. 'All right, thanks.' He hung up and turned to Genko. 'The patrol we sent to check out the Wilsons' farm found no body.'

Genko would have liked to argue that it was predictable

that Robin Sullivan would get rid of it. But he didn't, because Delacroix hadn't finished yet.

'But the police officers said there were signs of struggle in the house. And there were indentations in the hatch leading to the basement compatible with shots from a firearm.'

'Did they find Mrs Wilson's mobile phone?' Genko asked. 'If they did, you could trace her last call.'

'No phone.'

No one said anything for a while, then there was a knock on the office door. Bauer went to open it.

'Excuse me,' a young policewoman said. 'Dr Green wants to speak to you.'

'I'm coming,' Delacroix said to Bauer. Bauer got the message and left them alone. Delacroix stood up. 'The man we're after is very dangerous,' he said.

'I think I know that,' Genko replied sarcastically, 'seeing how he tried to kill me.'

'Actually, you don't know.' He was serious. 'This isn't a warning or a piece of advice to be ignored. When I say dangerous, I mean he's capable of the kind of evil you and I can't even imagine ... Green has described him as "a virtuous sadist". He belongs to a category of psychopaths profilers call "comforters".'

Genko took in the word, he had never heard it before. He figured this Green was the profiler with rather unorthodox methods who was dealing with Samantha Andretti.

'The word "comforter" immediately made me think of it in a positive sense,' Delacroix continued. 'After all, Samantha's abductor kept her alive for fifteen years. It's almost as if he didn't have the courage to kill her, he took care of her and even felt pity for her. But I was wrong.' He bit his lip, apparently very absorbed in his story. 'Unlike a serial killer, a comforting sadist isn't content with killing: death is a purely marginal element.'

Genko thought of Bunny and how he had spared him.

'These psychopaths' main aim is to transform the victim into an abject creature,' Delacroix went on. 'In a comforter's prison, the victim undergoes cruel tests, kept in a state of fear, forced to commit abominable acts . . . It's the way they comfort themselves for being monsters.'

Genko didn't reply.

Delacroix stood up. 'If you make a mistake and end up in the hands of that monster, you'll be praying to die as soon as possible,' he concluded. Then he gave him one last reproachful look and left, leaving the door open.

There were police officers coming and going outside the room. Genko felt out of place among all these uniforms. Before going out, he took a deep breath, then snorted dismissively. He should have expected the two policemen not to believe his story. While considering the idea of a nice black coffee at the Q-Bar, he saw a large, shaggy dog walk down the corridor.

Hitchcock, he recalled.

Then he heard shouting and went to see what was happening. From the doorway, he saw Simon Berish almost coming to blows with Bauer. Police officers were struggling to separate the Limbo officer and their colleague.

It's my fault, Genko thought, remembering the phone call in which he'd passed himself off as Bauer to obtain information about the 'R.S.' file.

He noticed the large dog staring at him. He slipped out towards the exit before Berish noticed him, too.

19

'If you make a mistake and end up in the hands of that monster, you'll be praying to die as soon as possible,' Delacroix had said.

Genko didn't have a problem with dying as soon as possible. Because he was already dying as soon as possible.

All the same, when he'd heard that the category of monster to which Bunny belonged wasn't interested in killing his victims, something inside him had snapped. Because at the Wilsons' farm, when he was trapped by the closed door and knew the monster was right behind him, Bunny had hesitated to shoot him.

He wanted me alive, Genko thought as he walked to his Saab in the police station car park. He wanted to take me back to the basement. Drag me down there into the dark. And show me what he's capable of.

He got into the car and waited a while before starting the engine. How long had it been since he'd last slept? He was exhausted. He dismissed the prospect of a coffee at the

Q-Bar – he'd had his fill of police. He could drop by Linda's and ask her to make him some breakfast. Perhaps even lie down on her sofa for half an hour and rest, watched over by her unicorns. It didn't seem like a bad idea: she was probably concerned because he hadn't called her back. How could he have? Bunny had his wallet and his phone but, luckily, Genko had taken away the most important thing from the Wilsons' farm.

He put his hand under the passenger seat and took out the comic book. The friendly rabbit gave him a sinister smile.

Although he was no expert in this field, Genko noticed that the only thing on the cover was the title. He turned the book over and saw there was nothing on the back either. He examined it inside and realised that there was no publisher or printer listed. There was no sales price or even a barcode. Strange, he thought. He was convinced that something was concealed in the mystery of this little book's origin. He quickly forgot about Linda and her unicorns: now more than ever, he had to find out the meaning of the comic book.

Only children can see Bunny.

He started the engine and drove to the city centre.

It was just after six in the morning and the streets were gradually emptying. Vampires were going back to hide during the sunlight hours. He went across the outskirts and over the bridge. Usually, the traffic would already be unbearable by this time, the cars moving at a snail's pace. But the heat had purged the city of its chaos and frenzy: it took him under ten minutes to reach his destination.

The old Saab stuck out like a sore thumb in this trendy residential area with its tree-lined streets, once the bohemian meeting place of artists and intellectuals but now mainly the home of successful social climbers and descendants of the upper-middle classes.

He stopped the car next to a white early twentieth-century three-storey building. There was an elegant vinyl plate with prominent silver letters: M.L. – ARTS GALLERY.

The large windows overlooking the street were now covered with heavy grey curtains, probably to protect the artworks from yet another aggressively sultry morning.

Before knocking on the door, Genko looked at his clothes. In other circumstances, in such elegant surroundings his current look wouldn't help him obtain the information he was after, but this time he could rely on his acquaintance with the owner.

The door was opened by an elderly gentleman with white hair, perfectly combed back, and a pair of reading glasses on the tip of his nose. Despite the stifling heat, Mordecai Lumann looked impeccable, as usual: navy blue blazer, a shirt with a buttoned-down collar, red tie, grey trousers and black moccasins. He always wore a coloured handkerchief in his breast pocket. He examined Genko from top to toe. 'Mr Genko!' he exclaimed as soon as he recognised him. They hadn't seen each other for three years.

'I didn't wake you, did I?' Genko asked, although he didn't suppose the man went to bed dressed to the nines.

'I don't share this folly of night living. Besides, I suffer from insomnia.' He stood aside. 'Do come in.'

Genko followed him into the building, down a corridor with dark green walls and white panelling.

In the past, Lumann had come to him to solve a delicate family issue. A slightly wild nephew of his had stolen a very valuable piece in order to pay off his gambling debts. To avoid upsetting his sister, the uncle had decided not to go to the police. Genko had managed to find the young man in the hotel of a large casino. Having established that he was still in possession of the booty, he pretended to be an art dealer keen on investing his money. He had recovered the loot and taken the reprobate back home.

'Would you like a cup of tea?' Lumann asked. His tone was austere, his manner affected.

'Yes, please.'

They went into the spacious lounge where the works for sale were on display. Lumann was no ordinary gallery owner. He wasn't interested in painting or sculpture, but dealt exclusively in comics and graphic novels. Superhero sagas and Japanese Manga were the *pièces de resistance* in his exhibitions.

In a corner of the room, Lumann put the kettle on to make tea. Meanwhile, Genko wandered among the original exhibits on display. There were only five for sale at the moment, standing on easels.

'Few pieces but precious,' Lumann said, imagining his thoughts.

Genko approached one of the drawings to get a closer look. It was of a battle between a ninja boy with disproportionately large eyes and a few robots.

'It depicts humanity's ultimate battle,' Lumann said. 'The apotheosis of struggle, the final duel between man and the most sublime product of his intellect: the machine. Notice how the illustrator draws the robots: they almost look like divinities. And the young ninja is the bearer of a glorious, centuries-old heritage.' He walked up to him with two steaming cups. 'I realise this is not the best drink for this weather, but iced tea is sacrilege as far as I'm concerned.' He handed one to Genko. 'Now what can I do for you?'

'Nothing in particular,' Genko replied, downplaying the situation. 'An opinion.' Balancing the cup and saucer, he took the Bunny comic book from his jacket and held it out.

Lumann was about to take it, but froze. Genko noticed the astonished look on his face.

'I can't believe it,' he said, putting his cup down on a small table. He rummaged in his pockets and took out a pair of white cotton gloves, put them on and took the book gently, with the tips of his fingers. 'Come with me,' he said, adding nothing else.

Genko followed him to a small room at the back, his private office. He watched him place the comic on a bookstand, switch on an Anglepoise lamp and aim it at the cover. Then he started leafing through it attentively. 'I'd heard about them but never seen one personally.'

Genko still couldn't understand the reason for all this wonder, since the quality of the comic seemed mass-produced. But after that initial reaction, he realised it had been a good idea to bring Bunny to Mordecai Lumann instead of showing it to the nerdy sales assistant of just any comic-book shop.

The gallery owner's face was immersed in the pages, while he ran his fingers down the pictures with the admiration of a historian who devotes himself to precious miniatures, and the excitement of a child reading a comic he's just bought with his own pocket money. 'Bunny the rabbit,' he said, like a greeting. 'Many of my colleagues think he's just a myth ... I've also often harboured doubts about it.'

'Sorry to interrupt,' Genko said, breaking his concentration. 'Doubts about what? Could you explain?'

'It's very simple, Mr Genko: this comic should not exist.'

He was taken aback. 'What do you mean?'

'The quality of the print, the paper used and the binding method suggest it was published in the 1940s. In fact, Bunny the rabbit was a publishing experiment of that time. It was a period of turmoil in the world of comics, so in order to attract new readership, the publishers tried to find new paths.'

'I don't think I've ever heard of the character.'

'How could you have?' Lumann replied. 'Bunny had a rather short life: as often happened back then, its lack of success spelt his rapid decline into oblivion.'

'So in time copies become rare, sought-after items, right?' Genko asked, thinking that, over seventy years later, the value of the comic must have increased disproportionately thanks to the folly of collectors.

'That's not quite what happened,' Lumann corrected him. 'Bunny comics aren't rare at all, you could easily unearth them in a junk shop or on stalls at specialist trade fairs. But there is one exception, and that's the book you brought me today.' He turned to Genko, eyes glistening. 'It's an apocryphal object.'

'No author, illustrator, publisher or printer,' Genko said. 'No indication about its origin.'

'And, even more evidently in the case of a comic book, the serial number is missing,' Lumann added. 'That means it's not part of a series. It's a unique piece.'

'And that increases its value? I don't understand.'

'It's not a matter of money, Mr Genko.' He removed the

glasses from his nose, then took the handkerchief out of his pocket and began wiping them. 'Even though I'm sure some people would pay astronomical sums to own it, what's special about this object isn't the fact that it's unique . . . But its purpose.'

'To entertain children?' Genko said innocently.

'Are you sure about that? Didn't you notice anything in particular when you leafed through it?'

The question made him feel naive. 'In the story, only children can see the rabbit,' he replied. 'Adults aren't allowed.'

'And didn't you wonder why?'

Genko didn't know what to say.

Meanwhile, Lumann had gone to his desk. 'Don't you think it's very ugly?' he said, rummaging through some papers on the desk. 'The drawings and the dialogue are terrible.'

'True.'

Finally, Lumann found what he was looking for and returned to the book stand with a small, rectangular mirror. 'Every era settles on its own aesthetics and sometimes even ugliness can generate beauty. Do you agree?'

Genko thought of the Hans Arp collage in his apartment, in his office. Not everybody would have described it as a work of art. It took a particular taste or aesthetic. Maybe he had made the same error in judgement about the Bunny comic. 'Do you think this rabbit is art?'

Lumann turned serious. 'No, my friend, not at all.' Then he approached the bookstand with the mirror and placed it in profile and at a diagonal on a random page. 'See for yourself,' he said.

Genko slowly drew nearer and saw.

In the reflection, the coarse, childish drawings were

transfigured. Bunny's expression, gentle and smiling, had become ambiguous. The rabbit with heart-shaped eyes was now performing explicit sexual acts with a woman. Genko repeated the mirror experiment with other pages. Bunny was always portrayed in obscene situations spiced up with violence and cruelty. Fetishism, bondage, and other extreme sadomasochistic practices.

'Pornography,' Genko said, remembering the sense of unease he'd felt the first time he'd leafed through the book, not remotely imagining its subliminal content.

'Mirror narration was a graphic technique as early as the nineteenth century, but it became briefly fashionable in the 1940s,' Lumann explained. 'It's still being used in some graphic novels to conceal a parallel plot or a subtext. The publisher is often not aware of it, and it's mainly a prank on the part of the illustrators. Some collectors love to go hunting for these "anomalies".'

'Earlier you talked about a purpose,' Genko reminded him. 'What did you mean?'

Lumann took a deep breath. 'I've devoted a lifetime to comics because I think they're works of joy: my profession is about advising collectors on the acquisition of art objects, but I know their real motivation is the thrill of going back to their childhood or adolescence.' He paused. 'So, in all honesty, I don't know what can possibly induce someone to create something as ambiguous as this,' he added, indicating the comic on the bookstand.

Only children can see Bunny.

Lumann closed the book and handed it back to Genko. 'My curiosity ends here, Mr Genko. But if you'll take the advice of a friend, you'll get rid of it as soon as possible.'

I can't do that, Genko wanted to say. He had to honour his debt towards Samantha Andretti, contracted through her parents fifteen years earlier. But that also involved his facing his own past. And an envelope buried in a safe in Room 115 of the Ambrus Hotel. He'd asked Linda to destroy its contents after his death. But he'd changed his mind.

And so, while Mordecai Lumann saw him out, Genko decided that the time had come to open that envelope.

20

The Ambrus Hotel was a narrow dwelling wedged in the middle of a row of identical buildings near the railway bridge.

The structure was dilapidated and there were strange rumours about the hotel. One of them claimed that in one of the rooms, people would vanish into thin air. Genko didn't care. He'd chosen it as a place to die because it matched the scruffy image of himself he'd always offered the world. Nobody must know the real Bruno Genko – the scrupulous professional, the perfectionist, the man who had a fortune concealed abroad and a collage by Hans Arp on a wall in his apartment.

And above all, nobody must ever have access to his secrets.

It wasn't about what he had discovered during his delicate investigations: what he was trying to hide were the methods used for solving these cases. Genko wasn't proud of what he'd been forced to do.

He keyed in Linda's date of birth and the combination

clicked. He took out the envelope and assessed its weight with a glance. He didn't think he'd ever see it again. Then why hadn't he got rid of it himself instead of asking his friend to see to it after his death? The truth was, he'd kept it because he knew a moment like this could come, when every tool – however illicit – would be necessary to reach a goal. In that case, the contents of the envelope would turn out to be useful.

He put it in a canvas hotel laundry bag and immediately left the room.

Once he was home, he performed the usual ritual of removing his clothes in the hallway, never taking his eyes off the bag he'd temporarily put down on the floor. He was afraid, because, basically, he'd sworn to himself he would never stoop to making pacts with the devil.

He was streaming with sweat and would happily have had a shower but instead, he put on a tracksuit and sat down at the computer in his office. No classical music this time, and the Dadaist work on the wall in front of his desk no longer had the power to cheer him.

He broke the seals on the envelope and opened it with a paper knife. He took out a small silver box and connected it to the MacBook Air with a USB lead. Then he connected to the internet.

The object he had hidden at the Ambrus Hotel opened onto a secret passage.

After years on the job, Bruno Genko had learnt that there are places on the face of the earth where rules – all rules, without exception – are suspended until further notice. Places where evil prospers, unobstructed, and the secret nature of men can be let loose without limitations. In these deserts of egotism, life and death have a relative value and another person's suffering becomes a bargaining chip.

One of these places was the deep web – the dark internet inside the internet, the network beneath the network, no man's land. Thanks to bitcoin, the electronic currency accepted only online, you could buy and sell practically anything: weapons, drugs, and even people.

Women and children were the most sought-after items.

The deep web worked exactly the same way as the official internet. There were search engines like Dark Tor and Ahmia. And Grams, with an interface that was just like Google. You could use them to navigate through sites offering goods or services – a gun with its registration number filed off, as well as the hand that would pull the trigger. There were blogs with instructions on how to assemble a dirty bomb with items from the supermarket and video tutorials showing how to rape a woman without leaving traces.

For Bruno Genko, the deep web was above all the perfect forum for information. There was nothing sophisticated about the negotiations: it was more like a Sunday market, though one where subscribers sold sensitive data in their possession.

Genko's profession relied on the ability to dig out information that could be useful or valuable. In order to obtain it, a good private investigator would usually have to perform endless and often boring tasks. Walking the streets, talking to people, sifting through every piece of information and checking its credibility. It was a lengthy, laborious process. But on occasion the time available to close an investigation was so short and the stakes so high that you needed a shortcut.

Genko was an old-style investigator, he used tested informants and spread skilfully doctored news to obtain reliable information in return. The deep web wasn't his territory and he felt uneasy whenever he had to go to the dark side of the net. For years, he had simply observed this parallel universe without ever revealing himself. In this way, he had served a long apprenticeship, learnt how it worked and how to take precautions against possible dangers. And, before taking his first steps, he had adopted a code. It consisted of a single rule.

In the deep web nobody is safe.

He repeated it to himself even now, as a stopwatch counted down on a black screen. Access wasn't immediate but dependent on a series of stages. First of all, in the same way as you plan a trip to an unfamiliar country, it was always best to protect yourself. The vaccines for this web were powerful antivirus programs and firewalls. After erecting the barriers, the surfer had to undergo checks from other users. If he wasn't found to be sufficiently 'trustworthy', he was ejected like a foreign body.

Over the years, Genko had created various identities to circulate easily through the shadows of cyberspace. Whenever he sensed something wrong, he would eliminate the one he was using and move on to the next. It could just be a hunch, but it was enough.

At last, the stopwatch finished scanning and a central strip appeared into which Genko typed the name of a site. Naturally, the deep web also had social networks, and on HOL – Hell OnLine – you could meet an assortment of cursed humanity.

Genko was hoping to find Bunny there.

In other circumstances, he would have spent his time hunting down Robin Sullivan in the real world. But since his time was running out, he would look for the abductor's alter ego.

'A sadistic comforter', he remembered, making Delacroix's definition his own. 'A child of the dark', Tamitria Wilson had called him. Two expressions that meant the same thing: that Robin Sullivan was not in control of his own perverse nature, that he was a slave to his obsession. He would otherwise not have had the necessary perseverance to keep going with an abduction for so long.

He's well organised, Genko thought. Socially integrated, therefore above suspicion. We see the monster, but beneath Bunny's eerie appearance there's a human being.

A man with two masks.

The first – the rabbit – was just a joke, a lie. The second – his face – was the real mask because it concealed his true nature from the world around him.

Bunny let me go, he thought, remembering his experience at the Wilsons' farm. Maybe because he still wants to hunt me down.

HOL was the right place to discover if that was really the case. So Genko chose a nickname and started a new profile, as an accredited lover of bondage, decorating his page with pictures that left the purveyor in no doubt of his interests.

Then he began interacting with the social network.

The perverts that frequented it usually exchanged extreme pornography. It was the right place for revealing the sickest fantasies and unleashing the worst perversions. All types were represented there. The most popular ones were rapists who would announce their actions in advance and immediately afterwards post videos of their exploits to get enthusiastic comments and 'likes' from the community. You came across every kind of psychopath. From necrophiliacs to 'parasites' who followed ordinary people, who were totally unaware of it, then shared the photos taken surreptitiously. It was often they who, in this way, would provide so-called targets to groups of users who would then get together and go and beat up an innocent father on his way out of his office or else rape an unsuspecting female student alone at home at night.

Lately, the favourite topic on HOL was Samantha Andretti.

They were singing the praises of her abductor, calling him a 'hero' and thanking him for 'setting the example'. Moreover, there were endless coarse remarks about the victim, with someone going as far as to suggest breaking into the hospital where she was and 'finishing the job'.

Genko was disgusted by these vile creatures, squandering the sacredness of other people's lives as well as their own. He pictured them leading a normal existence. He wondered if they still had parents or if they had brought children into the world. He wondered what their nearest and dearest would think if they found out the truth. And what will happen to you when you're at the end of your time? How will you feel when you're nearing death? You'll take to your grave the monster inside you, but you don't yet know that it'll be your only company for eternity.

Genko dismissed these thoughts – he mustn't lose his concentration – and once again immersed himself in the sinister darkness calling to him from the screen. The time had come to throw the bait, so he wrote a message to the fellowship of hell.

I'm looking for Bunny, a friendly rabbit with heart-shaped eyes. I'll pay generously for any kind of news, even

indiscretions. If anybody knows anything, contact me
in private.

He'd used references which only someone with first-hand knowledge would understand. He'd started with the notion that deviants like Robin Sullivan weren't content with living their experience in secret but, sooner or later, sought a stage to show off their 'work'. Hell OnLine was perfect for this purpose.

If he has confided in someone, it'll come out. Then Genko looked at his hands, still suspended over the keyboard of the Mac. They were visibly trembling. It's exhaustion, I have to get some sleep.

Taking advantage of the fact that it wouldn't be night for a long time and that, in any case, he had no choice but to wait for a response from the deep web, he went into the bedroom and collapsed on the bed. He put his hands on his chest, closed his eyes and listened to his own heartbeat.

How many beats do I have left?

But before he could imagine a possible reply, he fell asleep.

A distant sound started to dissolve the darkness – a white drop in an ocean of thick, black water. Genko slowly emerged from sleep. For a moment, he thought he was dreaming.

But the sound was real. Perhaps it was singing.

He wasn't used to hearing human voices in this apart-ment. Only classical music and silence. Besides, this wasn't an ordinary voice. It belonged to a woman. And, thinking about it, it wasn't even singing.

Even though it was at times melodious, it was a lament.

Genko got up from the bed, still drowsy. What time was

it? Outside, it was already dark. A terrible migraine was preventing him from thinking straight. He was dehydrated and the nausea had returned. But he forced himself to go and find the source of the mysterious sound.

It was coming from his office. From his computer, to be precise.

There was a bubble of faint light around the Mac, emitted by the screen. Genko dragged his heavy legs over to it to take a look.

He sat down at the desk and immediately noticed that something had changed on his Hell OnLine profile page. Below the message he'd published a few hours earlier, a small window had appeared, with shapes moving inside it. He magnified the window and turned up the volume.

It was a porn video.

The camera, however, was filming the scene from an odd angle. Only parts of the two naked bodies could be seen in the semi-dark room. The song or lament he'd heard a little earlier was a woman's repetitive moans of pleasure.

She was lying face down and her partner, who could barely be made out, was penetrating her from behind.

Genko didn't give much credence to the clip and figured it had been triggered accidentally. He was about to close the screen but froze because he had noticed something. The shadow on the wall behind the woman wasn't human.

It really looked like that of a giant rabbit.

Genko didn't imagine that Bunny was appearing in person, but couldn't work out what he was watching. What was the meaning of this video? What was it trying to show him?

The moans grew in intensity. The woman was about

to reach her climax. A female hand appeared in the foreground and inadvertently pushed the camera, which fell on the floor. Even so, it continued filming the scene from that position.

Genko tried to see other details in the video: it would have been useful to know where it had been filmed. There was something in the background, but it wasn't in sharp focus. He strained to work out what it was. He enlarged the frame. It looked like animals. Dogs, perhaps. And they were watching the scene. Absurd, he thought. No, they weren't dogs, but horses.

Genko suddenly felt cold. Once again, he'd been wrong.

They were unicorns.

He automatically reached for the phone on his desk, although his fingers still hovered over the keyboard.

Linda's number is in my address book. He took it. That's how he found her.

But now was not the time to think about this. He had to know if Linda was all right. *Nobody is safe in the deep web.* He wracked his brains for the damned number. One at a time, the digits began to emerge. He started to dial them but his mind kept tripping. So he hung up and started again. *Nobody is safe in the deep web.* Think: it's like a nursery rhyme: numbers in a row that have their own rhythm. He hesitated over the last two digits. A seven and a four. He dialled them and waited. Endless moments went by.

The Bunny video kept playing before his eyes. Meanwhile, the telephone started ringing. What shocked Genko was that he could hear the ringing in the computer in front of him.

It wasn't a recorded clip.

It was live.

The sound seemed to rouse the rabbit man. The filming suddenly stopped. In the final, fleeting frame, Genko saw the glowing blade of a knife.

21

The door of the apartment was ajar.

Genko stood on the landing for a few seconds, looking at it. He knew it could be a trap. Bunny could have devised a way of luring him there to kill him.

If that's the way it has to end, then fine.

He pushed the door open carefully with his left hand while pointing the pistol straight ahead with his right. It was dark inside the apartment, the only light coming from the shop signs in the street. Genko had a little torch but kept it in his jacket pocket for the moment.

He walked in and immediately checked the blind spots in the hallway to avoid being ambushed by his adversary. Then he took small steps towards the living room.

There was no sound in the apartment. Even the air conditioning was off and it was unpleasantly hot. Everything seemed in its place. The white sofa and carpet, the black lacquered furniture, the unicorns. Even though there were no obvious signs, Genko knew something terrible had happened. He could sense negative energy in the air – like static crackling on his clothes.

He carried on to the bedroom. The first thing he noticed as soon as he stepped in was the smell – pungent, raw, unmistakable. Blood had soaked the carpet and was dripping from the bed.

Linda lay lifeless in the dark.

Genko went to her, carefully in case there was a surprise awaiting him. She was lying on her back, naked, her stomach slashed with stab wounds. Her eyes stared blankly, still filled with fear. He took her hand and tried to find her pulse. Nothing. So he leaned down and put an ear to her chest.

For as long as there's air in your lungs, he thought. But his friend was no longer breathing.

He was on the brink of tears. How could this have happened? The arms and legs were covered in scratches. A sign that she hadn't given in straight away, that she had struggled. Genko felt proud of her. On the bedside table, he saw the wallet and mobile phone stolen at the Wilsons' farm. Bunny didn't need them any more. He'd taken away the only person for whom Bruno Genko wasn't just negligible human detritus. The only one who loved him.

He grabbed the phone, but as he was dialling the emergency number his gaze met that of the electronic eye the murderer had used to film the sex scene which had culminated in slaughter: the webcam was still on the floor. Why had he left it there? Genko wondered if Bunny was watching him at that very moment. Perhaps the monster was now the spectator.

That was when he heard the noise.

A sharp sound, like a blow. It wasn't his imagination,

he'd heard it clearly. It was coming from the other side of the apartment. The only rooms he hadn't checked were the kitchen and the bathroom.

He stretched his arms before him, so the handgun would lead the way, and went into the corridor. He stopped by the kitchen door and waited a few seconds in case the sound occurred again. Then he burst in. Nobody was there, so he continued towards the bathroom. He'd been to Linda's apartment many times so he knew it well and tried to remember the layout of the bathroom. It wasn't very large and there was a bathtub. Now the door was ajar. He approached it and tried once again to pick something up with his hearing.

He could sense somebody's presence.

Genko reached out for the handle but as soon as he put his hand on it he felt something slimy. It was covered in blood. His ailing heart was sending him unequivocal signals – he didn't think he could bear the tension. He had to make up his mind and go and see what was hiding behind the door, but he needed a diversion.

The torch, he thought.

He took it out of his pocket and held it together with the gun. Then he counted to three, kicked the door and immediately pointed the weapon inside, at the same time switching on the torch in order to blind the target.

It took him a few seconds to take in the scene before him.

Bunny the rabbit was there, slumped on the floor, naked, his back against the wall and one arm on the toilet. The knife he had used to kill Linda was plunged in his stomach. He was bleeding heavily. There was only laboured breathing, like a rattle, coming from the mask. Linda hadn't just defended herself, Genko thought. She'd seriously wounded her murderer.

But that wasn't enough for Genko. He found the prospect that this bastard could get away with it repugnant. He was brimming with anger and decided that if he were to finish off what Linda had started, he would never pay for his crime. What can they do to me? Sentence me? They wouldn't even have time to put him on trial: a higher, more inexorable justice was already acting on him. So he took a step towards the monster and aimed. 'Take off that fucking mask,' he said. 'I want to see your face.'

The rabbit didn't move at first. Then, with difficulty, he raised an arm, grabbed the long ears with his fingers, and pulled. As the grotesque animal semblance came off, a human face emerged. Under fifty, just as Genko had expected. Clean shaven, with an ordinary nose and high cheekbones. Deep, sad brown eyes that for a second broke his heart. A receding hairline. Robin Sullivan, a normal person.

But Genko wasn't taken in. *You and I are not the same. We never will be.* He wanted to kill him with his bare hands, tear off his limbs and torture him with his own knife. Instead, he cocked the gun and took another step, ready to shoot.

Sullivan closed his eyes, his face contracted with fear. He was shaking. 'Let them go . . . please.'

This threw Genko off track. What was he saying?

'I beg you . . .' the man continued, starting to cry.

'What the fuck are you saying? I don't understand.' He was furious. 'It's over, Robin. It's over.'

'I did as you said . . . Now let them go.'

Genko froze. It sounded like a bluff but the man was losing blood. If it was a lie, it made no sense. A suspicion wormed its way into his mind, an idea he didn't like at all. 'Did someone send you here?'

The man was startled. He, too, probably thought he was addressing somebody else.

Genko took the torch away from his face so that Sullivan could see him. 'Who was it?' he asked although he knew the answer.

'He came into our house. He locked my wife and daughters in the cellar. He told me to do as he said or he'd kill them.' He burst into tears. The sobs were shaking his chest while the blood ran from the wound in his stomach.

Who was the man lying at his feet? 'Where do you live?' he asked.

'Lacerville, 10/22.'

It was a nice residential area made up of detached houses, a place where middle-class people lived. It could be a lie, and something told him not to trust this man. But then he lowered his gun, took his phone and called the police. He requested an ambulance then added, 'You have to send someone immediately to Lacerville, 10/22, a woman and her daughters may be in great danger.' He waited for them to take note of this at the other end of the line, then said, 'I also want you to put me in touch with officers Delacroix and Bauer, tell them Bruno Genko needs to speak to them urgently.'

'He was wearing a mask, but I know him . . .' the wounded man murmured.

Genko forgot about the phone call. 'What did you say?' He wanted to make sure he'd heard correctly.

The man looked at him. 'I know who he is.'

22

Five quick knocks, then two slow ones.

It was a sound that cheered her up. The door opened and Dr Green walked in, pushing a trolley with an old television set on it. He had a cunning smile on his face.

'I have good news,' he announced. 'The police have managed to track down your father and he's already on his way to you.'

She didn't know how to react. She should have looked happy but couldn't even recall her father's face. So as not to disappoint Dr Green, she just smiled.

Fortunately, the doctor immediately changed the subject and indicated the television. 'I've borrowed this from the nurses' room,' he confessed, as proud as a child who's just pulled off a big prank. 'I'd like to show you something.' He positioned the device in front of the bed.

While he was fiddling with the cables, trying to connect the TV to the wall sockets, she sat up, intrigued, to watch the proceedings more easily.

Once Dr Green had finished, with a theatrical gesture he produced the remote control he'd put in the back pocket of his trousers and, like a cowboy in a gunfight, aimed it at the television. 'Let the show begin,' he announced.

Images broadcast live from a news channel appeared on the screen. It was evening and you could see people gathering around a bank of candles, soft toys and flowers. Some were singing and there was a festive atmosphere. There was a hospital in front of them.

'What are these people doing?' she asked, surprised.

Instead of replying, Dr Green turned up the volume.

'. . . the police have repeatedly attempted to discourage them but they keep coming,' a commentator was saying. 'They're driven by a need to bring a sign of their affection to the woman admitted to Saint Catherine's.'

Were they really there for her sake? She couldn't believe it.

'Today Samantha Andretti is a daughter and a sister to each and every one of us,' a female voice added. 'But she's also a heroine to all the women who, every day, suffer abuse and violence in the street, in the workplace and in their homes. Because Sam has made it through: by saving herself she has defeated her tormentor.'

She was moved. In the labyrinth, she had tried to hold back her tears as much as possible because crying would have meant admitting that the monster was winning, that he was weakening her defences and that she would soon yield control to him. But now she could finally let herself go. It was liberating.

Once again, the commentator spoke on the screen. 'The woman is providing the police with a series of clues that could lead to the arrest of the abductor in the next few hours . . .'

This last sentence upset her. Perhaps Dr Green noticed, because he immediately switched off the television.

'Why does everybody expect something from me?' she asked. It was a genuine question. Why wouldn't they leave her alone?

'Because nobody can stop him except you,' Dr Green said, then sat back down in his usual seat. 'Some time ago, a young girl disappeared in a little village in the Alps called Avechot. Then, too, people gathered outside her parents' house and brought gifts and prayers. But what happened next won't be easily forgotten.'

'Why are you telling me this story?'

'For a simple reason, Sam.' Dr Green leaned towards her. 'I want you to get rid of this nightmare once and for all. You know better than I do that if we don't catch him, once you're out there you'll never manage to lead a normal life.'

She looked at the yellow telephone on the bedside table. The doctor was right: she didn't want to be scared of everything. If, a little earlier, the mere ringing of a phone had frightened her to death, what would happen in the outside world? There wouldn't always be a policeman outside the door to protect her. And even if they gave her a new identity and a safe place to stay, she would spend every day fearing that he could return. 'What do you want me to do?' she asked, looking determined this time.

'I'd like to try something a little more ... radical,' he replied, glancing at the wall with the mirror, as though seeking the approval of those who were watching the scene from behind it. 'If you're willing, I'd like to speed up the administration of the antidote to the psychotropics,' he said, pointing at the drip connected to her arm.

She followed the doctor's eyes and looked at the bottle with the clear liquid. 'Is it dangerous?'

Dr Green smiled. 'I would never put you at risk. The only side effect is that afterwards you'll get tired more easily so we'll have to pause our chat for a while to allow you to recuperate.'

'All right,' she said without hesitation. 'Let's do it.'

Dr Green stood up and started tinkering with the drip. He turned the small valve that regulated the flow of the drug and said, 'Now you must choose a spot in the room – any spot – and focus on it.'

'I won't lose control, will I?' she asked fearfully.

'I'm not going to hypnotise you,' he reassured her, switching on the recorder. 'It's just an exercise to help you relax.'

She searched with her eyes for a sign or an object – a neutral place. She settled on a light patch of damp on the wall next to the bed. It had a regular shape and reminded her of a heart.

A wall with a heart. It made her smile. 'I'm ready,' she announced.

'Sam, was there ever a moment in the labyrinth when you felt happy?'

What kind of a question was that? 'Happy?' she repeated, offended. 'Why would I have been happy?'

'I know it sounds odd, but we must explore every possible experience . . . After all, you spent fifteen years in there, so I don't think all you felt was fear and anger. You wouldn't have survived this long.'

'Habit,' she replied, not knowing where the word had come from. The armour that had kept her alive was made up of small rituals with which she filled her days. Getting up, combing her long hair, eating, going to the toilet, folding her clothes, making the bed, going to sleep.

'You see, Sam, horror is a perfect hiding place for monsters; memories are overpowered by emotions. If we want to discover something about your abductor, we have to look for him somewhere else. Not only in horrible things but also in pleasant ones.'

Even if there had been some good times, she was ashamed to admit it. It was like confessing to having been the accomplice of her own torturer. She stared at the heart on the wall and searched inside herself . . .

She is kneeling on the floor, her hands plunged in a bowl of cold water. She's washing underwear. She's angry because she's had to sacrifice one of the small canisters the bastard leaves for her every now and then, and which she usually has to sip from slowly in order not to die of thirst. But she has her period and she's got only one pair of panties left. Son of a bitch. She's completed two sides of the cube and asked for sanitary towels: she's screamed for them all over the labyrinth, hoping he'd hear her. What does a pack of sanitary pads cost you, you arsehole? She mumbles insults only she can hear because she is, after all, always afraid of reprisals. Her nose is itching and she pulls a hand out of the water to scratch it with the tip of her finger. For that, she has to look up.

A shadow creeps past the doorway.

She screams with fear, jumps back and ends up with her bottom on the floor. What the fuck was that? A rat? Oh, gross. She figured there were some around, since the labyrinth is certainly underground, but she's never seen one. The image flashes into her mind of a large, slimy, hairy rat climbing into the toilet and popping back out. She remembers that the few supplies she has left are also stored in the next room. The tins aren't a problem but the creature could always nibble at one of the bags of sliced bread or else have a go at the plastic tubs with that disgusting ham in jelly that the bastard buys in large quantities whenever there's a special offer at the supermarket. If it were up to her, the rodent could eat the lot. But that food is fuel – that's what she keeps telling herself whenever she has to swallow something she doesn't like. She needs it to resist and survive.

Survive one more day. Resist one more game.

That's why, despite her revulsion, she has to go and check the next room. So she gets up and realises she doesn't have anything for hunting down the rat. She doesn't have a stick or shoes to throw at it. But she could use the pillowcase, put some food in it and make it a trap. That's right, she could do that. She steps into the corridor and looks around, searching for the animal. Nothing. She heads in the direction in which she saw the shadow slip by. She checks every room until she reaches the one she uses as a pantry.

The tins, the cans and the rest of her meagre supplies are stacked up in a corner. She looks at them but hesitates in the doorway. Then she takes a step inside.

Something does, in fact, move in the small stack.

'Hey!' she says, as if that were enough to intimidate a sewer rat.

In response, a tin falls from a stack and rolls to her feet.

She shouts again but then picks up the tin from the floor and brandishes it like a weapon. She's going to smash its damned head. She takes one step at a time and approaches slowly. She can't see any other movement but lifts her arm anyway, ready to strike. She freezes.

It's not a rat in the midst of her supplies, but a kitten watching her with large, inquisitive eyes. It mews.

She can't believe it. She puts down the tin and reaches towards the kitten with her arms. She's so happy she starts crying. All she wants is to pick it up and stroke it. 'Come here, baby . . .' she says, encouraging it. It allows her to grab it. She picks it up and lifts it to her breast, hugging it gently so as not to hurt it. She kisses it on the head and it responds with a purr.

'Was it really a cat?' Green sounded amused by this.

'Yes,' she said, also laughing. 'I would never have forgiven myself if I'd thrown that tin at it.'

'And you kept it?'

'I used to feed it and it slept in my bed. We played a lot and I'd talk to it.'

'I like cats, too,' Dr Green said. 'I imagine it grew big.'

'A beautiful big cat,' she replied. It was a pleasant memory, and she was grateful to Dr Green for having helped her retrieve it.

'What was it like? I mean, what did you feel?'

'I didn't expect to find something to love in the labyrinth. So it was rather strange.' She thought a little. 'Because at the time I didn't like myself any more. I was always angry. I'd become coarse, foul-mouthed. He'd made me like that . . . But thanks to that kitten, I found a little joy in life again.'

'Did you give it a name?'

She thought. 'No.'

'Why not?'

She frowned. 'I didn't have a name there, nobody called me anything any more . . . There's no need for names in the labyrinth, there's no use for them.'

Dr Green seemed to take note of this. 'How did you explain the presence of the kitten?'

She paused. 'At first I thought it was yet another of his cruel games. That he'd given it to me just to force me to do something dreadful.'

'What made you change your mind?'

'I realised the gift wasn't from him. That's why I kept it hidden from him.'

'Wait a second, how is that possible? Earlier, you said that the labyrinth "was watching" you, that "it knew everything".'

She didn't like Dr Green's sceptical tone. 'That's right,' she replied, annoyed.

'Sam, are you sure there was a cat with you?'

'Are you trying to say I just imagined it?' She was so angry she felt like crying. 'I'm not mad.'

'That's not what I'm saying, but I am puzzled all the same.'

She found him irritating even though he still spoke gently. 'What's puzzling you?' she asked defiantly.

'It's one of these two things: either the cat wasn't real . . . or *he* wasn't.'

'What do you mean by that?'

Dr Green looked confident. 'Please explain something to me, Sam,' he said politely. 'You always seem to know perfectly well the rules of the labyrinth, as if someone had trained you well. But how is it possible that he never spoke to you? At times you sound like you know him well and yet you keep claiming you never saw him.'

That question again. She was tired of repeating that he had never shown *himself*. 'Why won't you believe me?'

'I do believe you, Sam.'

She looked away from the doctor and once again focused on the heart-shaped damp patch on the wall. 'It's not true.'

'But I *do*. Only I'd like you to ask yourself something . . . If the abductor didn't bring the kitten into the labyrinth, then how did it get in?'

The heart on the wall started throbbing. *It isn't possible.* And yet she'd seen it clearly, she hadn't imagined it: it had moved.

'I know you have the answer, Sam.'

Another beat. *There it is again.* Then a third and a fourth. She could feel it accelerating. It would inflate and deflate. The wall was throbbing with her.

'Sam, I'd like you to lift your nightgown,' Dr Green said. 'I'd like you to look at your stomach.'

'Why?'

Dr Green said nothing.

She hesitated, but then did as he said. Before pulling up her nightgown to look, she slipped her hands under the fabric and explored her skin with her fingers. Touching herself around her navel, she found something. Her fingertips felt a slight depression. A hard, linear groove. She ran her fingers along it and realised it ended on her lower belly. A scar.

'Are you sure it was a cat, Sam?'

Dr Green's voice was covered by the thumping in her ears. The heart on the wall was beating, beating fast . . .

She is kneeling on the floor, her hands plunged in a bowl of cold water. She's washing underwear. She's angry because she's had to sacrifice one of the small canisters the bastard leaves for her every now and then, and which she usually has to sip from slowly in order not to die of thirst. But she has her period and she's got only one pair of panties left. Son of a bitch. She's completed two sides of the cube and asked for nappies: she's screamed for them all over the labyrinth, hoping he'd hear her. What does a pack of nappies cost you, you arsehole? She mumbles insults only she can hear because she is, after all, always afraid of reprisals. Her nose is itching and she pulls a hand out of the water to scratch it with the tip of her finger. For that, she has to look up.

A shadow crawls past the doorway.

She gets up and runs after it. She hears it laughing as it tries to run away. It's a game, the only nice game in the labyrinth. She goes after it and it turns and looks at her with large, inquisitive eyes. And smiles at her. Then it reaches out to its mother with its arms. She picks it up. She is so happy she cries. All she wants is to stroke her. Her little girl. 'Come on, baby . . .' she says, encouraging her. She holds her tight against her breast, kisses her forehead and she responds by putting her head on her shoulder.

Her birth has changed everything. She has become the most important reason for keeping going. Fortunately, the worst is over, when the baby wasn't growing enough because there's no sunlight down here. There was never enough powdered milk and she had to ration the baby food. And then there was the cold and the persistent cough. She's constantly scared she'll get ill, because she's so small and frail and nobody can help her if anything happens. As they sleep together on the mattress on the floor, she puts a hand on her chest to check she's breathing. And she can feel her tiny little heart . . .

The heart on the wall stopped throbbing. 'Why did I forget this?' she asked, her eyes brimming with tears.

'I don't think you forgot, Sam,' Dr Green said to comfort

her. 'It's the fault of the drugs the abductor pumped you full of in order to control you.'

She was scared to ask the next question but she had to know. 'What do you think happened to the child?'

'I don't know, Sam. But maybe we'll discover that together.' He stood up, went to the drip and once again turned down the flow of the antidote. 'But now you must sleep. We'll resume our conversation later.'

23

To a sadistic comforter, death is a purely marginal element.

Genko repeated to himself Delacroix's words during their meeting at the police station, when he'd tried to warn him against the danger of the kind of psychopath they were dealing with.

That's why Bunny had used a stranger to kill Linda. The bastard got his own hands dirty only when necessary, like in the case of Tamitria Wilson, because she knew his real face. From the monster's point of view, inflicting death was no fun. But broadcasting it live was, Genko thought, remembering the images that had unexpectedly appeared on the deep web.

'I'm sorry for your boy,' Bauer said.

Genko shook his head, more incredulous than annoyed. The bastard really couldn't bring himself to refer to Linda as a woman. He wasn't being nasty, just sloppy. And that, for Genko, was far more unforgivable than cruelty.

He'd seen her being carried past him on a stretcher. She'd

gone past him in a black bag, heading for the morgue. And now, while the place was teeming with patrol cars, their lights flashing, he sat on the pavement, having to put up with the ridiculous condolences of a policeman who hated him.

He thought about the last time they'd spoken, when Linda was worried about him. She couldn't have imagined that her end, too, was nigh.

Actually, when you come across somebody who's about to die, the last thing that occurs to you that it could happen to you first.

Delacroix approached. 'How are you?' he asked, apparently sincere.

'I'm OK,' he simply said. But it wasn't true because he felt responsible. Linda was dead because he hadn't done a good job of protecting her.

Besides, if you find out you're about to die, you certainly don't think somebody else can drop dead before you.

'Who's the man?' He meant his friend's murderer.

'His name's Peter Forman,' Delacroix replied. 'He's a dentist. A wife and two blonde little girls, Meg and Jordan.'

'Did he tell the truth? Did someone really force him to kill Linda?' Genko couldn't get the images of the live feed out of his mind.

'Unfortunately, yes,' Delacroix replied. 'A team just broke into the Forman house in Lacerville. They found the wife and daughters locked in the basement, terrified but unharmed. The woman claims she didn't register much of what was going on: she's in shock and keeps saying that a man with a rabbit mask came into their house while she was asleep.'

'Have you found any of the man's prints at the Formans'?'

'Forensics are just starting now, so I don't think we'll hear anything for a couple of hours.'

Genko was furious. 'If you'd checked up on Robin Sullivan straight away, maybe we wouldn't be here.' He was trying to unload his own sense of guilt on them, because he hadn't prevented Linda's death.

'Your Robin Sullivan is dead!' Bauer shouted.

'What?'

'We did check,' Delacroix said. 'He had a road accident almost twenty years ago.'

Genko was shocked. Until that moment, he'd thought Sullivan was Bunny. Then who was Tamitria Wilson talking to on the phone? Who was the man with the rabbit mask who'd rushed to the farm in the middle of the night just for him? Genko couldn't organise his thoughts. The only thing certain was that he'd followed the wrong lead. 'What's going to happen to Forman?'

'For now we've charged him with murder. The doctors at Saint Catherine's say he's lost a lot of blood but that he's not in such a bad shape: they're operating on him and he should pull through.'

'Let me get this straight – you've put him in the same hospital as Samantha Andretti?'

'It's the safest place since we're already guarding it in force,' Bauer explained with his usual arrogance, as if it was the most natural thing in the world. 'Why? Do you have any objections?'

'No, on the contrary: you made the wisest decision,' Genko replied. 'If I were you, I'd hold on nice and tight to that upright citizen.'

Bauer didn't like the dig but Delacroix stopped him

before he could respond. 'What do you know that we don't?' he immediately asked, suspecting Genko's game.

Genko shrugged. 'Nothing,' he said, although he meant the exact opposite.

'The first patrol car arrived ten minutes after you called, so you and Forman were alone together for quite a while. Are you trying to tell me that you didn't talk during all that time?'

Genko looked at them both. He wanted to make them suspect that he had something up his sleeve but was still assessing the situation. His head was spinning, though, and he was too heartbroken to keep up the charade. 'The dentist might know what the rabbit-man really looks like.'

'He might, or do you know that for sure?' Bauer asked with less patience.

'That depends . . .'

'I'm sick and tired of this arsehole,' he snorted, addressing his colleague. 'Let's wait for Forman to wake up after the anaesthetic in a couple of hours and we'll get him to describe him.'

'Forman recognised the man by his voice,' Genko said.

'Seems rather unlikely,' Delacroix immediately replied sceptically.

Bauer agreed. 'How does a man in a state of shock because there's a masked lunatic in his house concentrate on a voice?'

'That's what I thought,' Genko replied. 'But all we have to do is ask the wife: she knows him, too.' He let them absorb that twist. 'It's someone who regularly visits them at home. But the woman doesn't know that he and the rabbit-man are the same person, otherwise she would have said so.'

He had Delacroix's attention again. 'Who is he? A family friend? An acquaintance?'

'Don't pay attention to this arsehole,' Bauer interrupted, trying to pull him away. 'He's just taking us for a ride.'

'I'm sure Forman's wife will be able to give you clues for an identikit.' Genko indulged in a pause for effect to allow the other two to weigh up what he was telling them. 'All it takes is for someone to put the woman on the right track . . .' he finally added, referring to himself.

'What do you want in return now?' Delacroix asked.

'I want to see the identikit.'

'And what will you do with it? Are you going to try and look for him? To play the solitary vigilante?' He seemed amused.

No, he had no intention of avenging Linda. He rummaged in his pocket and handed them the talisman.

Delacroix opened the paper and began to read the medical report.

'I'm tired,' Genko said. 'I just want to get out of here.' Out of this crappy world, he wanted to say. 'To leave this place with peace of mind.'

Delacroix handed the page to Bauer, then turned to Genko again. 'And to look the sicko in the face will make you feel at peace?'

'Exactly,' he replied. 'I'll tell you the rest only in Mrs Forman's presence. You've read the report, right? You won't need to threaten me or throw me in prison for obstruction of justice. The only thing that terrifies me is already about to happen. So now we'll do as I say or else fuck off.' He was acting tough, but he'd already decided to give these two the comic book and tell them about the origins of Bunny's mask. After all, after learning of Robin Sullivan's death, his only lead had been exhausted and he no longer needed the little book. But what Delacroix said next changed his mind.

'Strange that you should want to see the dentist's wife,' he said. 'Because she's also asked to see you.'

24

They drove him out of the city. It was still night but according to the indicator on the dashboard it was thirty-eight degrees outside. Despite that, Genko began to feel cold.

Death was trying to let him know that it hadn't forgotten about him.

They reached a motel. Even though it was located in an area with nothing touristy about it, the sign announced, HOLIDAYS FOR ALL THE FAMILY. A ring of bungalows stood around a swimming pool full of liquid sewage, and the general maintenance of the place left something to be desired. It was being guarded by the police at least as heavily as the hospital where Samantha Andretti and Peter Forman had been admitted.

Bauer parked in the yard and opened the rear door to let Genko out. Genko looked around: a hundred police eyes fixed on him, immediately making it clear that the stranger wasn't welcome.

'This way,' Delacroix said.

The small apartment set aside for Mrs Forman was the most central, which made it easier to watch. When Genko stepped into the bungalow, he immediately noticed the bureau's psychological support team. Experts were helping the woman and her daughters, who were still in a state of shock from their experience.

Meg and Jordan, both blonde and both under ten, were sitting at the kitchen table. A psychologist was trying to distract them by getting them to draw. The two girls seemed calmer than their mother, who was lying on the bed in the room next door, unable to stop crying while a doctor took her blood pressure. She sat up as soon as she saw them come in.

'How's Peter?' she asked anxiously.

'He's in good hands, Mrs Forman,' Delacroix said reassuringly, then signalled to the doctor to leave the room and shut the door behind him.

'Mrs Forman, can you tell us again what you said earlier?' Bauer said.

'Of course.' She began biting nervously at her red-painted fingernails.

Perhaps it was an old bad habit, Genko thought, which she had overcome with costly manicure sessions. But fear had the power to make one forget appearances.

'I've always had trouble falling asleep, even as a girl. I take a sleeping pill before going to bed, which means that I sleep soundly ... When the girls were born, it was Peter who got up at night to give them their bottle or change their nappies.'

The woman was trying to justify herself for not having watched over her daughters, Genko thought.

'Did you take your sleeping pill last night?' Delacroix asked.

'This crazy heat and also this thing of sleeping during the

day have messed me up . . .' Her eyes wandered around the room, searching for a memory. 'I think it was about two in the afternoon. I must have heard one of the girls calling me, so I opened my eyes. I couldn't work out if it had been a dream. The shutters were closed, but peering into the semi-darkness I realised Peter wasn't next to me in bed. I assumed he'd got up to check on them and was about to go back to sleep when I heard Meg again: I hadn't imagined it, she really was calling me. Except that her voice wasn't coming from their bedroom . . . It was further away and scared.'

Genko noticed that her face was starting to become distorted. Only terror could disfigure someone like this.

'I got up to check,' Mrs Forman continued. 'Meg and Jordan weren't in their beds. I started calling them but they wouldn't answer.' She sniffed, about to cry. 'I went around the whole house, I was desperate. But then I saw that the cellar door was ajar.' She paused. 'The girls know they're not allowed to go down there, that it's dangerous. I thought they'd disobeyed us or that they'd fallen down, but instead—' The woman froze, looking lost.

'Then what happened?' Delacroix said, prompting her.

Mrs Forman ignored him and looked up at Genko. 'As I was going to the door, that – that – appeared right in front of me . . .' She didn't know what to call him, so she carried on. 'He was wearing a mechanic's overall and skiing gloves. At first, I wasn't scared, more surprised. I thought, isn't he hot wearing all that stuff?'

Nothing unusual, Genko thought. The mind takes a while to process odd events and always tries to rationalise horror.

'Then I saw his mask.' The woman burst into tears. 'I was sure he'd harmed the girls.'

Genko waited for her to calm down. 'Your daughters are fine,' he said to reassure her, figuring she needed someone to say that to her again.

'The man grabbed me by the arm and forced me to follow him down into the cellar.' She caught her breath. 'He'd tied up the girls, then did the same to me and left us there.'

When she'd finished telling the story, Delacroix looked at Genko, as if to say it was his turn now. 'Mrs Forman,' he said to attract her attention. 'Before he lost consciousness, your husband told me he recognised the masked man's voice.'

She was startled, apparently upset. 'I don't know . . . I had no idea where Peter was . . .'

Off killing Linda, Genko thought but kept it to himself.

'Mr Forman mentioned your gardener but couldn't tell me his name.'

The two police officers took a mental note of this new piece of information and looked at the woman, waiting for a reaction.

She thought about it for a while. 'I don't know it either. He's not an employee, he just comes every so often.'

'Do you happen to have his number?' Delacroix interrupted.

Genko noticed that the special agent was impatient, excluding him from the exchange now that he'd obtained what he wanted.

'No, my husband went to look for him at the shopping centre car park,' she replied. 'Peter said that unemployed people usually gather there, waiting for someone to offer them work.'

Genko pictured that miser Forman going among those wretches in his saloon car, promising to pay in cash, under the table.

'Can you at least remember the kind of car the gardener drove?' Bauer asked.

'I think it was an old Ford van, pale blue.'

'Can you describe the man?'

'Yes, I think so.' The woman froze, as though suddenly remembering something important. 'There is something . . . He had a large, dark birthmark right here,' she said, covering her right eye entirely with her hand.

Shortly afterwards, they sat in the bungalow's living room and the woman began to describe the gardener in minute detail.

Since the result depended mainly on the interaction between the witness's memory and the artist's imagination, in order to increase the chances of obtaining a portrait resembling reality, Forensics would usually use three different specialists to draw at the same time. At the end of the process, every sketch artist would show Mrs Forman their identikit, and she would choose the one with the best likeness.

It was a long, complex procedure.

While Delacroix and Bauer watched up front, Genko kept his distance. He stood against a wall, arms crossed, observing the artists at work as Bunny's face gradually took shape. The three identikits had many details in common. This was a good sign, and meant that the woman had a clear memory.

When the time came to reconstruct the birthmark on the face, Genko saw a dark stain appear that covered a large area of the right-hand profile, from the cheek to the eyebrow.

That's why he wears a mask, he thought. He must have been the butt of so many jokes, so much abuse even as a child, because of this distinctive feature. Maybe his total lack of empathy towards his victims came from his having experienced the ruthlessness of human nature at first hand.

The artists had almost finished their work, but Genko could already look into the face of the monster who'd taken Linda away from him. He had a bland, indifferent expression, although that was typical of all identikits. As he tried to decipher the mystery of that face, he felt dizzy and breathless again. He turned to the kitchen and saw that only one of the Forman girls was still sitting at the table. It must be the younger one, Meg. The other one must already have gone to bed. Just like the artists, Meg was drawing. But her sheet of paper didn't have the very ordinary face of a monster but a boat in the middle of the sea on a beautiful, sunny day. Genko wished that the afterlife might be as peaceful as Meg Forman's drawing. Yes, that was a really nice place to go. The little girl looked up as if she'd read his thought, and smiled at him.

'Yes, that's him,' Mrs Forman said with a broken voice.

The artists had shown her the results of their work and she had immediately burst into tears.

Delacroix looked around for Genko and motioned to him to approach. 'There's one more thing to clarify,' he said, addressing the woman. 'After we freed you, you asked to meet Mr Genko.' He indicated him. 'Here he is.'

'Did you ask to see me, Mrs Forman?' Genko asked gently.

She sniffed and shuddered. 'It wasn't my idea. It was the man in the mask who ordered me to do it.'

Bauer and Delacroix exchanged a look. 'What exactly did he order you to do?' the former asked.

'To give him a message.' She paused. 'In person.' She

stood up from the sofa and, before the astonished eyes of those present, walked across the room towards Genko.

He watched her approach, and even though he didn't know what would happen, he didn't move.

When the woman was standing right in front of him, she leaned towards his ear and whispered, 'Robin Sullivan sends his regards.'

25

Building number four was grey and anonymous. Located in the west wing, it was the most decentralised police department.

In the basement, there was Limbo.

That was what policemen called the Missing Persons Bureau. Genko had always wondered why, but he understood the moment he walked in. The impact on entering the first room was emotionally chilling.

Thousands of little eyes aimed at him all at once. The other walls, which had no windows, were completely covered in photographs of faces.

Genko immediately noticed that they were not impersonal images, like mugshots of criminals. There were cheerful people, often pictured on festive occasions, like birthdays, trips or Christmas. He wondered why these had been specifically chosen. It would have been more logical to display their ID pictures, for instance. Or else a shot in which their faces wouldn't be distorted by a smile.

Every image had a caption. Name, place where last seen, date of disappearance. There were women, men, old people. But it was the children that particularly stood out. There was no distinction of gender, religion or skin colour: an absolute democracy of silence governed Limbo.

Genko took a few steps into the room and the eyes that were watching him from the walls followed him. He felt that, for all the joy stamped on their faces, they envied him. He, too, would shortly move into the world of shadows. But, unlike all of them, he would know that he was dead.

Whereas the residents of Limbo don't know what they are. They live and die every minute in the imagination of those who are still waiting for them. And that is why they cannot find peace.

As he formulated this thought, the sound of someone approaching began to impose on the room as an echo. He stepped back, anxious. Almost immediately, he saw a galloping creature advancing quickly towards him through the door at the back. Genko was about to be assaulted. But then he heard a voice.

'Down, Hitchcock.'

On command, the large shaggy dog stopped and immediately sat down in front of Genko. A few seconds later, a tall silhouette emerged against the light from the same door through which the animal had come.

'Can I help you?' a male voice asked.

Genko recognised the special agent with whom he had spoken on the phone when he had called Limbo to request Robin Sullivan's file. 'Officer Berish?' he asked.

The man came forward, holding a small bottle of water because it was stiflingly hot in here. Once again, he was unusually elegant, wearing a navy blue suit and matching tie.

Genko didn't think he looked anything like a policeman. 'My name is Genko, I'm a private investigator.'

'Yes, I'm Simon Berish,' he said, introducing himself. Then he looked at him more closely. 'Are you all right?'

Not at all, he wanted to say. 'I've seen better days.'

Berish seemed content with the reply. 'Come in and sit down.' Accompanied by the dog, he led him to the offices.

'You're a bit short-staffed,' Genko commented, walking past two empty desks. It wasn't surprising: Limbo wasn't a place you aspired to, given the percentage of cases destined to remain unsolved.

'I don't work here,' Berish said, leading him to a third room. 'I've been coming lately to help with the filing.'

Genko, though, realised he was trying to distract him from something. Before going in, he stopped in front of a whiteboard on which the results of a recent case were recorded.

A spiral of road maps, various notes and pictures of places he had never seen. The key point was the ruins of a mill abandoned after a fire. There was a note in red felt pen on the picture: 'Location of last sighting'.

As he studied this strange collage, he became aware that Berish was standing behind him. 'Who's the missing person?'

'It's not yet certain that it's a missing person case,' he replied. 'The head of Limbo is following a lead undercover.'

Surprised, Genko turned to look at him. 'María Elena Vasquez,' he recalled.

'Mila,' Berish corrected.

The Whisperer case, the little girls who'd been abducted and mutilated – that was where he'd heard the name. It had happened a few years earlier and Mila Vasquez had been involved in the investigation. Everything was suddenly clear to Genko: Berish's arguments with Bauer and Delacroix, the near-scuffle at the police station, his words that carried an accusation against his fellow police officers. 'When will you start looking for her?' he'd asked without obtaining a reply. Berish seemed to be tackling the issue on his own.

'You said you were a private investigator,' he said abruptly, going into the next room. Genko followed him and sat down in front of the desk, where Berish had already taken a seat. The dog went and lay down next to him.

'I don't want to waste your time, Officer Berish,' Genko said, partly because he didn't think he had much of it left himself. 'I'm used to putting on an act when I deal with policemen.' The trick was making them believe that you didn't need them but that they, on the contrary, needed you. 'But I have nothing to offer you for the request I'm about to make.'

'I appreciate your honesty.'

'And I the courtesy with which you've received me.'

'We're not squeamish here,' Berish said, smiling. 'Officer Vasquez's philosophy is always to work with anybody. Unlike other sections of the department, cases in Limbo risk languishing for years without making the slightest progress. We lack the means, the resources and the political will to take care of the missing. Because more often than not it's a lost battle from the outset. And nobody likes losing.'

Genko knew something about this. Fifteen years earlier, he'd accepted the Samantha Andretti case, even though he'd thought she was already dead. 'I'm dealing with a disappearance that goes back to the mid-Eighties: a ten-year-old boy called Robin Sullivan.'

Berish, who was tearing a sheet from a notepad on the table, stopped. '"R.S."' he recalled. 'So it was you on the phone the other night.' He didn't seem all that surprised, though.

'I'm sorry I pretended to be Officer Bauer,' Genko said. 'You worked that out straight away, didn't you? And yet you helped me.'

Berish looked at him for a long time, then burst out laughing. 'Bauer is an arsehole. Besides, I know what it means to have to deal with the stupidity of some of my colleagues.'

He was probably experiencing it with Mila Vasquez's case, Genko thought. At the base camp in the swamp, he'd complained to Delacroix: 'Nobody answers my calls any more.' Perhaps that was why Berish had been so helpful to him. 'So you'll help me again?'

Berish nodded. 'I think we established on the phone that the mystery of the disappearance was solved after three days, when the boy came back home of his own accord. What else is there to know?'

'After Robin reappeared, he was no longer the same,' Genko began. 'The parents were given back a problem child with strange disorders and drives, he'd changed beyond recognition. So they decided to send him away and put him into care with a foster family.' *The children of the dark*, he recalled. According to Tamitria Wilson, Robin's mother and father were no good. 'Nobody realised that the monster had secretly inculcated him.' *He was infected by the dark*, the old woman at the farm had said. 'During his childhood, Robin Sullivan nurtured the shadows he was carrying inside him:

abandonment, indifference and violence were a dangerous incubator for what he eventually became.'

'And what did he become?' Berish asked.

'The abductor of Samantha Andretti,' Genko replied, to the amazement of his interlocutor. Suddenly, perhaps for the first time in his life, he felt he could trust someone. The fact that it was a policeman was surprising. So he told him in detail about the origin of his private investigation and what had happened up till now.

Bunny, the rabbit-man. The mysterious apocryphal comic in which the drawings, when reflected in a mirror, turned into pornographic scenes. The 'sadistic comforter' capable of turning an ordinary dentist into Linda's ruthless killer. Peter Forman, who had recognised the man who had taken his family hostage as his own gardener. Finally, the message Mrs Forman had conveyed on behalf of the monster.

'Bauer and Delacroix were convinced that Robin Sullivan had died in a road accident over twenty years ago. But he probably staged his own death. Now the police are after him; they have the identikit of a face with a large, dark birthmark covering the right cheek up to the eyebrow.'

'And you're conducting a parallel enquiry without anyone else knowing,' Berish said perceptively.

'Let's say that your colleagues have a different approach to the issue,' he said, trying to justify himself. 'I'm happy to leave the manhunt to them but I need to know.' It sounded more like a desperate plea for help than a reason.

'Why? What's there to know?'

'A couple of hours ago, I was ready to drop the investigation and I'm not sure how far I'll get.' *Little Meg Forman's drawing – the sea, the sun, the boat. That's where I'm going.*

'But if my initial plan was to catch Samantha Andretti's abductor, now all I want is to go and see her in hospital and at least try and tell her who the man who stole fifteen years of her life from her really is.' He paused. 'It's fine if the police catch Sullivan, I don't care: the future is no longer my concern. I'm part of the past now, Officer Berish. But I want to find out what happened to Robin during the three days when he went missing at the age of ten.'

Berish looked at him and perhaps sensed that he didn't have much time left. 'What's your request, Mr Genko?'

Genko thought about the room with walls covered in photographs. 'I'd like to see the face of that little boy.'

They went down into a narrow basement filled with filing cabinets and minimal lighting.

While the large dog called Hitchcock immediately started patrolling the place, his owner stood in front of an old pc standing on a small desk. After a brief search on the terminal, Berish went down a tunnel of shelves and vanished from Genko's sight.

'I warn you, it won't be easy,' Genko heard him say after a while from the depths of the archive. 'It's a real mess here, especially in the cases that go back to the Eighties.'

The minutes passed and Genko remembered Mila Vasquez. After brilliantly solving the case of the Whisperer, she could have chosen any position in the department, but had buried herself in Limbo. 'Has it been a long time since you last heard from your colleague?' he asked as he waited.

Berish's voice sounded muffled, as though he was speaking from inside a tin. 'Three days. But Mila sometimes disappears for weeks while following a case,' he added reassuringly. 'It's happened before.' He didn't sound particularly nonchalant and Genko sensed he was concerned for her.

'What exactly was she dealing with when she fell off the radar?'

Berish didn't reply. Soon afterwards, he returned with an open file in his hands. 'You said Robin Sullivan has a birthmark on his face, didn't you?' He detached a photo from the top page and handed it to Genko.

There were two little boys of around ten posing next to each other. They were wearing the uniform of a football team. One of them had a ball under his arm, but it was the second one who attracted Genko's attention.

A dark stain covered half his face. He looked sad.

Tamitria Wilson had described Robin Sullivan as a frail child who needed a lot of love, a compassionate child. He thought again about the choice of the last word. Because the old woman had then concluded that Robin was the perfect prey for anyone with ill intentions.

He was infected by the dark.

The 'compassion' mentioned by Mrs Wilson was the passage, the lesion through which something evil had gone in and contaminated his heart. 'Strange,' he said.

'What?' Berish asked.

'Seeing the predator in the guise of a child.'

'Don't call him that, it would be a mistake,' Berish said. 'My friend Mila is always saying that . . . They don't know they're predators, they think they're normal people. If you're looking for a predator, you'll never find him. But if, instead, you think of him as an ordinary man, like me or you, then you have a hope.'

They don't know they're predators. Genko memorised this

piece of advice. Then he looked at the second child in the picture, a little fellow with curly hair who was missing a front tooth – the smiling friend with one arm around the ball and the other around Robin's shoulders. 'Why are there two children?'

'You'll have noticed the room you came in through: they call it the Waiting Room. It's a collection of the last pictures of the missing before they're swallowed into the void.'

That's why they're smiling, he thought. 'People take pictures at happy moments, never imagining they'll end up on these walls.'

Berish nodded. 'There's often a relative or friend, or a stranger, in the photo.'

Once again, Genko studied the picture of the two friends. One happy, the other sad. Two children, two destinies. 'I don't suppose there's anything else in the file?'

Berish leafed through the few pages. 'There is something else: apparently, Robin Sullivan grew up in the same district as Samantha Andretti.'

26

Talking to Simon Berish about the case had been almost cathartic.

Providing the details of the investigation had also allowed Genko to share the anxiety he'd derived from Robin Sullivan's story. Now that he had partly got rid of the negative energy he had accumulated, he felt able to start again.

They don't know they're predators.

Genko kept repeating to himself those words of Mila Vasquez as reported by Berish, as he drove in the Saab along the streets of what had once been a working-class district with brick buildings and tree-lined avenues. A place where everybody knows everyone else, where you could have a quiet life, raise children and imagine a peaceful future. Then the first recession at the end of the 1970s had destroyed dreams and good intentions. Subsequent economic turbulence and, above all, the crisis in the manufacturing industry had swept away all illusions and the place had changed and quickly turned into what he had before him at present.

Another suburban ghetto.

This kind of place looked familiar to Genko. Even though he'd never set foot there, he'd already seen it in the drawings that came with the psychiatric report on 'R.S.'.

This is where it all began, he thought. And probably where everything ended.

At around midday, beneath the cloak of sultriness stifling the city, Genko kept the window open, looking around, even though the view was one of desolation. Shops that had closed down, rubbish everywhere, graffiti on the walls. The apartment blocks had turned into dormitories and too many men were loitering despite the heat. A sign that there was no work and the only way to keep going was to be involved in illegal trades or resort to drink.

The district was already in bad shape when Robin Sullivan was a child, let alone when Samantha Andretti lived there. After she had vanished, her father had gone elsewhere to look for work. Genko wasn't surprised that both abductor and abductee came from the same environment. All predators pick familiar locations as their hunting ground. Basically, it was a law of nature.

As a private detective, Genko was all too familiar with people's tendency to return to their origins. Dangerous criminals, fugitives wanted by half the police forces in the world, crooks so cunning they outwitted powerful organisations: they all had one thing in common.

No one could resist the call of home.

Many had had terrible childhoods, in and out of young offenders' institutions. Or else they'd emerged from terrible, violent family experiences. But no matter how much they may have hated the places where they'd been born, there was always something pulling them back. It was like a rite of reconciliation, as though they were afraid to forget who they really were and where they came from.

Once, Genko had been looking for a guy who'd devised a well-conceived fraud at the expense of a powerful multi-national company and who, in the end, had reaped several millions in loot. The firm had immediately turned to three different investigators to recover the lost money. They had less than twenty-four hours to catch the swindler before he erased his trail. As in the case of every professional crook, his plan no doubt included a safe escape route, complete with change of identity and throwing any pursuers off the scent.

While his colleagues were going after the fugitive, picturing every kind of scenario in order to be one step ahead of him, Genko researched his past, before he was a skilled con artist but just an ordinary neighbourhood thief. He discovered from an old photo that he'd grown up with his paternal grandmother, who'd been dead for years. He went to the cemetery where she was buried and waited. After several hours, when it was already getting dark, he noticed a man in a raincoat, hat and sunglasses wandering alone among the headstones. Before leaving, the stranger walked past the grave Genko was watching and casually dropped a flower. Genko saw that and unmasked the fraudster.

It was true: you can leave the place where you were born but the place where you were born never lets you go.

That was why, whenever he had to track anyone down, the first thing Bruno Genko would do was to contact the friends and relatives of the wanted man and ask to see family photo albums and school yearbooks. He always found among the pictures a detail which no disguise or plastic surgery could erase. And that was why he had also gone all the way to Limbo to get a childhood photo of Robin Sullivan. The police were hunting a gardener who drove a pale blue Ford van and had a dark birthmark on his face. He, on the other hand, had come to look for the little boy who loved to play football.

He's still here, he thought.

If, fifteen years earlier, Robin had chosen his own native district to procure his young prisoner, all the more reason why it was now the best place to seek shelter and accomplices.

He knows the territory, he knows where to hide here.

Genko had assured Bauer and Delacroix that he wouldn't go hunting for the monster. But something had changed after his visit to Limbo. Something he hadn't taken into account, which kept the spectre of his death at bay and made him feel still alive. An age-old predatory instinct.

The hardest animal to hunt is man. And he, like Robin Sullivan, was a hunter.

Something told him that the ultimate truth about Bunny wasn't far from these derelict houses and that stench of rubbish. Maybe he sent his regards through Mrs Forman to let me know he's nearby, he thought. Maybe he's watching me even now and is just waiting for the right moment to appear before me.

They don't know they're predators.

While picturing what it would be like to find himself face to face with his adversary, he noticed a small football pitch that looked exactly like the one in the photo of Robin and his friend with the curly hair and the broken front tooth.

It was behind a church which, according to a plaque fixed to the gate, was dedicated to Divine Mercy.

Next to the presbytery, there was also a garden with two swings and a slide over which stood a large lime tree. Genko saw a young priest with the sleeves of his cassock rolled up to his elbows trying to fix an external pipe with a spanner. He drew up beside him and got out of the car.

'So you grew up here,' the priest said, bending over the pipe he was trying to repair.

'It's been such a long time – my parents left here when I was fourteen,' Genko replied in support of the lie he'd told when introducing himself. 'I'm in town on business and suddenly felt like coming back and taking a look.'

'I've always lived up north, I got transferred here just two years ago.'

'Of course, I remember there was another priest in the Eighties,' he lied.

'Father Edward,' the priest replied as he struggled to tighten a valve. 'He passed away in 2007.'

'That's right, Father Edward,' Genko said, even looking sorry. 'Did you know him?'

'No, unfortunately not, but the bishop who assigned me here told me a lot about him. Father Edward was a parish priest here for so long that everybody in the district remembers him.'

He dropped the spanner into the toolbox, straightened up and started rolling his sleeves back down.

'Father Edward was an institution around here,' Genko agreed. 'If he died in 2007, I imagine he would have still been in service when that girl disappeared – the one they're talking about on TV . . . Samantha Andretti.'

The priest frowned. 'Father Edward would undoubtedly

have been glad to know that she's still alive. The parishioners told me that he never stopped believing, which was why many people thought he was mad. You know, every year he would say mass for her and invite everybody to pray for her return home.' He began picking up the cans and paper strewn on the garden lawn. 'He hoped until the end that someone would reveal something to him in the secrecy of the confessional. Perhaps a relative of the abductor who even just had a suspicion, or else an accomplice.'

'I've heard that the Vatican has an archive that collects the sins evildoers reveal during confession,' Genko said, in order not to appear too interested in the subject.

The priest shook his head, amused. 'Every time I hear another story about the secrets of the Vatican, I think about how easily people forget the mission of charity Christ entrusted to His Church.'

'You're right,' Genko said apologetically, even feigning embarrassment.

The young priest finished clearing the little garden and put the collected rubbish into a black plastic bin. Then he wiped the sweat from his forehead with the back of his hand and turned to him. 'Is there anything else I can do for you, Mr Genko?'

'Well . . . I'd love to see my old friends, if they're still here.'

'I don't know if I can help you: as I said, I haven't been here long.'

'Wait,' Genko said, rummaging in his pocket. 'I've brought an old photo of two of my football teammates. We always used to play on the pitch at the back there.' He took out the snapshot he'd taken from Limbo and showed it to the priest.

He took the picture and studied it attentively. 'I'd

remember the one with the birthmark if I'd seen him before,' he said, but sceptically.

Genko was disappointed but thought he could still find Robin's friend, the curly one with the broken tooth. 'What about the other one?'

The priest shook his head. 'I'm sorry,' he said, returning the photo.

Genko put it back in his pocket. 'All right, thanks all the same.' He turned to leave.

'You might like to see the oratory again,' the priest said, perhaps to make up for his disappointment. 'There's a glass cabinet with the football team's trophies and more photos.'

They walked across a room with a ping-pong table and a pungent smell of stuffiness and gym shoes. There were posters of football players, modern or past champions who shared the walls with images of Jesus.

'Only little ones come here now,' the priest said, down-hearted. 'As soon as they're eleven or twelve, they're already on the road to trouble. And the worst thing about it is that every year, the age of adolescents who get into trouble with the police gets lower and lower.'

While the priest talked, Genko headed for the trophy cabinet.

It was in a passageway, opposite a sliding door with a sign saying, EDWARD JOHNSTON LIBRARY.

Genko stood in front of the cabinet and bent down to get a better look at the framed team photos in among the cups and medals. He was looking for pictures from the 1980s and hoping that the priest would recognise in some old friend of Robin's an adult able to provide a lead.

He saw Bunny's curly friend, photographed when he still had both front teeth, but was very surprised not to see Samantha Andretti's future abductor among the other players posing.

'This year we came last in the championship,' the priest complained behind him. 'I don't know if we'll even be able to form a team next year.'

'I understand,' Genko said absent-mindedly, realising he'd failed once again.

'Father Edward, on the other hand, was brilliant at involving the boys,' the priest continued. 'His greatest asset was the library.'

Something about that last sentence immediately sounded odd to Genko. How did Father Edward manage to get children to read? At that very moment, he heard the priest behind him opening the sliding door of the room named after his illustrious predecessor. Intrigued, Genko turned to look. He froze at what he saw.

Father Edward's library had only comic books in it.

Entire shelves lined the walls all the way up to the ceiling. Dumbfounded, Genko started looking through them. There were some for every age group, from characters appropriate for small children to superheroes.

'I guess you also spent a lot of time here when you were a child,' the priest said.

Genko just nodded, his mind all the while trying to fit the clues together, searching for a solution.

A priest children trust unconditionally. A comic book library. Bunny the rabbit. A book with pornographic images. And, finally, the three days during which Robin went missing from home.

Nobody ever found out where he'd been and he'd never told anyone what had happened to him in that brief space of time. *He was infected by the dark.* Who would ever believe a child who accuses a priest? That was why Robin hadn't said anything.

Father Edward, he thought, trying to imagine the kind of wickedness he could have done to innocent children under cover of his cassock. A man above suspicion, a benefactor. He, too, when it came down to it, was a monster with a mask.

Genko began to hate him for what he had done, a long time ago, to a child who was only ten. He now had the confirmation that Robin hadn't been born a monster but had become one. So what Samantha Andretti had gone through was also Father Edward's fault.

'Do you know if there's anyone else I could ask about my two friends in the photo?' Genko asked. His tone had changed. It was no longer polite but resolute. He was determined to find Robin's friend at least.

'Let me think,' the young priest said. 'The only one who might know something is Bunny.'

The name sent a chill through him. He turned slowly and looked at the priest. 'Who?'

'The old caretaker. He used to do the maintenance. His name's actually William but the kids must have given him that nickname ages ago. He's been here for years. Don't you remember him?'

'Yes, of course, I'd forgotten him,' Genko said calmly, trying to take it all in. 'Bunny.'

'Ever since he's been in hospital I've had to fix everything myself.' He smiled. 'That's why you saw me working in the garden earlier on.'

'He's in hospital?' Genko asked to make sure he'd heard correctly.

'He has a terrible illness,' he replied, turning serious again. Perhaps he'd noticed anxiety on the visitor's face.

Genko looked at him. 'And where is Bunny usually?'

The priest pointed downwards. 'Down there, in a room next to the boiler.'

27

He had made a bad judgement call.

If Genko hadn't been put right by the young priest's providential intervention, he would still have been cursing the late Father Edward instead of standing at the top of a stone staircase leading into the basement of the church of the Divine Mercy.

The home of Bunny the caretaker.

'Do you mind if I don't come down with you?' the priest said.

'Not at all,' Genko replied, focusing on the darkness awaiting him down there.

No sooner did the priest leave than he reached out for a switch. A faint yellow light came on in the basement. He slowly went down the steps, greeted by the humid coolness rising from the foundations of the church. It would have been a pleasant sensation in the torrid morning heat, but he shuddered, as though there was evil in that atmosphere.

Something was lurking down there and he had stirred it with his presence.

He turned right at the bottom of the stairs. There was a lightbulb hanging from the low ceiling, crackling as though about to blow. Genko tapped it a couple of times with his fingertips and it vibrated as though on the point of going out, but then the light suddenly turned very bright, like a dying star. It was making an electric sound, like an extended note. It accompanied Genko in his exploration of the underworld.

There was a long corridor in front of him, with different-sized pipes running along the ceiling and climbing the walls. There was a smell of kerosene and turpentine. He saw a tall metal mesh at the end of the corridor and walked towards it.

The mesh marked out the perimeter of a small room.

Next to the entrance stood a work table with a stool and an Anglepoise lamp. Genko switched it on to get a better look. Along with the light, the crackling notes of a blues song started up. They were coming from a transistor radio on a shelf, assembled in a shoebox with parts from other devices. Judging by the tools lying on the work table, it was sure to have been made by Bunny.

The room wasn't just a repair workshop, however. In front of the table there was a folding bed with immaculate sheets, a thin pillow from under which the neck of a whisky bottle stuck out, and a perfectly tucked-in dark brown blanket. Over the bed there was a shelf on which the caretaker kept items of minimal value that looked as though they'd been rescued from the rubbish: a ceramic vase haphazardly glued together, a bedside lamp shaped like Marilyn Monroe, a hand-winding alarm clock stuck at 6.28.

Genko looked through the junk then went over to a small metal cupboard and opened it. It contained only four hangers with a couple of shirts, faded jeans and a winter jacket hanging on them. There was also a black suit with a matching dark tie that smelt of incense. It was probably used during funerals at the Divine Mercy, when the caretaker helped the undertakers carry the coffin and sounded the death-knell. There were two pairs of shoes on the shelf beneath the clothes. Work ones and a pair of black ones with laces. Next to them, an old Super 8 projector. Genko hadn't seen one of those for years.

He closed the cupboard doors and concentrated on the bedside table. All the caretaker kept there was a small mirror and comb, a bank book with yellowing pages containing a record of his meagre savings and, finally, a few articles cut out of a sports newspaper.

The world of William the caretaker, alias 'Bunny', was all there.

Exhausted, Genko sat down on the folding bed. The blues song on the radio ended and another one began. How can you live like a rat? he thought. A hidden, solitary existence. He thought about himself. All he had to do was compare the Hans Arp collage on his office wall with the junk on the shelf behind him, replace the blues with Bach . . . and hey, presto.

His life was just like this man's.

Both had chosen to vanish in the eyes of the world. Only one thing could make a man obliterate himself like this.

A secret.

In Genko's case, it was basically connected to his job as a private investigator. But what about Bunny?

You did something to Robin Sullivan. You hurt him. You infected him with your darkness and turned him into a monster. Just like you.

Genko realised that he didn't have to search too far to

understand the man's essence. All he had to do was think of himself. Since he kept a Dadaist work and the Glenn Gould CDs at home, he was sure that William, too, would want to keep what he loved most near him. So he instinctively slipped a hand under the bed on which he was sitting, seeking something in the dark. His fingers finally found it and he quickly pulled it out.

The cardboard box was there, at his feet.

Genko lifted the lid and immediately recognised the familiar smile of the rabbit with heart-shaped eyes. But this time he wasn't on his own, because there was a stack of comic books.

Genko began to study them. No author or publisher, no serial number. They were apocryphal, just like the specimen he carried in his pocket of his linen jacket. And they were identical.

He reached out for the mirror he'd noticed in the drawer and checked that the books contained the same evil trick. They did. He wondered how many young boys like Robin Sullivan had been lured with that sneaky tool then initiated into abominable practices at an early age.

Filled with anger, Genko started putting the books back, not even knowing what he'd do with them. Then he noticed something else in the box.

A small metal case.

He picked it up, trying to work out what it was. When he opened it a roll fell into his hand.

A film.

He remembered the Super 8 projector he'd seen in the cupboard.

28

The heart on the wall was throbbing. *Ba-bump, ba-bump, ba-bump.* She had forgotten her little girl. *Ba-bump, ba-bump, ba-bump.* In her dream she saw her taking her first hesitant steps with the precarious balance typical of babies as she went about exploring the labyrinth. But every time Samantha tried to reach her to look at her face, she would vanish. All that was left was her tinkling laugh evaporating in the echo of the underground prison.

Ba-bump, ba-bump, ba-bump.

Being unable to see her daughter's face was the punishment for having replaced its memory with that of an imaginary cat – she knew that now.

Ba-bump, ba-bump, ba-bump.

'Did you give it a name?' Green had asked about the animal.

'No,' she had answered.

'Why not?'

'I didn't have a name there, nobody called me any more.

There's no need for names in the labyrinth, there's no use for them.'

Ba-bump, ba-bump, ba-bump.

Where was that girl with no name now? Green had promised her that they would look for the answer together. Except that she was also scared of discovering it.

Ba-bump, ba-bump, ba-bump.

She was struggling in an agitated half-sleep. Every now and then, she would open her eyes, recognise the hospital room and try to stay afloat in reality, but then her tiredness would suck her back in and she would feel as though she was falling into the bed, as if through a black hole, a secret passage that took her straight back into the labyrinth.

No, I'm safe now. Nothing can happen to me here, there's a policeman outside my door.

Ba-bump, ba-bump, ba-bump.

During one of her confused waking moments, she felt a warm hand gently resting on her forehead. She thought she saw a figure dressed in white next to her bed. The tawny-haired nurse turned away to change the drip. 'Rest, dear,' she said softly. 'Rest.'

The pounding finally stopped. Her eyelids grew heavy and darkness embraced her.

She suddenly opened her eyes.

It felt like just a moment but quite a long time must have passed, because the nurse wasn't there any more and Dr Green had reappeared instead. He'd fallen asleep in the chair, legs stretched out, feet and arms crossed, head leaning to the side. His glasses had slid down to the tip of his nose.

She had a closer look at him. A still attractive sixty-year-old with a stylish taste in clothes – matching tie and navy blue shirt. She wondered if his wife picked out his clothes. Perhaps she took them out of the wardrobe herself and laid them out for him on the bed every morning. This gentle, banal thought made her think about her own situation again. Fifteen years had been taken from her – an ordinary, conventional, maybe even mediocre life, but a life nonetheless. She wondered what had changed in the world in the meantime. Luckily for her, they'd put her in the burns unit at Saint Catherine's, because at least that way there was no window in her room. She was scared of going out through that door. It was like having hibernated for a long time or else travelled into the future. She didn't know what awaited her past the threshold.

Or *who*.

'I want you to get rid of this nightmare once and for all,' Dr Green had said. 'You know better than I do that if we don't catch him, once you're outside you won't be able to lead a normal life.'

It was hard enough as it was – she couldn't, in addition, live with the terror that he might want to take her back to the labyrinth.

Dr Green straightened. He squinted, pushed his glasses up, noticed that she, too, was awake and smiled. 'How are you feeling?' he asked as he stretched.

'Was it me who took the little girl into the labyrinth?' she asked on cue. She was worried she might have involved another innocent in the nightmare, however unwittingly. And her own daughter at that.

Dr Green settled on his chair and switched on the recorder. 'I don't think you were already pregnant when you were abducted. After all, you were just thirteen.'

'So how was it possible?' She was confused.

'The real question is not how the little girl got into the labyrinth but how she got inside you . . . You do understand the difference, don't you, Sam?'

Of course she understood. She wasn't eight years old. 'I know how children are born. Somebody put his seed inside me.'

'And do you have any idea who that "somebody" could be?'

She paused to think. 'Someone who was with me in the labyrinth,' she replied because this was the most logical thing to say. She immediately sensed that Dr Green wasn't satisfied, though.

'Could you possibly be more specific?'

She tried. 'Another prisoner, perhaps?'

'Apart from the little girl you mentioned, I don't think there were any other prisoners, Sam.'

'How can you be so sure?' She saw Dr Green trying to find a way of explaining, and that annoyed her. I'm not stupid, she wanted to say.

'You see, the man who abducted you also chose you.'

'What do you mean?'

'That you fulfilled some criterion of desirability . . . In other words, we all know what we like and what's best for us, don't you agree?'

'Yes,' she replied, not knowing what he was getting at.

'Think about ice cream. Do you have any favourite flavours?'

'Cookies and cream,' she replied, not knowing where this memory came from.

'Good. So if you like cookies and cream you won't ask for chocolate or vanilla.'

She nodded, although the conversation struck her as idiotic.

'We're highly unlikely to choose something we don't care for, right?' Dr Green continued. 'That's why we tend to repeat the same preferences, because we know ourselves. And the abductor's behaviour suggests that he focuses his attentions on girls. He takes children, Sam. Girls, not boys.'

Why this prevarication? 'What are you trying to say?'

Green took a deep breath. 'That the only male present in the labyrinth was your abductor. And it doesn't make sense that you haven't seen his face if he's the father of your child.'

Why was Dr Green going on about this? Why was he so intent on hurting her? 'It's not true,' she said obstinately. 'That's not what happened. There has to be another explanation.' Except that she couldn't think of anything.

'I want to help you, Sam.' Dr Green approached and took her hand. 'I really do,' he said, looking into her eyes. 'But if you won't accept the reality of it, I'll never be able to make you remember what happened to your child.'

She felt her eyes fill with hot, heavy tears. 'It's not true,' she said again softly, in a broken voice.

'Why don't we try that exercise again? The one we did earlier. You could concentrate on a spot in the room again and relax. It worked earlier. Maybe your daughter is still down there, Sam. Waiting for you . . . Just waiting for her mum to rescue her.'

Once again, she stared at the light, heart-shaped patch of damp on the wall. A throbbing heart, her child's heart. Did I abandon her? she wondered. Did I run away and leave her there to save myself?

'Be brave, Sam,' Dr Green began. 'Tell me about when he would come to find you in the labyrinth . . .'

'The dark,' she said, then froze.

'Good, go on, Sam . . .'

'I called it the game of the dark . . .'

The strip lights start to quiver. She knows what it means. It's happened before. And it will happen again.

It's a signal that the game of the dark is about to start.

If she wants to save herself, she must follow a procedure. She's perfected it over time. It doesn't always work but sometimes it does. First, there's no point looking for somewhere to hide: there are no nooks or crannies in the labyrinth where she can seek refuge. The trick is camouflage. To blend in, become one with her surroundings. But in order to do that she must wait for the last possible second.

She goes out into the corridor and starts running in one direction then the other. Meanwhile, she keeps an eye on the fluorescent lights. The strips are crackling more and more. It's about to happen, it won't be long now. She counts. 'Three, two, one . . .'

Dark.

She slips into a room and stands flat against the wall. She's out of breath and her heart is pounding but she just needs a few seconds to calm down. She starts to regulate her breath, her heartbeat slows down. She doesn't move.

She waits.

An apparent peace reigns over the labyrinth. Her ears can only hear a continuous whistle – the sound of silence. Then she thinks she picks up on something. It's like a shuffling sound, along with a metallic noise. It could just be the fruit of her imagination but she knows it's not.

He's here now. He's come down to pay her a visit.

She doesn't know where he's coming from or where he ever

comes from. But he's here now, here with her. She hears his footsteps – slow, patient. He's looking for her.

He can't see anything either, that's the point of the game. That's why he walks with his arms stretched before him, touching everything around him – she can hear the rustling sound of his hands as they caress the grey walls, like a creepy-crawly. Meanwhile, she knows he's hoping to catch a sound, any sound that will reveal where his prisoner is.

He's not far, he's coming closer.

She can hear him: he's walking past the door to the room. Don't stop. Don't stop. Good, he's gone past it. But then he stops.

What is he doing? Why doesn't he keep walking?

Instead, he turns back. He's standing there, outside the door, wondering. He's making up his mind whether to come in or not.

Go away. Go away.

He comes in. She can hear him breathing – a monster's breathing. But she doesn't stir, she stays where she is. She's not going to try and run away because it's happened before that he's come near his target and, for some unknown reason, didn't bother or changed his mind. But this time she doesn't feel she's going to be so lucky. This time luck is on her adversary's side. She hears him approach her cautiously.

He stops, as though he can see her through the darkness.

She knows something is about to happen but stays very still. He brings his face close to hers, just a few centimetres away, and she feels the warmth and smell of his breath. Sweet and bitter at the same time. A monster's breath.

Then a hand gently touches her cheek. It's not love, she tells herself and stiffens – she doesn't want to yield. He caresses *her neck, travels down to her shoulder, then lingers on one of her small breasts. He slides over her stomach and insinuates himself under the elastic of her pants. His fingers explore her hair and stop when they find living flesh. She doesn't close her eyes – she doesn't want to cover darkness with darkness. In any case, she wants to see his face, even in the dark. I'm no victim, she keeps telling herself. I'm not yours. Meanwhile, she tries to think of something so that she's ready down below. Because last time he took what belongs to him, he hurt her . . .*

'You wanted to know, didn't you, Dr Green? Well, that's exactly how it happened. Happy now, you arsehole?'

'No, of course I'm not,' Dr Green replied.

She sensed that he was genuinely sorry. And not just because he hadn't obtained the answer he had hoped for. He seemed upset for her, for what she'd had to suffer – the perverse games of an invisible monster. She felt guilty for having insulted him.

'All right, Sam, we'll find another way of retrieving your memories of the abductor,' he promised, switching off the recorder. He turned to the mirror and brushed with his fingers the carabiner of keys attached to his waist. It looked like an agreed gesture, a kind a signal to whoever was watching.

29

Meg Forman's drawing – the boat gently rocked by a calm sea, the warm sun. The place where Genko wanted to be, at the end of everything.

The perfect paradise in a little girl's mind.

That imaginary place was a yearned-for refuge but he couldn't go there yet. Because I have to stay here and see what's on the film, he thought.

He placed the projector on Bunny the caretaker's stool, put the film in and directed it at the wall. Then he switched off the lamp. He took a deep breath during the few seconds of darkness.

He started the show.

The first frames were empty but soon something started to appear. The shooting on Super 8 was amateur and the operator couldn't quite focus. Then the picture became sharper.

An interior: an elegant living room with leather armchairs, floorboards and dark wood panelling. The sepia light was concentrated mainly in the centre of the frame, while the top and bottom were in shadow. Consequently, the people were clearly visible only from their knees to their chins.

Men in elegant suits – pinstripe, with waistcoats, hand-kerchiefs in their pockets or carnations in their buttonholes. They were almost all holding drinks or smoking cigars. They were talking politely and smiling while waiters in white livery circulated among them with trays of glasses and canapés.

It was like a scene from another era, Genko thought. A club frequented by respectable people of high rank. Genko had feared the contents of the spool, imagining some vile scene. He was about to change his mind.

Then the setting suddenly changed.

Exterior. A dense wood. The camera was looking for something in the thicket. It found it, camouflaged in the bushes. A blonde, barefoot little girl. Her light blue dress was torn, her arms and legs scratched by the branches. All you could hear were her footsteps on the dry leaves. Then there was a sound and the little girl turned around, fright-ened. Someone laughed.

Genko leaned forward to try and work out who the girl was, but the film changed again.

Another forest, but this time it was a cartoon that seemed to be from the 1940s. A big rabbit with heart-shaped eyes, in the middle of a large field. Bunny was sitting on a tree trunk, explaining something to two children sitting on his large paws. A butterfly flew over their heads and the wind stirred the leaves of a tree.

A sudden break. Moans.

A naked woman having sex with two hooded men. She was lying on a large marble altar surrounded by candles and knives. The woman had her hair down to her shoulders and her skin was covered in a thin layer of sweat. She kept her eyes shut while the two men took turns penetrating her violently. There were incomprehensible words concealed in her moans. A kind of invocation or prayer.

Another cut, another place.

A room in daylight, an empty chair. The word 'Love' written on the wall. For some reason, the cameraman lingered on the scene. Then the room grew dark. A naked man was tied to the chair, his head leaning forward. The writing behind him was barely visible. The cameraman quickly approached the prisoner, holding something in his hand, a knife perhaps. The man lifted his head and screamed.

Genko pulled away as if it was happening to him. But the scene returned to daylight. The chair was empty again. All quiet.

Another cut.

A school courtyard. Young children running after one another. The cameraman was following them at a distance, concealed behind a wire mesh. He focused on one of the children. He was different from the others. An albino. The boy stopped as though alerted of danger by a sixth sense. He looked around then carried on playing as though nothing had happened.

Quickly edited sequences. An elderly woman breastfeeding a baby. A circus tent in the middle of a deserted plain. The word 'Red'. A man without legs dragging himself along, singing. A TV set showing an old detergent commercial. The word 'Orgasm'. Two women with black hoods caressing each other and removing their clothes. The word 'Light'. A funeral in the rain. More pornography. Blood.

Death symbols. Genko was dazed by the constant scene changes, but also deeply disturbed by the images. He wondered what he was watching exactly and why the caretaker of a parish would have this footage.

Another scene.

An indefinable place, pitch darkness pierced by the dusty ray of a torch. The cameraman was walking on an uneven floor, you could only hear the sound of his rough, heavy steps, lost in the echo of a large, empty room. He was looking for something but there was nothing around him. He stopped and listened. You could hear the buzz of small, distant voices. The cameraman turned right and the torch moved quickly, searching the surroundings. As the beam ran along a brick wall, Genko saw a cluster of something briefly appear. The torch stopped and turned back to frame it better. In a corner, it unearthed a small group of frightened eyes. Little children with bare torsos huddling together, trying to get away from their persecutor. Seven-, eight-, maybe ten-year-olds. The cameraman walked calmly towards them, only this time he was not alone.

Dark shadows appeared from behind him. Human shapes that walked past him towards the children . . .

The projector swallowed the last piece of reel and the images vanished from the wall, leaving Genko with a heap of questions and an unpleasant feeling in his soul.

What he had witnessed was surreal, to say the least. And evil – yes, evil. What kind of twisted mind had created something like that?

In the basement of the church, in the dark, Genko felt sorry he had started this investigation, felt sorry he had set his mind on honouring a pact he'd made fifteen years earlier with Samantha Andretti's parents, and with her, too. This was not how he wanted to end his own life. He would have preferred not to know the absurd, painful truth. That human nature was capable of genius and beauty, but also of giving rise to dark, nauseating abysses like the one that had just closed before his eyes.

Fortunately, men die, he thought. And William the caretaker was dying. But before the black goddess could get them both, Genko had to have a chat with Bunny.

30

The place where he was going was located in the most distant corner of the district.

From the murals on the buildings, Genko sensed that street gangs shared every centimetre of what amounted to an enclave. In fact, no sooner had he driven past the junction, where there was an abandoned school, than he felt as though he had just crossed an invisible boundary. A car carrying three young men wearing bandanas and sunglasses immediately started tailing the Saab. The sentries had signalled the presence of a stranger, he thought, and those three had the task of escorting him and keeping an eye on him.

No wonder. A year earlier there had been a gang war, which, after just over a week, had left almost twenty people dead on the streets. Drugs or territory – it could have been either. The victims were always extremely young, twenty at most. Life was worth so little around here that mothers knew they would survive their children the moment they gave birth to them.

Soon this will no longer be your concern, he thought. The world of the living, with its damned contradictions, could go fuck itself.

Genko was driving with his hands in full view on the wheel to let anyone watching him know that he had no hostile intentions. There was a bottle of whisky he'd bought from a liquor shop on the passenger seat. He'd arranged on the dashboard the rudimentary map the young priest at the Divine Mercy had drawn on a piece of paper to explain how to reach his destination. Satnavs would get lost around here and internet maps showed just a large white spot where the area should be.

He reached the building he was looking for, parked next to a bench, picked up the bottle of whisky and got out of the car. The midday sun was beating down, feeling like a weight heavy on Genko's skull. He looked around, partly to allow his watchers to get a better look at him. Then he slowly walked towards the entrance of the building.

He went in and was overwhelmed by the smell of cooking and disinfectant. In the hallway, there were a few odd plastic chairs and a table strewn with information leaflets on medical and sanitary topics – from preventing venereal diseases to advice on oral hygiene. In what looked like a waiting room, there was just a homeless man sleeping on the floor right now. He had probably sought shelter from the heat and nobody had sent him away.

The place looked like a clinic but, from what the parish priest who'd sent him here had said, it was a lot more than that.

They called it 'the harbour' because people mainly went there to die. The poor, vagrants, those who had nobody in the world to look after them. Relatives didn't want them and they couldn't afford to stay in a hospital.

Genko couldn't find anyone to ask, so he hid the bottle of whisky under his jacket and began to climb the stairs leading to the upper floors. The steps inspired no confidence and the railing was frighteningly rickety. As soon as he walked through the glass door of a ward, Genko realised that his own imminent death was not a misfortune in comparison with what awaited the human wrecks relegated here. The ceiling fans couldn't cool the air but only spread the miasma in the room. There weren't enough beds for everybody so they made do with camp beds and some even had to content themselves with wheelchairs.

What struck Genko most, however, was that nobody was complaining.

There was almost total silence in the aisles. As though they had all long ago accepted their end with dignity. That or patient resignation, he corrected himself.

At last he noticed a presence. It was a middle-aged lady, not too tall, with short grey hair and wide hips. She was wearing a pair of old All Stars, a knee-length skirt and a T-shirt two sizes too large for her, printed with one of those big Rolling Stones tongues. She had a pink plastic rosary around her neck.

The woman saw him and, not even knowing who he was, gave him a beautiful smile and came towards him. 'Good day,' she said, welcoming him.

When her clear blue eyes came to rest on him, Genko immediately felt an unusual sense of wellbeing. 'Good day to you,' he replied, forcing himself to return her cheerful greeting. 'I'm looking for a man staying here: the caretaker of the Church of Divine Mercy. His name's William but he's known as Bunny.'

She seemed suspicious. 'Yes, of course,' she said. 'Are you a friend?'

'Yes. I heard Bunny's not well and I wanted to come and say hello.' He immediately felt she didn't believe him. Maybe she'd noticed the whisky concealed under his jacket but she said nothing about it.

'That man has no friends,' she replied in a whisper, as though reluctant for the others to hear her.

'Sister Nicla, could you come here a moment?' someone called from the ward entrance.

She turned to a very pretty young woman who was carrying a bowl with towels. Genko was surprised to learn that he was with a nun.

'I'll be right there,' she replied, then brought her attention back to him. 'You shouldn't be here,' she said very gently. Then she lifted her arm and stroked his bristly cheek.

He was overwhelmed by such tenderness. He got the mysterious certainty that she had sensed he didn't have long left and wanted to let him know that everything was all right, that he needn't be afraid.

'You're not a believer,' she said. 'Pity.'

'I've learnt that the world is evil,' Genko replied: it was pointless to go on with the act. 'And if God made the world then He is, too. All you have to do is take a look at what He does to his beloved children,' he added, indicating their surroundings.

Nicla looked compassionately at those who were there waiting. 'I called this place "the harbour" because it's the last landing stage. In actual fact, their journey hasn't begun yet and the place where they are bound looks like a huge, warm ocean.'

Genko remembered Meg Forman. This woman had read into his heart, he thought. 'An ocean drawn by a child's hand,' he said, not knowing why.

Nicla liked the description. 'God is a child, didn't you know? That's why He doesn't realise it when He hurts us.'

It was Genko who smiled this time, envying such strong faith.

The nun turned serious again. 'The man you're looking for is in the last room at the end of the corridor.' She pointed out the direction then looked at him, worried. 'Be careful.'

31

The door was ajar. Genko pushed it open. Despite the over-crowding in 'the harbour', the man lying in the bed was the room's only occupant.

A faint light filtered through the closed shutters, falling ruthlessly on the white sheet wrapped like a shroud around the patient's gaunt limbs. All that protruded was his head and his skinny arms.

Judging by the smell, William the caretaker had begun to decompose while still alive.

The old man had his eyes shut and was struggling to breathe. But then he roused himself and tried to work out who the intruder was who had disturbed his sleep.

'Hello, Bunny,' Genko immediately said.

At first, the man studied him in silence. 'Who are you?' he asked.

Genko pulled out the bottle of whisky. 'The angel of death,' he replied.

Bunny hesitated for a moment, then gave him a smile

through yellowed teeth. 'Come in,' he said, inviting him with a gesture of his bony hand.

Genko took the only chair, which stood against a wall, and brought it close to the bed. 'Do you mind if we have a little chat?' he asked as he sat down.

'Not at all,' the man replied in a croaky voice. Then he coughed and a lump of phlegm came up in his throat. 'Are you a policeman?'

'Not exactly, but I do have a few questions for you.' He noticed the old man looking at the whisky like a thirsty man at a desert oasis. 'If I get what I want, I'll leave you alone with this,' he promised.

Bunny laughed heartily. 'What did you come to ask me?'

'If you know, why don't you just start telling me about it? The sooner we finish, the better for everybody.'

The old man looked at the wall, as though searching for a way to begin. 'Would it surprise you if I told you my name isn't William?'

'Not at all.'

'I was a caretaker at the Church of Divine Mercy for forty years, but only so they wouldn't find me.'

'Who wouldn't find you?'

'The police. Or folks like you.' Another cough shook his chest. 'But I think by now I've fooled them all.' He laughed again.

'Why were we supposed to be looking for you?'

'Because as far as you're concerned, I'm the devil.'

Perhaps he'd said it to feel sorry for himself, but Genko sensed a hint of pride. 'And you're not?'

'In reality, I'm just a servant, my friend.'

'Whose servant?'

The old man was lost in thought for a few seconds.

Genko prompted him. 'What was your task? Luring little boys with those comic books? Brainwashing them? I've seen the film, by the way.'

'You couldn't understand,' the old man said with contempt. 'None of you can.'

The sunlight quickly ebbed away. Dark clouds gathered outside the window. The room was plunged in a grey half-light.

'What's there to understand? Why don't you explain it to me?'

'No point.'

'Try.'

'Listen to me, don't bother.' Another laugh, another bout of coughing. 'Just keep living your wretched life, like you have done so far, trust me.'

Genko was furious but didn't want to show it. 'Who are you covering for?'

'No one.'

Genko knew he was lying. 'What have you earned from this, Bunny? Besides living in a basement ...' His tone was mocking.

'When I was asked to choose, I did,' the old man said.

Outside, there was a thunderclap, heralding a storm.

'What do you mean? What does "choose" mean? You'll have to explain.'

The old man looked at him with his liquid, inscrutable eyes. 'Instead of wondering who I am, you should ask yourself *what* I am.'

Genko thought for a moment, then understood. 'You're also a child of the dark.'

The old man nodded.

Genko realised that, despite his apparent reticence, Bunny wanted to talk, to pour out a story he'd carried around with him for heaven knew how long. All he had to do was wait and the answers would come of their own accord. And indeed, before long, the old man started to speak.

'One day, while I'm playing in the street, a man comes up to me. He calls me over and says he wants to give me a present. Then he shows me a comic book. The main character's a rabbit, but he says there's also a big secret. He tells me what to do. "Take a mirror," he says, "and if you like what you see, come back to me."'

'And what happens next?'

'I go back to him, but only because I'm curious. He takes me away and shuts me in a kind of black hole. And leaves me there, in the dark. I was just a child, and scared to death. I don't know how long I screamed or how long I stayed there. Days or maybe months. Then the little door opened and someone reached out to me. It was a policeman. "You're safe," he said . . . But he didn't know that I couldn't be saved any more – never again. No one could imagine that I had a kind of curse on me. I didn't know that yet either. But I'd already been marked by the dark.'

'What was the man's name? – the one who abducted you.'

The old man looked away. 'Bunny, naturally . . . Or at least that's what he told me. Other people knew him by another name. He'd been the nightwatchman at a fertiliser warehouse for twenty years. He slept by day, so he didn't have any human contact. He didn't say a word at the trial, not even when the judge sentenced him to spend the rest of his days in jail.'

From the way he was telling the story, Genko noticed that the old man felt a kind of admiration for his jailer. He wanted to hear the rest of the story. 'That's not where it ends, right?'

'I was thirteen. One morning a prison officer comes to our house. He says Bunny's dead, but also that, some-time earlier, he made a will and made me his sole heir.' He wiped his dry lips with the back of his hand and chewed the clotted saliva thickening in his mouth. 'My mother didn't want a penny from that man, but we were too poor to be able to refuse. Except that afterwards it's not just money that arrives, they also bring his stuff. A few clothes, a Super 8 projector, a box of identical comic books and a strange film.'

'You watched it . . .'

'And I understood. It was like a message – "Pass the baton", or something like that.'

'Who started all this?'

'I don't know. But I completed my task, I was good.'

They don't know they're predators. The caretaker, too, thought he was normal. After all, from his point of view, William had merely done his job well. 'Are you trying to make me believe that you don't know who's behind this? Who it was you served with such devotion?'

'The dark,' the old man replied without beating about the bush this time.

There was another thunderclap, but still no sound of rain.

Genko was disgusted. 'Is that what you did to Robin Sullivan when he was still a child?'

Hearing his name, the old man roused himself.

'You abducted him for three days and took him with you . . . Into the dark?'

The old man smiled. 'I passed the baton.'

'How many were there before and afterwards? How many?'

'I don't know, I've lost count. But the others don't matter . . . It takes many attempts to find the right boy. After Robin I carried on for a while but I already knew he would make his choice. Just like I did when I was about his age.'

Genko rummaged in his pocket and took the photo from the Limbo file of Robin Sullivan and his friend with the curly hair and the missing front tooth. He showed it to the old man.

'There you are, son,' he said, recognising him immediately. 'How long has it been?' His eyes were shining.

'Who's the other boy in the picture? The curly one with the missing tooth.'

The old man looked at him, lost.

'This picture suggests he was part of the parish, so I'm sure you know him.' He waved the bottle of whisky in front of his face as encouragement.

The caretaker wet his dry lips with his tongue. 'Paul, I think. He used to live in the green house two blocks from the church.'

After his initial disorientation, the caretaker had been helpful. Genko couldn't explain it. It was quite likely he'd fed him a lie just to get rid of him. The only way to find out was to go and check personally by knocking at the door of the green house. First, though, he handed the promised prize to the dying man. 'Goodbye, Bunny,' he said.

'See you soon,' the old man replied.

Genko shuddered at the thought that they were both

bound for the same place. But the other man was right: he still had to earn the peace depicted in Meg Forman's drawing, and he didn't have much time left.

Another thunderclap. The storm was near.

32

The green house was behind a thick wall of water.

Genko got out of the Saab and headed to the porch in the rain. He reached the shelter of the projecting roof and pulled down the collar of his jacket. The thunderstorm had caught him on his way out of the harbour and was still going on; his hair and linen suit were soaked. He touched his forehead, feeling a fever. His heart was still beating in his chest, though, defying the doctors' prediction. It won't last, he thought. It was no use deluding himself. It wasn't a beat, but the tolling of a clock running backwards.

He tried to make himself more respectable, then read the name on the letterbox. 'Paul Macinsky,' he said to himself to memorise it. 'Paul,' he repeated. It tallied with the tip received from the caretaker.

But something didn't add up in his mind.

He tried to ring the bell, but it was out of order. He assumed there was a power cut because of the lightning. He knocked on the door and waited a while. Then he tried again, in case the noise of the teeming rain was preventing the occupants from hearing. Again, nothing.

He moved to a window and peered inside.

A living room with a sofa covered in newspapers and, opposite, an old television set and a shapeless armchair. Next to it, a small table on which stood at least ten empty beer bottles and an ashtray heaped with cigarette butts.

This mess – common among men who had no family – suggested to Genko that Paul Macinsky might be the only occupant of the house, and that he probably wasn't in at the moment.

He wanted to meet Robin Sullivan's old parish football teammate for a specific reason. If the monster had sought refuge in the district where he had grown up, he might well have turned to Macinsky for favours and a cover. Paul might even know where Bunny was hiding.

He's still here – I know it.

Genko realised he needed to make a quick decision. He could wait in the car or under the porch for the owner to return, or he could go in and take a look around.

The second option was the one he usually preferred.

He always tried to be prepared before questioning a source or a witness. Because the only way to encourage someone to talk was to know as much as possible about their lives.

For example, Genko had once needed a middle-aged woman to tell him where to find a female acquaintance of hers. If he had simply turned up and asked her outright, she would have been suspicious and told him nothing. People were always wary of strangers who asked questions: even if it was a matter of protecting someone they hardly ever saw, an automatic sense of solidarity would kick in. Genko didn't have time to strike up a prior friendship, so on that occasion he dedicated a few hours to watching the woman, and discovered that she spent a large portion of the day watching TV soaps. So he went to see her and asked where her friend was, saying he was madly in love with her. Moved by his story, the woman told him everything he wanted to know without any problems.

That was why, there and then, Genko tried the door handle of the green house. Having judged that it would be easy to get the better of it, he gave it a couple of nudges with his elbow and opened it.

Once inside, Genko's first impression told him many things about Paul Macinsky. First, that the former boy with the broken front tooth wasn't well off at all. The furniture seemed to have been picked up from a dump. The carpet may once have been beige but was now an archipelago of grease stains. There was dust and dirt everywhere. A blanket, two bowls and a lead were lying in a corner, but luckily there was no sign of dogs.

Genko closed the door behind him. The noise of the rain abated. The house was two storeys high, and he decided to start with the upper floor.

At the top of the stairs, there was a short corridor with three rooms. He approached the frosted glass door and figured it led to a bathroom. He opened it just a few centimetres and a black dog immediately barked at him fiercely. He quickly closed it again before he could be attacked. He cursed the animal, himself and even his heart pounding in his chest. He'd got a fright, but then laughed: it would have been a truly stupid way to get a fatal heart attack.

He continued inspecting the surroundings. The second room had only the rusty base of a double bed. Rainwater dripping from a crack in the roof had formed a puddle on the floor.

The wardrobe contained women's clothes that smelt of mothballs. He figured they must belong to Paul's mother and assumed Mrs Macinsky must have been dead for some time.

The third room, on the other hand, was still in regular use. Paul's bed was a mattress on the floor. There were a few posters of heavy metal bands on the black walls. It looked like a teenager's room from the 1980s. Except that the man who slept here was just under fifty years old. There was a small collection of LPs next to a record player. A small trophy stood in prime position on a shelf, with a brass plaque that said, PARISH TOURNAMENT 1982–83 – THIRD PLACE. Judging by his state now, this must have been the only moment of glory in Paul's existence.

Next to the bed on the floor, under a stack of porn magazines, was a ceramic bowl with all the necessities for rolling a joint. He also noticed that a section of the skirting board was coming away from the wall slightly. Genko easily removed it and discovered a cavity with a block of hashish inside. He felt its weight. It was a modest quantity, for a small-time dealer. He put it back where he'd found it.

At this point, Genko concluded that his brief exploration of the house hadn't given him any useful information with which to establish a friendly dialogue with Paul. It was difficult to find common ground with someone who basically enjoyed getting stoned and reading obscene publications. He would have to find another way of gaining his trust and persuading him to open up. Paul Macinsky was the closest person to Robin Sullivan he had managed to unearth.

If he knows where Bunny is, I could get it out of him. But how?

The dog in the bathroom was still barking, preventing him from thinking. He was getting a migraine. He shivered and his teeth started clattering. His temperature was rising. He went back downstairs.

He should have left the house immediately and sat in the Saab to wait for Paul Macinsky to return. But having come downstairs, he felt suddenly exhausted. He couldn't go back out there in the rain again. He removed the newspapers from the living room sofa but then decided to sit in the armchair, in what looked like Paul's favourite spot, in front of the TV, which was now off. There was even a blanket: it was dirty and full of holes, but he put it around himself all the same. His shivering showed no sign of stopping. He was also frightened, but realised he had to immediately dismiss the thought of imminent death. He tried to calm down. He had to think of something.

Once again he remembered the old caretaker and especially how readily he'd told him the name of the curly haired boy with the broken front tooth, standing next to Robin in the Limbo picture.

When Genko had accused him of having taken a poor, defenceless child into the darkness, William had justified himself with an absurd reason.

'I passed the baton,' he'd said.

He meant that Robin was a worthy disciple, and that was what didn't add up in Genko's mind. If old Bunny considered Robin as his heir – the new Bunny – why had he helped a stranger find him? He should have done more to protect the identity of the childhood friend who might supply information that would lead to the capture of his beloved pupil.

And yet he'd uttered Paul's name almost immediately.

He couldn't work it out. But at least his trembling had subsided and the dog upstairs had given up. Lulled by the silence and the old armchair, Genko looked at his reflection in the TV screen. He felt glad to still be here and not dead. He'd escaped once again. He felt grateful and relieved.

Without realising it, he fell into a deep sleep.

33

A tight grip at his throat, his mouth wide open – desperately – in search of oxygen. The worst way to wake up after a sleep as deep as death: discovering you're alive only to die again – and painfully.

The thug behind Genko wouldn't let go. He could feel the powerful forearm ruthlessly tightening its hold. Genko tried to tear that arm from his neck but his fingers kept slipping on the attacker's skin, which was wet from the rain. He would have liked time to explain to Paul Macinsky why he'd broken into his house like a burglar. To tell him he understood his reaction but that, given the situation, it was somewhat exaggerated. He wanted to say all this to the man about to kill him. But then he caught his reflection in the television opposite him.

The thug had a dark stain on the right side of his face.

It wasn't Paul Macinsky. It was Sullivan.

That's why the old man helped me. He sent me here and

somehow warned his disciple. Thanks to him, I've ended up in a trap.

Bunny no longer needed his rabbit mask and they were finally face to face. And Bunny, too, was looking at him on the screen. There was no hatred in his beady eyes, or even anger. Just a cold, lucid desire to kill.

Meg Forman's drawing – *the warm ocean, the boat, the sunshine*. The paradise imagined by a little girl. I've earned it, Genko decided, I deserve it. 'God is like a child, didn't you know?' the nun at the harbour had said. 'That's why He doesn't realise it when He hurts us.'

Genko began to accept the pain of the end.

Shining trails, like graceful fairies, began to dance before his eyes. His lungs were quickly emptying and he was now gasping for air. *The warm ocean, the boat, the sunshine –* he could almost see them. I'm coming, he thought. He felt himself being yanked upwards and threw his head back. It was an unquestioning reflex, but he managed to unwittingly give the assailant a blow on the nose.

Dazed by the unexpected reaction, Robin Sullivan loosened his grip. Genko took advantage of that to disengage himself and bounced up from the armchair. He fell forward and landed with his hands on the filthy carpet. He tried to breathe but only just managed it at the third attempt. He turned to check on his attacker: Bunny's nose was bleeding and his tears were impairing his vision, but that didn't stop him from rushing at Genko again. He grabbed his ankle, but Genko slipped his leg out and darted forward, away from the monster but also from the front door. He didn't know where he was going, acting like a fly that doesn't notice the gap in a window and remains a prisoner through its own stupidity.

He staggered into the kitchen, the only room in the house he hadn't checked out.

He felt relieved when, next to an old fridge with a door covered in magnets, he saw a door leading to the backyard.

Genko saw that Bunny had roused himself in the meantime and was coming at him again.

Being out of the house didn't mean being safe, but it was an excellent incentive not to admit defeat. He used what little strength he had left to rush to the door, hoping it wasn't locked like the one at the Wilsons' farm a few nights earlier, when Bunny had been behind him just like now.

He grabbed the handle and pulled: the door was open. He was about to step outside but hesitated. Everything seemed to be happening slowly. He felt the bullet penetrating his back, right between his shoulder blades. A piece of burning-hot metal digging through his flesh.

Yet he hadn't heard a shot. How is this possible? he wondered.

It felt like being shot through with a bullet. But when he looked down, he noticed that there was no exit hole in his chest. Before he could find an explanation, he felt his legs give way and fell to his knees. There was a deep, syncopated beat in his ears – it was his heart losing its rhythm.

Nobody had shot him.

It was the fatal heart attack he'd been expecting for days.

Bruno Genko let go of the door handle, swivelled slightly on his knees, leaned against the fridge door and slid to the floor, taking with him a cascade of coloured magnets.

Suspended between life and death, his eyes absentmindedly came to rest on one magnet in particular: a tropical palm. There was a drawing under it.

The style and colours were unmistakable. It had been done by a child.

It was the picture of a large rabbit with heart-shaped eyes, holding a little blonde girl by the hand.

But what surprised Genko was the signature at the bottom of the drawing. The diminutive of a first name.

Meg

34

Incredible how the brain of a man about to die can work so fast, Genko thought. Because he could now think at twice the speed.

How come the Formans' youngest daughter knows Bunny?

Genko looked up, assuming his attacker was about to give him the final blow. Instead, the man was standing still, looking at him. Maybe he was waiting for him to die of his own accord. But no matter what was going through his mind, Genko still had time to learn the truth. He made an effort and put a hand in his pocket. He took out the photo from Limbo and held it out to the man with the dark birthmark on his face.

The man hesitated for a second, then took it.

From his expression, Genko assumed he'd been right. 'You're Paul Macinsky, aren't you?' he asked.

The man said nothing, then reacted. 'What does this picture mean?' he asked nervously. 'Who are you? And what are you doing in my house?'

The last sentence was enough to tell Genko that this wasn't Robin Sullivan. The old caretaker lied to me, he thought. That's why he looked so lost when I asked him the name of the curly haired boy in the picture. He knew I was after the wrong person. Because I thought Robin was the sad one with the birthmark on his face. But that's not the case.

It's the other one – the cheerful one.

The old Bunny had thrown him off the scent, but the case of mistaken identity had begun earlier. The error had been generated by the dentist's statement: Peter Forman had recognised the voice of the man with the rabbit mask who, he said, had forced him to kill Linda by threatening his family. It was the dentist who had first pointed to the gardener.

How come the Formans' youngest daughter knows Bunny the rabbit?

'Tell me about Robin,' Genko said to Paul Macinsky in a whisper.

'Perhaps I'd better call you an ambulance, my friend.'

He looked genuinely worried but Genko shook his head. 'Robin Sullivan,' he repeated.

'He's not called that any more, he changed his name. We used to hang out together as kids, then I lost touch with him. Perhaps he thought I wouldn't recognise him when he came to ask me to go fix his garden but I immediately knew it was him.'

'Who?' Genko asked. 'Please tell me.' He needed to hear it from his lips.

'Robin … Robin Sullivan … He's got a nice house, an attractive wife and two girls. He calls himself Peter Forman and he's a dentist.'

How come the Formans' youngest daughter knows Bunny?

'Now tell me about this.' Genko pointed at the drawing under the palm tree-shaped magnet.

'I'm calling an ambulance,' the man replied, taking a mobile phone from his pocket.

'Please: the drawing.'

The man had dialled the number but paused to answer the question. 'The Forman girl – the youngest one – gave it to me. It was a week ago.'

The little girl had felt sorry for this solitary man who, in his childhood photos, expressed the sadness that would be with him his entire life. Genko had mistaken him for a monster, and felt guilty. 'Did Meg tell you what the drawing means?'

'No,' he replied.

How come the Formans' youngest daughter knows Bunny? Because she knows the man under the mask, Genko thought. *Bunny is her daddy.*

He remembered the scene at Linda's, when he'd found Peter Forman gravely wounded. That was when the monster had begun his act.

But why involve his own family by staging an abduction? 'He broke into our house,' the dentist had said, tearfully, when it was him who'd appeared to his wife in the Bunny mask and then locked her in the cellar with their girls. 'He said that if I didn't do as I was told, he'd kill them,' he'd said, sobbing. But why pretend with them, too? Why hadn't he just gone to Linda's home and killed her?

Because that, too, was a dirty trick, Genko thought. 'He was wearing a mask but I know him . . . I know who he is.' It wasn't just the start of an ingenious plan to throw everybody off the scent and divert suspicion onto the innocent gardener.

No, he had a specific aim in mind.

When Genko had found the man in the rabbit mask lying on the floor, naked and bleeding, he'd assumed that Linda had defended herself, that she'd gravely wounded her murderer. And he'd been proud of her.

It wasn't Linda who'd wounded him with the knife, he now thought. Bunny did that himself.

Genko had been surprised when Bauer and Delacroix had told him that Forman had been admitted to Saint Catherine's. 'It's the safest place, since we're already guarding it in force,' Bauer had said with his usual arrogance.

The safest place for Bunny was also the place where Samantha Andretti now was.

He wants to get her back, he thought. *That bastard wants to take her back into the dark.*

But no sooner did Bruno Genko have a complete picture of the plan than he died.

35

Dr Green returned to the room and quickly shut the door behind him. He was hiding something behind his back. 'Here you are,' he announced, producing a paper bag. 'I thought you might be hungry.'

She followed him with her eyes as he went and sat down in his usual spot.

'The hospital food is disgusting, this is much better.' He took two sandwiches wrapped in clingfilm out of the bag. 'Chicken or tuna?' he asked.

'Chicken,' she replied.

He gave her one of the sandwiches. 'Excellent choice: my wife's chicken sandwiches are unrivalled.'

She took it and looked at it.

'Aren't you going to eat it?' he asked, biting into his tuna sandwich.

'I'm sorry,' she said. 'I just thought of something ... How did my abductor manage to give me the drugs to keep me quiet?'

'The psychotropic drugs, you mean?' Dr Green stopped to think. 'I think he must have given them to you with your food.'

She turned her sandwich over. It had been a long time since she'd eaten anything prepared with love. 'Your wife must love you very much.'

'We've had our ups and downs,' Green confessed, 'but I think that happens to all couples who've been together for a long time.'

She turned to the mirror. 'Isn't my father here yet?'

'It'll take a little time yet, and then we'll bring him straight here.'

'I don't know . . .' She didn't feel ready to see him again yet.

'Nobody's forcing you, Sam. You can take all the time you need.'

'The fact is, I don't even remember what he looks like.'

'I can bring you a picture, if you want. It might help you remember something.'

The doctor's words had the effect of bringing her relief. She unwrapped the sandwich and attacked it greedily. Dr Green was right: it was delicious. 'Tuesday,' she said without thinking.

'What?'

Once again, she focused on the damp patch on the wall – the throbbing heart. 'Tuesday is pizza day,' she said . . .

Actually, she doesn't know if it's Tuesday. Or if it's day or night. Moreover, it's highly likely that what she calls 'Pizza Tuesday' occurs once a month or even less often. But that's what she's decided. One of the little conventions she has applied to the routine of the labyrinth.

It all started the first time she managed to complete the

third side of Rubik's cube. She was proud of herself, so pleased with her work that she immediately felt angry. Because she felt she deserved a prize. So she started walking around the labyrinth, holding up the cube like a trophy, marching and shouting, 'Pizza! Pizza! Pizza!' As well as claiming her rightful reward, she meant to annoy the bastard in the event he was listening. And she even got a certain pleasure from her rebellion.

In the end, she had obtained what she wanted.

In one of the rooms, she found a cardboard box with a soggy margherita pizza, a couple of days old. The bastard thought he'd punish her that way, but she'd gladly eaten it anyway. Ever since then, it had become a ritual.

Every time she completed the third side of the cube, there came another Tuesday. Stale pizza.

Where does the bastard get it? The box is plain, anonymous. No indication as to the shop. It might be a pizza chain or a small business that only does takeaways. She pictures a place with a perennial smell of fried food, white tiles covered in a layer of shiny, slimy grease no soap can ever wash away.

Every time she takes the first bite of the pizza, she wonders what the person who made it looks like. For some reason, she imagines a young man with strong arms covered in flour and a beer gut. A cheerful guy who likes hanging around with his friends, going to the cinema with them to see action films, or bowling. He doesn't have a girlfriend but there's a very attractive brunette in his life, a cashier in a supermarket.

The young man never wonders who his pizzas are for – why should he? He doesn't even suspect that the one he's preparing will end up in a labyrinth to feed a wretched prisoner. He doesn't know he's the only contact, however indirectly, that she has with the outside world. But he's the proof that there's something else beyond these walls. That humanity hasn't become extinct through a nuclear holocaust or an asteroid falling from the sky . . .

'I kept hoping I'd find a message for me in one of the boxes that arrived on my imaginary Tuesdays. Not a note, of course, but even just one word written in tomato sauce. A simple greeting, like a "Hi", for instance. Once there was a little artichoke on the pizza and I took it for a sign. But then it didn't happen again.'

'What bothered you most in the labyrinth?' Dr Green asked, taking one last bite of his tuna sandwich.

'The colour of the walls. That unbearable grey.'

'There's a theory that some colours influence our psyche,' Dr Green said, wiping his mouth with a tissue. 'Green gives confidence, which is why gambling tables are always green: to urge the players to take risks. Warm tones, on the other hand, trigger serotonin and make people talkative, for example, or sexually promiscuous.'

'What about grey?' she asked.

'It inhibits the action of endorphins. The rooms in psychiatric asylums are painted grey, as are maximum security prison cells.' Then he added, 'The cages at the zoo . . . In the long run, grey makes you meek.'

Grey makes you meek, she repeated to herself. He had seen her as a kind of animal whose instinct had to be repressed.

Maybe Dr Green noticed that the subject had upset her. To distract her, he scrunched up his tissue, turned to the wastepaper basket, aimed and shot it straight in. 'I was a playmaker in the university basketball team: I was amazing, though I say it myself.'

She couldn't help smiling.

But then she noticed that Dr Green had taken advantage of her moment of distraction to touch the carabiner of keys at his belt again. Again, that signal for communicating with the police behind the mirror, she thought. What did it mean? Perhaps there was no code, just her paranoia.

Dr Green noticed he'd dropped a little tuna on his navy blue shirt. 'My wife's going to hit the roof,' he muttered, desperately trying to rub the stain off with his fingers. 'I must try and get rid of it,' he said, getting up. 'I'll be right back.'

She was glad of the respite. She was desperate to pee and although she had a catheter she was embarrassed to do so in front of him.

'I'll bring you back a drink,' he promised before leaving. 'But don't lose your concentration, because we must get back to work.'

Left alone, she obeyed Dr Green and continued to stare at the heart on the wall. That was when the yellow telephone on the bedside table rang again.

Once again, that paralysing terror.

Dr Green's right, she thought. It's only someone dialling the wrong number. It's silly to be scared. But there was only one way to find out.

Answer.

The rings echoed eerily in the room and inside her head. She just wanted them to stop soon, but they didn't.

She made up her mind. She reached out to the bedside table. Her leg in the cast impaired her mobility but all the same she managed to touch the receiver with her fingers. She pulled it towards her, grabbed it and lifted it to her ear. I'll just hear a deep silence, she thought. And that silence will conceal breathing. 'Hello?' she said, and waited anxiously.

'You forgot the address,' a male voice immediately said.

She didn't understand, there was a lot of background noise. It was like Dr Green had said, a wrong number. She felt calmer.

'Hello?' the man at the other end of the line was growing impatient.

'I'm sorry, I don't know what you're talking about.'

'I need the address,' the man said. 'For the order.'

She stared and a shudder went through her, like an electric shock.

'The pizza,' the man on the phone said. 'Where are we delivering it?'

She threw down the receiver as if it had scalded her. Then she instinctively turned to the wall with the mirror. It was more than a simple gut feeling. As she looked at her own reflection, she had the distinct feeling that an evil shadow was concealed behind it and that it had heard her story.

And the purpose of this prank had been to let her know that it was nearby.

36

A single, consistent sound in the background.

'Clear!'

He was no longer in control of his body. He was there, but it was as though he was imprisoned in a diving suit made of flesh. He felt no pain, though. On the contrary, there was a strange sense of wellbeing.

He couldn't close his eyes so he stared and watched from a prime location as the rescuers busied themselves over him. The spectator of his own death – how cool was that?

'Clear!'

The paramedics were a man and a woman. He was a sturdy fellow, around thirty, with a crew cut and dark eyes. The kind of guy you'd have a beer or watch a game with. He was pressing an Ambu bag over Genko's nose and mouth. She was smaller but no less determined. Blue hair tied in a ponytail, fair skin, freckles and green eyes. At any other time, he would have asked her out. In a ballsy tone, she gave another command.

'Clear!'

The stout man took a step back and she placed the electrodes on Genko's chest again, then emitted another shock. Every time, it was as though someone had started a fire inside him. The flames would flare up and go out within seconds.

After a brief pause, the background sound changed and became rhythmical.

'Good,' Blue Hair announced enthusiastically. 'We've brought him back: now he's transportable.'

Nobody asked you to bring me back. You should have left me where I was.

They lifted him onto a stretcher. After travelling down the alley with a series of jolts, they put him into the ambulance. The doors shut and the siren came on.

'Now stay with us, mate, OK?' the man was saying to him in order to keep him awake. 'You've been lucky: your friend gave you a ten-minute cardiac massage. If it hadn't been for him we would have been no use. So start thinking of a nice present.'

He couldn't believe it: Paul Macinsky had – temporarily – saved his life. He wanted to tell the two paramedics that the man was innocent, that he'd had nothing to do with Samantha Andretti's abduction. That Bunny was actually . . . Who was Bunny? He'd forgotten.

Darkness.

A sudden bolt of lightning – like the magnesium flash of bygone cameras – that dissolved into a totally different setting. He was no longer in the ambulance. Hectic sounds and noises. A great bustle around him. He was lying down, a bright white light watching him from above. Indistinct voices. They were all naked.

'How's the oximetry?' a short girl with huge breasts asked.

'Dropping. Sixty-seven per cent,' a very hairy, bearded man replied.

'Asystole,' another one – all he could see of him was his large belly – said.

'I'll prepare an atropine injection,' a female voice said, before turning to reveal an attractive bottom.

They're naked because of the heat, Genko thought, unable to fathom this absurdity. While they were all serious, he started to giggle.

'Let's put the CPAP on,' said a young female doctor with black hair cascading softly over her shoulders. She was the only one wearing a white lab coat. But she had nothing on underneath. Oh, how he would have liked to take it off!

'How's the pressure?'

'Eighty-eight over fifty-nine.'

How about taking that coat off? I'm sure you'd fancy me, baby . . . He was no longer in control, but dying wasn't so bad after all. He was euphoric.

Meanwhile, someone was talking on the phone. 'Hello, this is the coronary department at Saint Catherine's. We need information about a patient . . . His name is Bruno Genko.'

I'm at Saint Catherine's, he thought. The same hospital as Samantha Andretti. And Bunny's here, too, he remembered. Who's Bunny? He couldn't think of his name. But Samantha was in danger. Hey, can you hear me? Something terrible is about to happen and you have to call the police immediately. Alternatively, bring me a tequila and let's party.

'What's he clutching in his right hand?' somebody asked; it was the bearded man, trying to prise open his fingers. 'It looks like a ball of paper but he's not letting go of it.'

'Leave it alone, as long as it's not an item he can use to hurt himself or us,' the pretty female doctor said. 'Get an adrenaline injection ready.'

Darkness.

Another bolt of lightning, but this time more akin to fireworks. The earlier sounds had subsided and now there was that rhythmical sound again lulling him – the electronic version of his heartbeat. He was still lying down, and a large plastic mask was pressing on his face, covering almost all of it, forcibly pumping oxygen into his lungs.

The young doctor with black hair and an older male doctor were talking in front of his bed. Strangely, they were both dressed.

'Who authorised you to resuscitate him?' The male doctor was holding a sheet of paper and sounded upset.

That's my talisman, Genko thought.

'The ambulance crew couldn't possibly have known and we didn't have time to search his pockets,' the female doctor replied in justification. 'How were we to know it was a terminal case?'

He was seriously pissed off by the way they were talking about him as if he wasn't there.

'Our unit has limited resources and you waste them on someone who at most can hope to live until tomorrow morning.'

Actually, I didn't particularly want to be brought back to life either – have you considered that, you arsehole? If I'd dropped dead, then at least I'd have been spared the sight of your ugly mug. Really, though, he was upset by the fact that nobody could care less about his death. Even though, when it came down to it, he was simply reaping the fruit of a solitary life. He hadn't had a family and had never thought of having children. He'd even taken that as a given. The 'get married and start reproducing' plan was one he'd never even considered.

The old Bunny has passed the baton to the new Bunny, he thought. Even the monster at the harbour had a descendant who would keep his memory alive. And the new Bunny had a wife and two blonde daughters. What was his name again?

Forman, he thought. *Peter Forman, and he's a dentist!*

Except that the thrill of this epiphany soon died down because there was no way of communicating it to the outside world.

Take off the oxygen mask, I have something to tell you!

'You've brought a vegetable back to life,' the elderly doctor said.

I'm not a vegetable, you moron. Take off this fucking mask and I'll prove it to you.

'I'm sorry, doctor,' the nice young woman said. 'It won't happen again.'

The elderly man looked at her sternly. Then he gave the talisman back to her and walked out.

The young woman shook her head and was about to fold the paper but stopped to have a closer look at it. Genko noticed that she wasn't reading the report but examining the back of it.

Bunny's portrait sketched by the poacher who had helped Samantha Andretti.

Then something happened. He heard a voice in his head. Linda – *his* Linda – was speaking to him. *Pass the baton.* But it wasn't easy. Genko concentrated. Unlike his mind, his body was already dead. But he had to do this. He visualised his right hand, fingers clasped around a ball of paper. *Pass the baton*, Linda said again gently. He started with his index finger, which moved slightly. Don't go away, he said to the doctor in his thoughts. Stay a little longer. Then it was his thumb – such an effort, like shifting a heavy boulder. *Pass the baton!* He felt Linda taking his hand and helping him. The middle finger, then the ring finger and finally the little finger. He didn't know if this was happening for real or only in his head. Linda's voice stopped. The doctor folded the talisman and put it in her coat pocket. She was about to leave. No, please, no!

The faint sound of something bouncing.

The doctor paused and turned to the bed. She looked down. Come on, come and look. And she did, indeed, go towards him. She bent down and picked up the screwed-up piece of paper that had slipped out of his hand. She opened it, an expression of uncertainty in her face. She glanced from the contents of the paper to him a couple of times. Then she took the talisman out of her pocket and compared the two sheets.

The poacher's depiction and that of the Formans' youngest daughter, which had been attached to Paul Macinsky's fridge with a magnet.

The same subject. A rabbit with heart-shaped eyes.

The doctor looked confused. She took something resembling a pen from her coat pocket. No, it was a little torch. She drew close to his face, lifted the lid of his right eye with her finger and flashed the bright beam into his iris. Then she did the same with his left eye.

Genko tried to move his lips, hoping she'd notice despite the huge plastic mask.

She noticed.

She hesitated, but then slowly lifted the rubber straps and uncovered part of his face. She came closer and put an ear to his mouth.

Genko used what little breath he had left to utter a few sounds.

The doctor waited, then straightened up. She put the mask back on his face and looked at him, disconcerted.

He wasn't sure he'd been able to communicate. He probably hadn't said anything to her because his mind was playing strange tricks – though he did enjoy the hallucination where they were all naked.

The woman headed to the door.

No, damn it, no . . .

But instead of going out, she picked up the phone and dialled a number. 'Yes, it's me,' she said to whoever was on the line.

Come on, darling, *pass the baton.*

'The patient in 318 might have a relative. We must notify him, he's just told me his name.'

37

You could already smell summer in the air on that late afternoon in mid-June.

He and Paul were returning home after a football game on the pitch behind the parish church, all sweaty and happy as you can be only at the age of ten. The sun was a red circle at the end of the street and you could hear voices blending with the laughter on television in the houses as people got ready to sit down to dinner.

Paul Macinsky was his best friend. At least that was what Father Edward had decided. He'd taken them aside and said, 'From now on you'll be best buddies.' Paul wasn't very bright so had just nodded without querying it. But Robin knew why the priest had put them together. There was a specific category for children like him and Paul; it didn't have a name, but the difference between those who belonged to it and all the others was immediately clear to anyone. Hardly anybody ever spoke to them, they were never invited to parties, were always the last ones to be picked for a football team and, above all, nobody knew their first names but only addressed them by their surnames.

Sullivan and Macinsky.

They weren't even entitled to be targeted by bullies, like swots or effeminate boys. They simply didn't exist.

Father Edward, who knew how cruel children can be to their peers, had summoned them to the sacristy. By decreeing their friendship, perhaps he wanted to spare them the embarrassment of a solitude which, at this carefree age, is the worst stigma of shame.

Despite the mark on his face, which was also the main reason for his painful shyness, Paul wasn't a bad sort. Of course, it was hard to get a word out of him. Robin gathered that he lived with his mother and had never known his father. He didn't want to embarrass him, so had enquired no further. But rumour had it that Paul's mother had had an affair with a married man and that was why she'd been abandoned by her family, who'd thrown her and the bastard she was carrying out of the house.

Even though Paul had his mother's surname, and was therefore seen as a child of sin, Robin envied him. Not a day went by without an argument at his home. Both his parents drank heavily and would come to blows. His mother had once stabbed his father in the stomach while he was asleep. He was OK in the end but as soon as he came back from hospital, he fractured her skull with an iron. Sometimes, Robin would get caught up in the middle of a domestic row, but Paul never asked him how he'd got his bruises.

After all, almost all the local kids had troubles at home. But, unlike these two, they knew how to survive in this world. It was as though God had provided them with a kind of armour but had forgotten to give any to him and Paul.

Perhaps that was all that united them. Was it enough to build a friendship on? Robin didn't think so. Father Edward had been too optimistic in hoping they could help each other. They had nothing in common and did nothing but spend their time throwing pebbles at empty cans and chasing after stray cats.

But then one day something happened.

They had ended up in the same football team, although always as reserves. Some kind of miracle had occurred on the pitch: they had unexpectedly formed a pair of formidable defenders. An insurmountable wall against attackers from the other team. From then on, things had improved. Outside matches, the other children still addressed them by their surnames and hardly talked to them, but they would treat them with respect during the game.

That afternoon in June 1983, as they walked down the street talking about the game they'd just played, Robin Sullivan and Paul Macinsky were practically strangers once again, because their friendship only really materialised on a football pitch. As they turned the corner at the back of the church, they came across Bunny the caretaker, who was bringing out a bucket filled with rubbish.

'Hey, how's it going, boys?'

Neither of them replied, but they slowed down. Back then, Robin thought the guy was simply weird. He had a smile made up of teeth stained from too many cigarettes and he seemed overly polite when addressing the ladies who came to mass. Even Father Edward was distant towards him, as though he didn't quite trust him. The caretaker usually kept to himself. If anyone mentioned him, Robin always pictured Bunny holding a broom in the churchyard. Once, when he'd cycled past the Divine Mercy, he turned to the façade and saw that the man had stopped sweeping and was staring at him. There was something in that look that followed him all the way down the block and made the hairs stand up on his arms.

'How was the game?' the caretaker asked, putting the bucket of rubbish down.

'Same as usual.' Strangely, it had been Paul who answered. Only several years later did Robin understand that his friend's courage was determined by the fact that he wanted to get rid of Bunny as quickly as possible, perhaps because he was scared of him.

'I've often watched you: you two are inseparable.' They didn't respond to what sounded like an anodyne remark, but Bunny hadn't finished. 'I see how you get treated by the other boys, but I like you two and I'm tempted to share with you something nobody else knows—' The caretaker stopped to cough, then spat a lump of phlegm on the pavement. 'You can keep a secret, can't you?' They didn't answer, but he felt compelled to carry on anyway. 'There's a comic I think you'll like very much. But it's not the kind Father Edward buys ... The comic I'm talking about is special.' His eyes glistened as he said this.

'What do you mean by special?' Robin asked, intrigued.

Bunny looked around, then took a rolled-up book from the back pocket of his trousers.

'A rabbit?' Robin sneered, seeing the cover. 'That stuff's for babies.'

'And what if I told you it's not like that at all?' the man

said defiantly. 'If you read it in a mirror, something happens you can't even imagine.'

Paul pulled Robin by the sleeve of his T-shirt. 'We're late for dinner.'

But Robin ignored his friend. 'I don't believe you,' he said to the caretaker.

'Well, all we have to do is go to my place and you can see for yourselves.'

'Why do we have to go to your place?' Paul asked suspiciously.

'Actually, you don't need to. If you have a mirror on you, I can show you right now.'

The man was obviously trying to provoke them, but Robin knew he was more cunning than him. 'You go and get the mirror while we wait for you here.'

Bunny couldn't think of a response. But then he smiled. 'Sorry, boys, I thought you'd be interested. Oh well, I'll show it to someone more on the ball than you.' Then he turned to go.

Paul started walking again, while Robin stood staring at the man as he left.

'So, aren't you coming?' Paul asked.

He followed him willy-nilly. Once they'd reached the corner of the street, it was time to go their separate ways. Paul would turn right, towards the green house. 'Are you OK?' he asked, seeing Robin looking pensive.

'Yes,' he replied.

'We're still friends, aren't we?' he asked timidly.

'Sure we are,' Robin replied.

They looked at each other silently for a few seconds.

'Bye, then,' Paul said, and walked away. After a few steps,

Robin turned to look at him again. A nasty little voice told him that Paul would never get along in the world. He knew that voice. It was his father's. For as long as Fred Sullivan drank there weren't too many problems, but as soon as the effect of the hangover started to wear off he'd turn cruel. If he didn't hit him, then he'd start picking on him even if he hadn't done anything wrong. More than anything, he'd suddenly remember that he was a parent and start sharing his 'pearls of wisdom'. Things like 'Women can only do one thing'. Or 'Don't let a black man screw you'. But his favourite was, 'Hang out with your betters.' It wasn't hard for Robin to work out who to 'hang out' with, since practically everybody was better than him. The difficult part was persuading them to hang out with him. But if he carried on spending time with 'monster-face Paul', there was no hope he'd ever be accepted.

That June day, as the afternoon drew to a close, he couldn't bear that even Bunny the caretaker allowed himself to make fun of them, implying they were cowards. Maybe the time had come to prove that he and Paul were different. That was why he waited for his friend to walk away down the street.

Then he turned back.

Once he'd reached the church, he knocked on the door that led to the basement. He was planning to teach the care-taker a lesson by stealing something from him and running away. Then he would show off his loot to the other boys and brag about his daring act. As his father said, if you want to learn how to tackle the strongest ones, you always have to start by picking on someone weaker.

'I see you've changed your mind,' Bunny said, finding him on the doorstep.

'Yes,' Robin said defiantly.

'Then come in,' he said, indicating the staircase behind him.

Robin followed him, but as soon as the wooden door closed behind him he had a nasty feeling. They went down into the basement, into the rooms where the boilers were. Bunny's den was a small room fenced off by a metal mesh. It looked like a chicken coop.

Robin glanced around.

The place where the caretaker lived made him feel uncomfortable. Sunlight couldn't reach down there, and there was a pungent smell of kerosene. A folding bed, a collection of junk with no value on a shelf, a work table and an iron cupboard. Bunny immediately switched on a transistor radio assembled in a shoe box, which broadcast cheerful, clear blues, in contrast with the environment.

The caretaker sat down on the bed, opened the drawer of the bedside table and took out a small mirror to show him the secret hidden in the comic. 'Come and sit next to me,' he said, giving the blanket a light tap. His voice had changed, and there was now a creepy softness in his tone.

At that moment, Robin felt afraid. He should have listened to Paul, because he didn't want to stay there any more. 'Perhaps I'd better go,' he tried saying.

'Why? Don't you like being here?' the caretaker asked, acting offended. 'I'm sure we'll become friends.'

'No, really . . . My mother's expecting me,' he stammered. 'She must already have made dinner.' At most, his mother would have scraped together a two-day-old roast chicken from the supermarket and slammed it down in front of him without even heating it up. But there and then Robin would have eaten any kind of rubbish just so he could get out of there.

'Would you like some milk and biscuits?' Bunny asked. He took a carton from the cupboard and started pouring milk into a dirty glass.

Robin didn't reply.

Bunny shook his head, annoyed. 'Why do you all do this? At first you're cocky, then you try to back off.'

'I'm not backing off, but perhaps I'll come back another time.' He started to retreat.

Bunny looked at him gravely. 'Sorry, boy, but I don't think that'll be possible.' He held out the glass. 'Now drink your milk.'

38

Thirty years after he had followed Bunny the caretaker to the basement, Robin Sullivan alias Peter Forman could not forget the details of that event. He could still smell the place, feel the underground chill, the muffled sounds. Even the echo of the blues track was intact.

The recollection his memory had projected on the white ceiling of the hospital room gave way to the pain from his stomach wound. The stitches were pulling at his skin but he'd done a good job inflicting that stabbing on himself. He knew the exact spot to plunge the blade because it was where his mother had once stabbed his father with a kitchen knife. Back then, the doctors had said that despite all the blood he had lost, the man had been lucky because there weren't any vital organs there.

His parents had been a terrible example to him for almost all his childhood, while Bunny the caretaker had been a good teacher. During the three days he'd kept him imprisoned, the bastard had taken advantage of him, but had also taught him that there could be a mysterious frisson in someone else's fear.

Because that was exactly what Bunny was after. A child's fear was his nourishment, his passion.

Seventy-two hours of torture, abuse and psychological torment. Robin had managed to escape by pure chance only because on the third night his torturer fell asleep, drunk, and forgot to tie him to the headboard of the bed. So he'd slipped out of his prison and asked a passing woman for help, and she'd immediately taken him to the police.

But why had he taken the rabbit comic with him?

His decision had also influenced his decision not to tell anyone what had happened to him. In the beginning, he'd thought it was out of shame, or else fear that the monster might take revenge on him. But that wasn't the case. There was a reason, and it was linked to what Bunny had planted in his mind with the comic as well as a strange film.

During his brief imprisonment, terror had dug a deep abyss inside him. A distant, unfamiliar place in which the grown-up Robin had collected unspeakable desires, dark urges, the seeds of violence. But when he was still only ten years old, he could not yet imagine that something was hatching in that chasm.

A presence.

There was someone inside him. He'd discovered it in his parents' eyes after he'd returned home. There was an evil rabbit reflected in his mother's eyes. And, for the first time ever, she and his father were afraid of him. That was why they had sent him away. He'd found a new kind of love at the Wilsons' farm, which he shared with other children like him, all the prey of unscrupulous men and women who'd taken their childhood innocence by means of force and deception. But Robin felt different from them, too, because he did not accept his own condition as a victim. Maybe that was why Tamitria Wilson was so fond of him, thinking that Robin simply wanted to free himself from a terrible experience or that he refused to be marked by it for the rest of his life. That was why she had helped him take on a new identity and get a qualification that would allow him to attend university.

Tamitria had hit a private investigator, Bruno Genko, on the head and locked him up when he'd shown up a few nights earlier to enquire after a boy called Robin Sullivan. Like a caring mother, she wanted to protect a son called Peter Forman who'd left a terrible past behind him.

He'd loved Tamitria, but had had to kill her all the same because she hadn't understood the most basic truth. That the little boy Robin Sullivan refused to feel like a victim because he already knew he belonged to the category of torturers.

Tamitria had been suspicious of the comic book he always carried around but had never grasped its true meaning. When he left the farm, he'd asked her to keep it for him because he didn't have the heart to get rid of it but especially because by then he'd decided that Bunny deserved to come out from its pages.

He was already secretly thinking about a mask that would give him a particular from. But not a human one. Because Bunny should be a kind of divinity.

He'd brought it with him even on the night when Tamitria had called him to tell him about that busybody. He'd buried the old woman's body behind the barn but wasn't pleased about having had to kill her. He actually got no pleasure from taking someone's life. Even though he was often forced to do it.

Unlike the old Bunny, *he* liked little girls.

He nurtured his fantasies by going hunting on the deep web. But the ones he then abducted and took into his secret lair never lasted long. They were like hamsters or canaries and, after a year at most, got ill. So rather than watch a sad, protracted end, he made sure the girls stopped suffering. When it came down to it, his was an act of pity.

But things had gone differently with Samantha.

He'd immediately realised she wasn't like the others. First, as fate would have it, she had spontaneously approached his van with the reflective windows on a very ordinary February morning on her way to school. Like a fly which, unaware that it's flying too close to a spider's web, Samantha Andretti, attracted by her own reflection in the shiny maze, had paid the correct price for her vanity.

He'd been certain that this small girl wouldn't last even a month in captivity. But then she'd become his pride. Not only had Sam held out for fifteen years but from the very start she'd also given him a motivation to improve his strategy for concealing Bunny from the rest of the world.

If Peter Forman had got married and had two lovely girls, he owed it purely to her.

Safely hidden in a normal family, with an apparently quiet life, the calm dentist could have two perfect lives. His wife didn't even suspect that he harboured another being inside him. He had to admit he'd actually had fun scaring her with Bunny's mask the night before and locking her and the little girls in the basement. That was where Meg had found him wearing the rabbit head. He'd managed to persuade her to keep her mouth shut by telling her it was a secret between father and daughter.

He always managed to be kind and in control of himself at home. But he'd been harsh too often with Samantha, probably because he loved her too much. Then there had been the issue with the child. He'd always been careful when having sex with her. Besides, Sam hadn't had a period for years, so he'd thought she wasn't fertile. But she got pregnant. Perhaps he should have killed her straight away, but he couldn't. He thought she would die in childbirth. But when the moment came, he'd helped her give birth to her little bastard girl. Thanks to his medical skills as a dentist, he'd managed to perform a rudimentary caesarian – the kind that would get you struck off the register. Then he'd left and had avoided going for almost a week to the place where she was imprisoned. He was sure that on his return he'd find two dead bodies. Instead, that extraordinary little bitch had pulled through and not died from loss of blood.

Taking the child away had been the hardest part.

She was three years old but looked half that. She wasn't growing and had various problems brought about by her captivity.

Sam hadn't forgiven him. Previous to that, she'd always stood up to him but after he'd taken away her only reason for living, she'd rebelled against him in the worst possible way. She'd started to ignore him. She no longer harboured anger towards him and her constant fear vanished.

Bunny didn't scare her any more.

Before she could let herself die, he'd decided to give her an opportunity to change her own destiny.

A game.

He'd put her in the trunk of his car and taken her to the swamp. There, he'd removed her clothes so as to admire her one last time in all her animal beauty.

Then he'd let her go.

He'd waited an hour then gone looking for her.

It had taken him ages to find her. When he finally saw her, she was on the edge of a road, injured. As he was walking through the wood towards her in his Bunny disguise, a damned pick-up truck had arrived. The driver, almost certainly a poacher, had rushed to help her. Robin had watched the scene, hiding behind a tree.

Sam had flung her arms around that stranger's neck.

Watching her hug another had torn his soul apart with jealousy. He knew it now: he was in love with her, and always had been. That was why, unable to bear the sight of this, he had appeared.

When the young man with Sam – *his* Sam – had seen him, he'd hesitated then run away.

Good for you, boy, Good for you.

As the pick-up drove away, Samantha had started to scream and he'd rushed to comfort her and tell her he loved her. But she'd uttered words that wounded him, hurt him deeply.

She'd whispered, 'Kill me.'

After all these years together, after sharing the experience of becoming the parents of a girl, after he'd confessed how he felt about her, that coward preferred to die rather than admit that they were bound by the same deep feeling.

He couldn't accept that. So, since her right leg was obviously already broken, he'd decided to abandon her to her fate. 'If that's what you want, then that's what you'll get,' he said, and walked away.

He hadn't turned to look at her again. But, under Bunny's mask, tears of pain were running down his face.

When he'd returned home, the television was broadcasting the news that she had been found. People couldn't believe it and were pouring out into the street to celebrate. He should have been afraid for himself because the police had forgotten about Samantha Andretti and therefore about him, too, a long time ago and would now start looking for him again. But, oddly, he didn't care.

During the hours that followed, he'd found it hard to play the role of the quiet dentist, especially with his family. He was constantly afraid that his sadness would spill over the wall he'd erected so ruthlessly and that Bunny's cry of pain would emerge from the abyss, that somewhere, deep in the dark, he was prey to despair.

But, before the sun set, he'd had a revelation.

She loves me, too. But, like all couples, we sometimes argue. That's what happened, a simple lovers' quarrel. Yes, just a squabble because of my absurd jealousy. He'd been too proud and had gone off offended but he should try and clear everything up immediately.

That was what he had to do.

He was sure that all he had to do was go and see her in hospital. If he could just talk to her, he'd explain and everything would go back to the way it had been. That was why even the prospect of injuring himself with a knife didn't frighten him. It was a love token and Sam would appreciate it.

He'd even managed to use old Paul Macinsky to complete his plan. A few weeks earlier, he'd gone looking for a gardener in the shopping centre car park where the unemployed would gather. He'd noticed his old childhood friend from the birthmark on his face. Of course, showing himself to him was risky, but he couldn't resist the curiosity of knowing whether or not Paul would recognise him.

No, he didn't – or so he told himself.

By a happy coincidence, that random encounter had turned out to be useful when he'd needed to divert the police's and that stupid private investigator's attention elsewhere. While they were focusing on Paul Macinsky, Robin could act undisturbed.

Ever since he'd been admitted to the surgery department of Saint Catherine's he'd started making plans for Samantha and himself. After running away from the hospital together, they would go and hide somewhere for a while. Perhaps in the old lair. After all, that was their love nest. Provided the police hadn't found it in the meantime, in the basement of the house where he'd grown up. The only inheritance his parents had left him after both dying of cirrhosis of the liver.

In any case, they couldn't stay there for long. So Robin planned to withdraw a large sum of money from the bank, buy a second-hand car and go somewhere else. They would travel around the country for a while, in order to erase their tracks. Then, one day, they would come to a quiet village in the mountains, where they could stay for the rest of their lives. Using false names, they could get a real house, find two respectable jobs and perhaps try and have a child again – or maybe even two.

Yes, it would be wonderful. Two fugitives in love.

He had to talk to Sam about it, tell her about his dream and ask her to make it come true together. But first he had to apologise to her, of course. Sam was intelligent and understanding: she had already forgiven him so much, she would again.

Robin looked again at the ceiling of the hospital room. His darling Sam wasn't far from him, in the burns unit. There were only two floors between them. He couldn't believe he had managed to resist for so long the temptation to go and see her straight away. With some difficulty, still in pain from the stitches in his wound, he sat up. He was happy.

Soon, he would finally be able to embrace the woman he loved.

39

The emergency exit leading to the fire escape was ajar.

Robin Sullivan had been keeping an eye on it for some time and noticed police officers going discreetly in and out. He approached and immediately caught the unmistakable whiff of nicotine. He pushed the door open and saw two policemen talking and smoking. As soon as they saw him, they stopped to take a closer look: all he was wearing was a hospital gown and a pair of towelling slippers. He greeted them with a nod and they resumed smoking and talking as though nothing had happened.

He leaned on the railing. A breeze was making the heat more tolerable and there was a beautiful starry sky. It really was the perfect night. He breathed in and out deeply, still listening out for what was going on behind him. One of the policemen extinguished his cigarette butt by crushing it against the wall and threw it into the void, then left his colleague to go back to his duties. Once they were alone, Robin put a hand in his pocket.

The second policeman also finished his cigarette.

He was about to follow his colleague but as soon as he turned to the wall to extinguish his cigarette end, Robin took out a syringe he'd prepared earlier in the medicines room. He quickly stabbed the man's neck with it, then immediately stepped back. The policeman put a hand to his throat, turned to him, staring in surprise, and reached out to grab him with his other hand, but the powerful barbiturate injected right into his jugular had already reached his central nervous system. He staggered and fell to his knees.

Robin made sure he was unconscious, and began to remove his uniform.

The burns unit was on the top floor of the hospital. The patients' rooms were concentrated in the internal part of the building and had no windows because sunlight and heat could be harmful to the patients' skin. Clever of them to admit Samantha there, he thought. That way they could keep a closer eye on her.

He used the service lift. As soon as the door opened, two policewomen came towards him but he lowered his head so that his face would be better concealed under the visor of his cap. They paid no attention to him and walked past.

There were only doctors and nurses in the corridor. The bulk of the police were concentrated outside the hospital and there was only one patrol between the floors because the rooms had to be kept sterile for the other patients.

He walked through the rooms, looking for Samantha's. He was sorry to be going to her empty-handed. He would have liked to take her something, flowers, perhaps, but he didn't want to risk attracting attention. He already knew what he would do: he would kneel before her and ask for forgiveness.

He identified the door to her room because of the police officer guarding it. He went up to him.

The policeman noticed him approach and looked at him, probably wondering why he was there. 'What's going on?' he asked.

'I don't know,' Robin replied. 'I've been ordered to come here.'

The policeman glanced at his watch. 'Strange, my shift doesn't end till two.'

Robin shrugged. 'Those were the orders.'

The policeman took the radio attached to his belt. 'Let's ask the sergeant.'

Robin stopped him. 'It's probably a mistake. I'll go back down and tell them.'

'All right.'

'How's it going in there?' he asked, indicating the door as though merely curious.

'Dr Green's taking a break, and I think the girl's sleeping.'

Robin nodded and started to walk away, but then turned around. 'Since I'm here, do you want to have a cigarette or get a drink of water? I can stay for five minutes.'

'Heck, yes,' the policeman quickly replied. 'Thanks, you're a pal.'

Robin watched him leave and turn the corner of the corridor. He waited another few seconds then leaned with his back against the door and reached out for the handle. After making sure nobody was watching him, he opened it and quickly went into the room.

*

It was dark and the only faint light was coming from the medical equipment arranged around the bed. He waited for his eyes to get accustomed to the semi-darkness and the objects gradually started to emerge in his field of vision. He could hear breathing – regular and calm – coming from the bed.

My love is asleep, he thought. She'll be so happy to see me. After all, fifteen years together is a kind of marriage.

He started drawing closer. He wanted to wake her with a kiss.

Once he'd reached the bed, he stopped and smiled. He reached out to stroke her but couldn't find her.

The bed was empty.

'Hello, Bunny.'

The male voice had come from behind him. He instinctively made to turn around.

'Don't move,' the man said.

He heard clearly the heavy sound of boots walking in the room as the men took up their positions around the target. He pictured shotguns and their night viewers, aiming at him. They've sent a special team, he thought. He was flattered by so much attention. He shook his head in disbelief that he had reached the climax, and began to raise his hands as a sign of surrender.

'On your knees,' the voice said.

It wasn't peremptory but calm and patient. He found that comforting.

'Hands behind your head.'

He obeyed. As he did so, he could feel his heart breaking and a tear ran down his face. It wasn't the prospect of it all being over that was painful, so much as the thought that he would never see his love again. They grabbed him and handcuffed him. 'Can I at least know who's arresting me?' he asked.

The voice introduced itself. 'Special Agent Simon Berish.'

40

After discovering that Sullivan's bed was empty, they'd immediately realised that the monster was circulating around the hospital undetected. A manhunt would have endangered too many innocent people, which was why Berish's suggestion had been welcomed.

It hadn't been necessary to move Samantha Andretti. All they'd had to do was place the police officer on watch outside the door to another room and wait inside for the trap to click shut.

In the end, they arrested Sullivan. He cried like a baby as they took him away. His first request was somewhat peculiar. Milk and biscuits.

Berish kept thinking about it as he walked to the operations unit's camper van. He'd had to leave Hitchcock in the square outside. Fortunately, somebody had placed a bowl of water next to him. It was three in the morning but as hot as midday and the dog was clearly suffering from the crazy weather more than everybody else. 'We're going home soon,

OK?' Berish said, stroking the hovawart's muzzle. In the meantime, he also tried to call Mila, but without holding out much hope. Her mobile was still switched off.

Vasquez, where the hell are you?

He had no idea about the case she was investigating or why she had disappeared. The last time he'd spoken to her, five days ago now, she'd mentioned a very promising lead. When he'd asked what it was, she'd rudely dismissed him.

'Leave me alone, Berish.'

This wasn't unusual for Mila, but this time he'd vowed he wouldn't forgive her. His friend forgot about her duties as a mother too often: Alice was still very young and needed her. But as soon as she was back from her damned mission, he'd tell her straight out what he thought – all of it.

'Your call is being transferred to an automated voicemail,' the recorded voice announced on the phone. Berish was about to leave a message but stopped.

Bauer and Delacroix were coming towards him.

'So, can you explain?' Bauer asked. 'What's your connection with Bruno Genko?'

'He came to Limbo last night and that's how we met. He was looking for information about the disappearance of Robin Sullivan.'

'And you gave it to him?' Bauer opened his arms in disbelief. 'You're not even on duty there and you offer help to anyone who just asks you?'

Berish couldn't stand it. 'Look, guys, let's make one thing clear: are you looking for somebody to take the blame for your failing to solve the case?'

Bauer was about to respond when Delacroix intervened.

'Nobody has any intention of putting anybody on trial here, we just want to understand what happened.'

Berish assessed the situation before replying. 'Genko told me what he'd discovered: the comic, Bunny, the man with the birthmark on his face . . . I think he had a desperate need to resolve this.' He remembered Genko's pale face, caused by the evident effort he was putting into this business. 'And so, without intending to, that's how I came to acquire all the elements of the case.'

'And what did you give him in return?' Bauer asked, increasingly agitated.

'A photo,' Berish replied without hesitation. 'Genko wanted to know what Robin Sullivan looked like as a child. The snapshot kept in the Limbo file showed him standing next to a childhood friend.'

Bauer sneered. 'How very touching.'

Berish ignored him and carried on talking to Delacroix. 'A couple of hours ago, I got a call from a doctor at Saint Catherine's: she said a patient in a serious condition had mentioned my name – she thought I might be a relative or a friend. When I arrived, they told me he'd been given first aid by a Paul Macinsky, who'd come with him to the hospital. They pointed him out and I realised there had been a case of mistaken identity, that the boy with the birthmark on his face in the Limbo picture wasn't Robin Sullivan, which meant that the dentist had lied.'

Delacroix studied him, perhaps trying to work out if he was telling the whole truth.

Berish knew he didn't have a good reputation among his colleagues and had been a kind of pariah for years. Maybe that was why he'd felt comfortable with Bruno Genko. 'You should thank Genko,' he said. 'Without him Samantha Andretti would have been in great danger.'

'He died twenty minutes ago,' Bauer said abruptly. Then he turned his back on him and left.

The news caught Berish unprepared. He hardly knew this man but he felt sorry all the same.

'He said that when it was all over he wanted to meet Samantha, I think he wanted to apologise to her for something.'

Delacroix put a hand on his shoulder. 'It would have been no use, anyway.'

Berish stared at him in surprise. 'Why not?'

'The chief is calling a press conference in half an hour's time.'

What the hell was Delacroix talking about?

'There's a piece of news we haven't circulated yet. And it concerns Samantha Andretti . . .'

41

She pulled the sheet over her head. She didn't want to be watched by the mirror any more. And she no longer wanted to hear the yellow phone on the bedside table ringing.

He knows I'm here and he's coming to take me back to the labyrinth. She thought again about the prison with grey walls and no way out.

'The rooms in psychiatric asylums are painted grey, as are maximum security prison cells, the cages at the zoo . . .' Dr Green had said. 'In the long run, grey makes you meek.'

Where was the doctor? At least an hour had passed since he'd gone to remove the sandwich stain from his shirt. He'd said he'd be back straight away, and instead he had left her alone.

The sheet was a cocoon, the last defence she had left.

At first it had worked, and had been enough to calm her down. But then something had sneaked into her refuge. Alongside the familiar hospital sounds, the heartbeat on the wall had returned.

The heart of the baby girl born in captivity, whom she couldn't remember at all. The heart of her daughter. Who was also the monster's daughter.

Stop beating. I beg you, stop. But it wouldn't stop.

The obsessive beat was driving her insane. She realised she had to do something or it would never leave her alone. So she plucked up the courage and slowly emerged from under the sheet.

They'd told him that he could watch her from behind a fake mirror, so all that separated Simon Berish from Samantha Andretti now was thin glass. Apart from the poacher who had saved her, the policeman, the profiler who was treating her and, naturally, the monster who'd kept her prisoner, nobody out there knew what she looked like as an adult. Most people remembered her as she was at thirteen. As far as the rest of the world was concerned, Sam was still a young girl.

Berish was among those who'd been allowed to witness the truth.

All he could see was a frail, defenceless creature. Delacroix had told him that Samantha had broken a leg while escaping because her imprisonment had weakened her bones. Her immune system was also compromised, which was why she had been placed in a sterile environment.

Were there really men capable of doing something like that to an innocent girl?

The heart on the wall had become enormous and was still growing.

It's only a stain, she kept telling herself. It's a hallucination.

It's the psychotropic drugs that bastard gave me. It'll soon disappear, as soon as the antidote in the drip has cleansed my blood and my brain.

The throbbing was like a drum beat. It was calling her.

It's my little girl, she just wants her mummy to stroke her. Her mummy, who abandoned her. She felt like crying. Don't trust her, she's the monster's daughter, she just wants to take you back to the labyrinth. You know she's still there, waiting for you. If you don't want to go back there, you have to ignore her.

No, I can't. I'm her mother, I can't.

She pulled the sheet off determinedly and sat up in bed. She spread her legs, pulled off the catheter and threw it down. A puddle of urine formed on the floor. She looked at the drip and carefully took the needle out of her vein – she would reconnect it later. She wasn't sure she had enough strength to stand up, she still remembered how she'd tried it the first time and ended up on the floor – Dr Green had immediately rescued her, smelling of cologne. So she moved her right leg first and put the foot on the floor, then grabbed the one in the cast with both hands, lifted it and tried moving it to the edge of the bed, a little at a time. When she reached the very edge, she gave it a push with her hip and slowly eased it until it touched the floor. Finally, she propped herself on the mattress with her arms, took a deep breath, and heaved herself up.

At first, the room spun around her, but she managed nevertheless not to lose her balance. Good, she thought. Then she aimed straight for the heart on the white wall.

She had to prove to her brain that it didn't really exist, that it was a trick, a false perception. She moved her right foot first, brought her chest forward, then dragged the leg in the cast. She calculated a distance of a couple of metres between her and the finishing line. She was confident she would make it.

She struggled, step by step. At the fourth, she stopped to catch her breath. Meanwhile, the throbbing on the wall had quickened. I have to get there. I have to stop it.

When she was less than a metre away, she smiled. She was very close to completing her small endeavour. Come on, one last effort.

Once she was close to the wall, she gave in and reached out with one arm. She put her hand delicately on the heart and it stopped beating.

At last, it had calmed down.

She felt something moist. There, I was right: it's just a damned patch of damp.

But when she took her hand away from the white wall, her own heart froze.

Berish was still watching the girl lying in the hospital bed, feeling infinitely sorry for her. 'There's a piece of news we haven't circulated yet. And it concerns Samantha Andretti . . .' Delacroix had said.

Her eyes staring blankly, a rivulet of saliva dripping from the corner of her mouth. All that was left was the semblance of a human being.

Berish could understand the bureau's resistance, because as soon as people out there found out the truth they would be angry with the police for not having saved Samantha Andretti in fifteen long years.

'I know what you're thinking,' a female voice behind him said.

Berish turned and saw a beautiful, very elegant black woman of about forty.

'Is it true what they're saying?' he asked. 'That she's in a kind of coma?'

'Not exactly,' the woman replied. 'She's in a catatonic state and alternates between moments of partial wakefulness and others in which she's completely absent.'

'Special Agent Delacroix used another expression to describe Samantha's state . . .'

'Oh, yes?'

'She's like someone trapped for ever in a nightmare, never able to wake up.'

The woman sighed. 'We had hoped she'd be able to provide useful information that would help us catch her abductor or find the prison where she was kept for fifteen years, but all our attempts have been futile.' She paused, then shook her head. 'The real prison is in her mind and now it's impossible to free her from there.'

He saw the disappointment on her face and wondered what her role had been in the Samantha Andretti case. 'I'm Special Agent Simon Berish,' he said, proffering his hand.

She shook it and gave him a faint smile. 'I'm the profiler responsible for the case – my name is Clara Green.'

The wall under the patch of damp was grey.

The palm of her hand, on the other hand, was stained with white paint. It can't be, she thought. A wave of terror swept over her. This isn't really happening to me. This isn't happening to me.

She had to tell someone immediately. The yellow phone, she thought. It was no longer hostile now, it was her friend.

She went to the bedside table as quickly as she could, heedless of how tiring it was to drag the leg in the cast. As soon as she'd reached the phone, she grabbed the receiver and put it to her ear. She dialled nine, as Dr Green had told her . . . But it was silent, there was no connection.

She wanted to scream, but restrained herself.

She turned to the door to ask for help. But if what was happening was true, then it was totally irrational to hope that anyone would help her.

Even so, she headed to the door in a state of frenzy but also in fear of discovering how things really were. She tried the handle: it wasn't locked. She took that to be a good sign.

She opened it and saw the back of the policeman on watch outside the door. She was so happy she could have hugged him. Her euphoria lasted only a second because her mind sensed that what she had in front of her was just an inanimate object.

A smiling dummy, like in a department store, wearing a uniform.

On a small table, amid syringes and medicines, stood an old portable stereo: a background of hospital sounds was coming from the loudspeakers. There was also the TV set on which Dr Green had shown her the live images outside the hospital, but she now realised that it was connected only to a video recorder.

There was a stack of old newspapers. On the cover of the one on top was an article about her unexpected reappearance. There was a tawny wig and a nurse's uniform lying on a chair. 'Rest, darling, rest . . .' the woman had said in a maternal voice while changing the drip.

At last she looked around. She recognised the grey walls

and iron doors of the rooms looking out onto the corridor. Her hope that she was wrong was swept away by reality. Now she knew exactly what it was.

A game.

She had never left the labyrinth.

'They told me about your friend the private detective,' Dr Green said. 'I'm sorry.'

'We weren't friends,' Berish said, wishing he could add that he'd have liked to get to know Bruno Genko better. 'But thanks, anyway.'

'Would you like a coffee?' she asked.

'I'd love one,' he replied. He glanced once more through the fake mirror and wondered how many Samantha Andrettis were being kept prisoner somewhere, without anybody being able to save them.

Then Berish thought again about the comic, the rabbit with the heart-shaped eyes. God knows how many children had been infected by the dark and had become monsters as adults.

God knows how many Bunnys were out there.

42

I'm not Samantha Andretti.

She felt crushed by this sudden awareness. She had to get out of here. She knew it was impossible, but her stupid brain refused to accept the notion that it had been just an illusion.

A monster's sadistic game.

She carried on down the corridor, dragging her plastered leg like a dead weight. *The broken leg is probably a trick, too. A way to keep me in bed, to stop me from getting around and discovering the truth. And there were no menacing eyes behind the mirror she's been so afraid of, just another damned wall.*

After walking twenty metres or so, she froze. Her attention was caught by a faint sound. It was coming from the third room on her right.

It sounded like a radio programme.

She headed in that direction and stopped just before the door. She listened: it was actually a conversation.

She decided to take a look inside.

Dr Green was standing with his back to her, the device on which he'd recorded their conversations in front of him. He was wearing headphones. The volume must have been loud because the sound was leaking out.

'*I don't know if I can.*'

She recognised her own voice, then heard the doctor's.

'*Listen, Sam: you do want that man to pay for what he's done to you, don't you? And above all, you wouldn't want him to do the same thing to somebody else . . .*' It was what he had said to her after she'd woken up remembering nothing, after he'd shown her the flyer with the picture of thirteen-year-old Samantha Andretti. '*As you might have gathered, I'm not a policeman. I don't carry a gun and I don't go around chasing criminals or being shot at. To tell you the truth, I'm not even that brave.*' She heard him laugh at his own joke. '*But one thing I can assure you: together we'll catch him, you and I. He doesn't know it, but there's a place from which he cannot escape. And that's where we'll hunt him down: not out there but in your mind.*'

Dr Green's last sentence made her shudder, as it had the first time around.

'*What do you say – do you trust me?*'

She remembered how she had put out her hand to take the flyer with the photo back. Without knowing it, she had started off the game.

'*Good, well done, my brave girl.*'

I'm not your girl. And I'm not brave either.

You're not a doctor. And you don't want to help me. You're *him*.

Now that she knew what he looked like, the monster seemed even more monstrous to her. Because the thought that such a normal man could conceal such evil inside him was worse than any nightmare. Monsters in fairy tales were so horrific that they generated in their victims the fantasy of being able to defeat them. Whereas with such a banal being there could be no hope of salvation.

Perhaps the chicken sandwich he had given her really had been made by his wife. And when he left here, he would go and lie down next to her in a warm bed, beneath the roof of a house like so many others. Maybe he had children or grandchildren, certainly mates or school friends who thought they truly knew him but actually knew nothing about him.

Only I know who he is.

That was when she noticed once again the carabiner at his belt.

Then she looked down at her belly and her fingers searched for the groove of the scar.

If I've survived this long, it means I'm stronger than I can now remember. So she decided the time had come to ask herself the question she had avoided until now.

Who am I?

43

'I have great news,' Dr Green announced, coming back into the room. 'We've managed to catch him: your abductor has been arrested!'

She pretended to be speechless with surprise. In reality, it was fear that prevented her from reacting. She hoped he hadn't noticed. 'How did it happen?'

'Unfortunately, I'm not yet at liberty to share the details with you, but rest assured that we couldn't have done it without your help.' He looked euphoric. 'You can be proud of yourself.'

'So then it's over?'

'Yes, dear,' he replied, taking his jacket off the back of the chair. 'Your father has arrived. We had a chat: I explained to him that it wouldn't be easy for you to see him straight away, and he said he'd wait until you were ready to speak to him.'

'And where will you go, Dr Green?'

He smiled. 'I'll go home but I promise I'll come and see you soon.'

'Do you have a nice house?'

'And a nice mortgage, for that matter.'

'What's your wife's name?' She immediately saw that he was taken aback by her question.

'Adriana,' he said after a brief hesitation.

I wonder if it's true, she thought. 'Do you have children?'

He looked at her, puzzled. 'Yes,' he simply said.

'And what are their names?'

'How come you're so interested in my life?' He laughed again but was clearly embarrassed. 'I'm not that interesting, you know.'

'I want to know,' she replied, not in the least scared.

He put the jacket back on the chair and sat back down. All of a sudden, he was no longer in a rush to leave. 'The eldest is Johanna, she's thirty-six. Then there's George, who's thirty-four. And finally, the youngest, Marco, who's twenty-three.'

She nodded, as if taking it in. But it wasn't enough. 'What do they do?'

'Marco's at university, he has three exams to go before graduating in Law. George has set up a small internet company with a couple of friends. Johanna got married last year, she's an estate agent.'

She was studying his face to see if he was putting on an act. No, it's all true, she thought. 'How did you meet your wife?'

'At high school,' he replied in a neutral tone. 'We've been together for over forty years.'

'Was it hard to win her over?'

'I was going out with her best friend and she introduced us. After seeing her for the first time, I wouldn't leave her alone until she agreed to go out with me.'

He was staring at her intently, but she didn't look away. 'Did you ask her to marry you straight away?'

'A month later.'

'With a ring?'

'I couldn't afford one. I just asked her, that's all.'

'What's in my drip?'

'A psychotropic drug.'

'Are my memories real?'

'Some are. Others are induced hallucinations.'

'How long have I been here?'

'Almost a year.'

'Why did you make me think I was Samantha Andretti?'

'It's a game.'

'Who are you?'

He didn't reply.

She fixed him with a defiant look. 'Who am I?' she asked.

He smiled, but there was something different in his expression now. Dr Green's gentleness had vanished.

'I'm sorry,' she said. 'This time I've won.'

The monster took a deep breath. 'Congratulations, you were good.'

'What's going to happen now?'

'What always happens,' he replied, then searched in his jacket pocket and took out a ready-to-use syringe. 'I'll inject you with some of this, and you'll have a good sleep. When you wake up you won't remember a thing.'

'How many other times have we played this game?'

'Countless times,' he said, smiling. 'It's our favourite.'

He approached the bed. She proffered her right arm to let him know she was ready. 'Let's get it over with.' He's scum – she remembered – he's just scum.

As he was about to give her the injection, she reached out with her left hand and suddenly grabbed the pole with the drip. She pulled it hard and the bottle fell on the back of the fake profiler's neck, shattering into a thousand pieces.

He let go of her arm and fell from the bed to the floor like a dead weight. He was stunned but not unconscious. She realised she didn't have much time: soon he would come to and go back on the offensive.

She dropped onto him and took the carabiner with the keys to the labyrinth from his belt. Then she stepped over him. Still breathless, her throat burning, she rushed to the door. The plastered leg was a weight. But she had to make it – she had to. One step at a time, but the weight made the distance from the door seem interminably long. She occasionally turned around to check the situation.

The coward was coming round. At first, he just put a hand on his head. Then he saw the keys and everything became clear. The mild-mannered Dr Green had vanished. Hatred was now dripping from his face like wax.

She saw him get up and lunge at her like a raging animal. His hands slapped her but were unable to grab her nightgown. She wouldn't be this lucky the second time around.

She reached the iron door he'd painted white to make it look like a hospital door and opened it as fast as she could.

She stepped out and pulled the handle towards her.

The infinitely short time during which the door was shutting stretched, slowing down every gesture. She felt as though she were experiencing déjà vu, like that time with the girl he'd sent to kill her – she wondered if that has been real or another chemically induced illusion. As the action moved inexorably to its end, she saw on the monster's face a series of expressions ranging from anger to contempt to absolute wonder.

With trembling hands, she searched for the key. She tried a couple but there were about at least twenty of them. I'll never make it. She even nearly dropped the carabiner on the floor. At her fourth attempt, she heard the key turn.

One, two, three turns.

Something hurled itself violently against the door. It was him trying to get out. She heard him screaming and hitting the iron. She was afraid he'd succeed in breaking it down, but then decided to ignore him and began her search because she was certain that salvation had always been close.

She tried every lock with the bunch of keys. After a series of empty rooms, she found one with a rusty ladder that led up to a manhole.

In order to climb up, though, she had to get rid of the cast on her leg. She began to kick the iron door until she made a few cracks. She stretched them open with her fingers and tore bits out.

Then she climbed without knowing what she'd find on the other side. Perhaps even another labyrinth – after what she'd been though, she wasn't sure of anything any more.

At the top of the steps, she turned a kind of safety valve on the manhole with both hands. It took a lot of strength to lift it just a little. But as soon as she succeeded, she was rewarded with a gust of cold air and the pale light of day.

She pushed as hard as she could until the lid of the man-hole fell outwards with a metallic clang.

She pulled herself up and tried to work out where she was.

Above her were the ruins of an abandoned mill and what remained from a fire. Around her, there was a landscape of snow-covered woods as far as the eye could see.

Not a sound, no human or animal presence. No point of reference. As far as she knew, this place could be anywhere. How did the monster come all the way here every time? She'd thought she would find a car. He parks it a long way from here – he's careful. She didn't even know where there was a road – or *if* there was one. She was wearing just a light shirt and she was barefoot. I won't survive in this temperature for long, she thought. If I don't find help, come nightfall I'll die of exposure. The alternative was to go back down and get better prepared for the expedition, perhaps even postpone it until she'd built up her strength.

But she just wanted to get away from here as soon as possible. Whatever the cost.

Before starting on her walk, however, she lifted the iron lid again. The screams of the man in the labyrinth were still echoing in the hole beneath her. She let the lid drop heavily on the manhole. The sound quickly faded in the air. The monster had got the fate he deserved.

Buried alive.

At this point, she walked into snow that came up to her shins. She was cold but felt free. She realised that these conditions, uncomfortable as they were for her body, were having a beneficial effect on her mind, because fragments of memory suddenly came back to her.

The scar on her belly: I'm the mother of a little girl but I never gave birth in the labyrinth. She's at home, safe.

The monster didn't abduct me: it was I who came looking for him.

I'm a policewoman and I work in Limbo. My name is María Elena Vasquez.

But I've always been called Mila.

Acknowledgements

Stefano Mauri, publisher – friend. And, along with him, all my publishers around the world.

Fabrizio Cocco, Giuseppe Strazzeri, Raffaella Roncato, Elena Pavanetto, Giuseppe Somenzi, Graziella Cerutti, Alessia Ugolotti, Tommaso Gobbi, Diana Volonté and the inevitable Cristina Foschini.

You're my team.

Andrew Nurnberg, Sarah Nundy, Barbara Barbieri and the extraordinary associates of the agency in London.

Tiffany Gassouk, Anais Bakobza, Ailah Ahmed.

Vito, Ottavio, Michele. Achille.

Gianni Antonangeli.

Alessandro Usai and Maurizio Totti.

Antonio and Fiettina, my parents. Chiara, my sister.

Sara, my 'present eternity'.

ALSO BY DONATO CARRISI

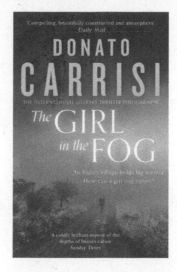

SIXTY-TWO DAYS AFTER THE DISAPPEARANCE . . .

A man is arrested after a road accident in the small town of Avechot. His shirt is covered in blood. Could this have anything to do with a missing girl called Anna Lou?

Detective Vogel is on the case, but his eccentric methods start to unsettle the locals. When a media storm hits Avechot, Vogel is sure that the suspect will be flushed out. But the clues are confusing, and may lead him even further from the truth at the heart of the town.

'A thoroughly disconcerting, addictive thriller' METRO

'A coldly brilliant exposé of the depths of human nature' SUNDAY TIMES

'Compelling, beautifully constructed and atmospheric' DAILY MAIL